Cemetery Tours

Jacqueline E. Smith

Wind Trail Publishing

Cemetery Tours

Copyright © 2013 by Jacqueline E. Smith

Wind Trail Publishing
PO Box 830851
Richardson, TX 75083-0851
www.WindTrailPublishing.com

Second Paperback Edition, January 2020

ISBN-13: 978-0-9896734-0-2
ISBN-10: 0989673405

Library of Congress Cataloguing-in-Publication Data
Smith, Jacqueline E.
Cemetery Tours / Jacqueline E. Smith
Library of Congress Control Number: 2013944772

Cover Design by Wind Trail Publishing

Printed in the United States of America.

For my mom, my dad, and my sister, who have always believed in me no matter what.

CHAPTER ONE

It was a lazy Saturday morning, and as usual, Michael Sinclair was trying to decide how to spend it. Throughout the long work week, he would compose a mental list of things he would rather be doing; reading one of the several books he'd accumulated over the years, taking advantage of his apartment complex's great swimming pool, or even making another pathetic attempt at learning to ride a bicycle. But by the time the weekend actually rolled around, he was so worn out, all he wanted to do was sleep in and spend the rest of the day lounging around in his pajamas, eating cereal, and catching up on *Doctor Who*.

Today was no exception.

He was rummaging through his near-empty pantry, kicking himself for forgetting to go to the grocery store yet again, when a movement out of the corner of his eye distracted him.

"New neighbor alert," Brink, Michael's friend and occasional roommate, announced and heaved himself onto the couch, propping his long legs up on the coffee table.

"Next door?" Michael asked. Mrs. Riggs, his mean old property manager, had been trying to rent out the apartment next to his for ages. It was no secret around the Riverview Apartment complex that Building 17 was some kind of cursed. All tenants of the two-story building, at one time or another, had complained of strange noises, power failures, unexplained cold spells, and an overall feeling of unease and ill-will. Only Michael Sinclair of apartment #1723 seemed immune.

It was for that very reason that Mrs. Riggs figured he must somehow be the source of her other tenants' discomfort. Fortunately, she didn't have any sort of evidence to support her claims. Otherwise, she would have had him evicted right from the start.

"Yep. Young couple. Bat-Lady probably gave them a discount or something." Although the entire building suffered from "technical difficulties," Mrs. Riggs had a much harder time keeping the second floor inhabited than its lower level counterparts. Especially the apartment next door to #1723. "Wonder how long they'll last?"

Before Michael could offer an estimate, a muffled thud, accompanied by a yell and the sound of shattering ceramic dishware, resonated through the hallway just outside his front door.

Cereal forgotten, Michael hurried to the door and pulled it open to see a young man sprawled across the landing. Next to him, broken plates and metal dining utensils spilled out of an old, flimsy cardboard box, held together by a substantial amount of duct tape.

"Dammit…" he muttered to himself as he scrambled to collect the shards of plates that had scattered across the landing.

"Are you okay?" Michael asked.

"Fine. Just tripped," the young man replied gruffly.

"Here, let me help," Michael dropped down next to his new neighbor and began to gather pieces of broken plates and silverware that had gone astray.

"Gavin?" a new voice called. Michael turned to see a young woman with dark blonde hair sprinting up the stairs. "What happened? Are you all right?" She knelt down in front of Gavin and placed a hand on his shoulder.

"I'm fine, Kate. Can't say the same for our dishes, though." Gavin rose up on his knees and dropped a handful of shattered plate into the box.

"Oh well, they were secondhand anyway." For the first time, she acknowledged Michael. "Hi, I'm Kate. This is my brother, Gavin."

"I'm Michael. I'm uh, your new neighbor." *I'm also*, he realized looking into her pretty hazel eyes, *still in my pajamas.*

"You look really familiar to me. Have we met before?"

"Um, I don't know," Michael replied, though he was sure they hadn't. Most of the women Michael knew, he met through his job at the local library. Besides, he would have remembered a girl as pretty as Kate. "Maybe we passed each other when you came to check out the apartment."

"Maybe," Kate said, gathering up the box of broken dishes.

"Kate, let me." Gavin took the box from her. As soon as he stood up, Michael noticed his bloodied, scuffed up knee through his torn jeans. Kate saw it too and gasped.

"Gavin, you need to get a Band-Aid on that."

"It's fine. Just a scrape. Besides, all our first-aid stuff is buried in one of the boxes."

"I have some Neosporin if you need it," Michael offered.

Gavin answered, "No, it's all right," as Kate asked simultaneously, "Do you mind?"

"Not at all."

Michael quickly retreated back to his apartment, where he immediately shed his plaid pajama bottoms and white undershirt and replaced them with a pair of jeans and a polo shirt. Then, he grabbed the yellow tube of Neosporin and a handful of Band-Aids from his bathroom drawer. Less than a minute later, he headed back across the landing where Kate and Gavin had left their door open. He knocked once before poking his head in. Kate and Gavin sat on the floor in the middle of the near-empty living room, sorting out the silverware and plates that were still intact. A few boxes sat on the sidelines. They were obviously still in the early stages of the moving process. Kate looked up at him.

"Thank you so much," she said as she stood to greet him. He handed her the Band-Aids and Neosporin. "Can I get you something to drink? We have... water."

"I'm all right, but thanks," Michael answered.

"I'll go to the store once we get my truck cleared out," Gavin announced, taking the medical supplies from his sister. "I need some more of those little energy drinks."

"You've got to start weaning yourself off of that stuff. It's not good for you," Kate said.

"Do you have a sister, Michael?" Gavin asked.

"No."

"You want one?"

"I'm serious," Kate crossed her arms. "You throw those back like an alcoholic at an open bar. Gav, that stuff is going to *kill* you."

"Kate, you're paranoid. And exaggerating," Gavin told her, applying Neosporin to his injured knee. Although Michael agreed that Kate was being a little extreme, she may have been onto something. Gavin didn't look very healthy at all. Although he couldn't have been more than a year or two younger than Michael's twenty-seven, his light hazel eyes were sunken and surrounded by dark shadows. His messy hair and five o'clock shadow were the same dark blonde color as Kate's, but his complexion was much paler, even a little gray in comparison to her rosy glow. He looked almost like someone going through some sort of withdrawal.

"No, I'm not! Your addiction to that stuff is probably the reason you're so tired all the time. It's like being hooked on over-the-counter pain medicine. Eventually, it's going to make the problem worse."

"Says the girl who can't function without three cups of coffee every morning. Caffeine addiction is no joke, Kate," Gavin patronized.

"Fine. Drink your little energy drug. But don't come crying to me when you need a new kidney."

"Kate, do you work in medicine?" Michael asked.

"She's an interior decorator," Gavin remarked. "An overprotective, germaphobic, control-freak of an interior decorator."

"I'm *not* a control-freak. I just think you need to take better care of yourself."

4

"I do take care of myself. But we've been moving stuff since 6 AM. If I don't get some sort of energy boost, I'll be unconscious by noon."

"Well, it's 11:10 now. Guess we better get a move on."

"Do you have anyone helping you?" Michael asked.

"No. Our father's out of town and our mother has a bad back. We had a few friends come over last night and they helped us haul some of the heavier stuff down to the trailer we rented, but they all had plans today," Kate explained.

"Do you need an extra hand?"

This time, it was Kate who said, "Oh Michael, we couldn't ask that of you," while Gavin replied, "We'll pay you."

"You don't have to pay me. I don't have anything to do today. If I wasn't here, I'd be wasting the day in front of the television."

"Well, we can at least buy you lunch," Kate said. "Is Subway okay?"

Michael wasn't sure what it was about her, but he had a feeling he would have agreed to anything she offered him.

"Subway's great," he told her.

An hour later, they'd just about cleared out Gavin's truck and all three were starving. Kate and Michael assured Gavin that they could handle the last few boxes while he got ready to run to Subway and the supermarket.

Michael was making his way back down to the truck when he noticed something. A stack of laminated flashcards, hooked together on single silver ring, lay in the middle of the sidewalk. Michael stooped down and picked them up. The word *RED* was scrawled in red marker across the top card. Below that card, the word *ORANGE* in orange marker, *YELLOW* in yellow marker, and so on. Michael was so busy wondering what they were for, he barely noticed Kate approaching him.

"What's that?" she asked.

"Nothing. I think a neighbor kid must have dropped them," Michael showed them to her.

"Actually, those are mine," Kate admitted, taking the cards from him and stuffing them in her pocket. She must have seen the curious look in Michael's eye because she explained, "About a week after New Year's Eve, I was in a car accident. I hit my head pretty good and when I woke up, I couldn't remember the names of any of the colors. I still recognize them. I know that the color of a fire truck is the first color in the rainbow. I just can't for the life of me remember the names. The doctors call it Color Anomia. Ironically, I have no trouble remembering that."

"I've never even heard of that," Michael told her.

"Brain injuries are funny things," Kate replied, climbing into the back of Gavin's pick-up truck and handing Michael another box. "Anyway, that's the reason Gav and I moved in together. Our parents didn't want me living alone after my 'head trauma' and since I really didn't want to move back in with them, Gav offered to be my roommate." Kate grabbed the last box and duffel bag and jumped down next to Michael.

Once they reached the apartment, Kate dropped the box and duffel and collapsed onto the floor, right in front of the giant box fan that Gavin had set up amidst the plastic bags and cardboard boxes heaped all around the living room.

"You know what's going to be a lot of fun?" she asked, closing her eyes and savoring the blast of cool air emanating from the fan. "Dragging that couch up here."

"I'm trying not to think about that," Gavin muttered from the kitchen counter as he scribbled down a list of things to get at the grocery store. "Kate, what do you want to drink?"

"Gatorade. I need electrolytes."

"What kind?"

"This one." Kate held up her *BLUE* flashcard.

"Got it," Gavin jotted it down. "Michael, do you want some Gatorade?"

"I'll take some red, thanks," he said.

Once Gavin was gone, Michael took a seat on the floor next to Kate. She'd had the right idea, settling down in front of the fan. Even with the air on high, the apartment still felt stuffy in the mid-June Dallas heat.

"So Michael, tell me about yourself," Kate said, gazing up at him from her spot on the floor.

"Um... not sure what there is to tell," Michael replied honestly. He really wasn't a very interesting person.

"Where do you work? How long have you lived here?"

"I work inventory and shelve books at the library. Exciting, I know," he said. Kate grinned. "I've lived here for five years, ever since I graduated from college."

"Where did you go to school?"

"UNT. I majored in Interdisciplinary Studies and minored in Psychology."

"That's pretty cool," Kate told him.

"Sort of," Michael shrugged. "What about you? I know Gavin said you were an interior decorator."

"Yep. I graduated from SMU two years ago with a degree in Art and Design. Got my job as a decorator about a month later and that's what I've been doing ever since."

"Do you enjoy it?"

"Yeah, I do."

"I hope you don't mind me asking, but is it difficult? You know, with the color thing?" Kate stared at the ceiling as she contemplated her answer.

"It was pretty annoying at first, but my boss has been so wonderful about the whole situation. If she ever needs something in a specific color, she describes it to me. Like, instead of asking for a," she flipped through her note cards until she found the one labeled *GREEN*, "green vase, she asks for a grass-colored vase. It's not a perfect system, but you know, any time I start to get frustrated, I remind myself how lucky I am just to be here and that it could have been a lot, *lot* worse."

"I'm glad you're okay," Michael told her. She glanced over at him and smiled. He hoped she didn't notice the blush creeping up his neck as he cleared his throat and asked, "So uh, what about Gavin? What does he do?"

"He's actually between jobs right now. He used to work as a sound technician for one of the local theaters, but about two months after my accident, he started getting sick a lot. He never had a fever or anything, but he'd feel drained and exhausted; his head would hurt, he'd get the chills... I really thought he had mono, but for some reason, he just refused to go to the doctor. It wasn't until he got so dizzy that he fell over that he finally made an appointment."

"What was wrong with him?" Michael asked.

"Absolutely nothing," Kate replied. "They ran all sorts of tests. Blood tests, MRIs, even a lumbar puncture. He was perfectly healthy. No mono, no anemia, absolutely no physical explanation for any of his symptoms."

"So what did they do for him?"

"Since there was technically nothing wrong with him, they really couldn't prescribe him anything. They advised him to take it easy and get plenty of rest. Unfortunately, about a week later, someone broke into our apartment. Neither of us slept well after that."

"Are you serious?" Michael asked.

"Yeah. Suffice it to say, it has not been a fantastic year for the Avery family. Luckily for us, they didn't take anything. Or if they did, it was something we didn't use very often because we haven't noticed it missing."

"Why bother breaking in then?" Michael asked.

"Whoever it was, it looked like they were on some sort of rampage. The entire place was trashed. Furniture was moved, tables were knocked over, mirrors and picture frames were shattered. It was one of the scariest moments of my life, coming home and finding the apartment like that. I was convinced whoever had done it was still inside."

"Did you call the police?"

"Yeah, but they didn't find anything that could help them," Kate explained. "I just hope that whoever it was didn't target us specifically. I hope they just picked a random apartment and when they couldn't find anything of real value to steal, they decided to trash it. Gavin thinks I watch too many crime dramas, but I just have this horrible feeling that it was personal." Michael wasn't sure what to say. He was certainly no stranger to mysterious circumstances, but he'd never felt like he was being targeted. "That's one of several reasons I'm glad to be living in a gated community now." Kate looked at him. "I can't believe I told you all of that. I just met you. I should be telling you about the book I'm reading or asking you what kind of movies you like. Not dumping all my personal crises on you."

"I really don't mind," Michael told her. "But if you really want to know, I enjoy historical fiction and psychological thrillers."

"Oh! Have you seen…"

By the time Gavin returned with food and drinks, their conversation about movies had evolved into a debate over whether the Hollywood adaptation of *Shutter Island* did the novel justice. Gavin also brought with him about five bottles of Super-B Energy. Kate frowned as she watched her brother down one in a single gulp.

As they ate, Michael thought back to everything Kate had told him about the break-in, about how scared she was that whoever it had been was still out there. Although they'd never had a break-in at the Riverview Apartments, he nevertheless felt he should warn her about the strange things that happened in Building 17. He was almost certain that if someone had told her about the "curse," she'd never have signed the lease.

Then again, he had no idea how to tell her without seeming like he was trying to scare her. Besides, what if he told her and nothing happened? Then he would have scared her for nothing. No, it was probably better just to keep all of that "curse" business quiet for now.

Of course, if the last six months were any indication, Kate and Gavin Avery might have been under a curse of their own.

Once they finished eating, they decided to tackle the trailer that was hooked up to the back of Kate's Land Rover. Inside the trailer, Kate and Gavin had stashed their bed frames, mattresses, a few small tables, and a couch.

They decided to start with Kate's bed. It was the smallest and the easiest to maneuver out of the packed trailer. They didn't have too much trouble getting the frame or the twin mattress up the stairs and into her room. Gavin's bed proved to be a little more of a challenge. It took all three of them to haul the full-sized mattress up the stairs. Once they made it to the living room, Michael and Kate shoved it through the apartment while Gavin ran into his room to clear a pathway through his scattered belongings.

"Oh, it feels good in here," Kate remarked, noting the sudden drop in temperature inside Gavin's room. "Gav, where do you want this?"

"Just set it against the wall for now," Gavin answered. Michael barely heard him. His attention had fallen on the man standing in the corner of the room, clenching his fists, and staring at Gavin with murderous eyes.

Eyes that had long since looked their last.

CHAPTER TWO

He'd seen them for as long as he could remember.

They'd never scared him, really. When he was younger, he hadn't known that there was anything different about them. By the time he was old enough to figure out that no one else could see them, he was also old enough to realize that being dead didn't turn people into monsters. It just meant that most of them were lonely.

This guy scared him.

He was tall, almost as tall as Michael, who towered above most people at 6'2, and muscular, something that Michael couldn't boast. His dark hair was buzzed short, like an army crew cut, and he wore dark navy jeans, a gray T-shirt, and an old black jacket. As intimidating as his physical appearance seemed, however, nothing compared to the fury and repulsion with which he stared at Gavin Avery.

"Michael?" Kate's voice snapped Michael out of his stupor. "Are you all right?"

"Yeah, fine." He wasn't fine though. His voice had gone hoarse, the same way it always did whenever he tried to choke out a lie. He cleared his throat and assisted Kate and Gavin setting the mattress against the wall. No matter how he tried to convince himself otherwise, he could feel the stranger's eyes boring into the back of his neck. Although he didn't think the ghost had noticed him staring, he didn't want to draw any sort of attention to himself.

This was the reason he never complained about the strange noises or feelings of discontent that plagued the other residents of Building 17. He'd always been a terrible liar, and anyone observing him too carefully would realize that when he

11

said he had no explanation for the weird things that happened, he wasn't telling the truth.

Once ghosts figured out that he could see them, they followed him home. Over the years, he'd gotten better at ignoring them, tuning them out, but there was always the occasional slip-up. He'd respond to an otherwise unheard voice, or accidentally make eye contact with someone who'd grown accustomed to being invisible. That was when the trouble started.

Michael had learned the hard way that nothing good came from interfering in the affairs of the afterlife. He'd always been careful not to let anyone know what he could see, but everyone, from his classmates to his own mother knew there was something off about him. Their suspicions were somewhat confirmed after he was arrested as a suspect in a murder investigation at the beginning of his senior year of high school. The charges were quickly dropped, but still, the damage had been done.

Now, whenever spirits followed him home, he ignored them. This was frustrating for all parties involved, but especially for the ghosts. They knew he could see them, but when he didn't acknowledge them again, they grew agitated. Some of them went crazy, throwing pots and pans around or heaving books off of shelves in desperate attempts to get his attention. They usually gave up and moved out after a week or so of being ignored. But some of them, the more annoying ones, tended to linger. Some acted out of spite, some out of boredom. Some flat out refused to move on for reasons that Michael could never figure out. Maybe they were waiting for someone, or maybe they were scared of crossing over. Michael could accept that. Still, he would have preferred they not make his apartment building their halfway house.

Thinking back to everything Kate had told him about Gavin, his mysterious ailment, even the break-in, Michael knew he should have realized that those were the products of a haunting. He'd experienced the same symptoms of dizziness and exhaustion on multiple occasions. Spirits thrived on energy. It was how they moved heavy objects, or manifested themselves to those who otherwise wouldn't be able to see them. They took this energy from any source they could find; electricity, radio waves, even the living. Especially the living. Michael had always been particularly susceptible to their attacks. He had a theory that since his mind was already so open to the spirits, it made it easier for them to drain his energy.

He wasn't sure if that was what was happening or if all the physical exertion was finally catching up with him, but all of a sudden, he felt dizzy and lightheaded. He broke into a cold sweat and without warning, the ground began to tilt.

"I need to go," he announced abruptly. He concentrated all that remained of his energy on not falling over as he stumbled out of the room.

"What's wrong?" Kate asked, eyeing him with obvious concern.

"I'm sorry Kate, I'm just – I -" He took a deep breath and willed himself to stay conscious. "I really don't feel well, and I need to go. I'm so sorry." He turned to leave and in doing so, brought on such an intense wave of vertigo that he tripped over the leg of one of the bedside tables he'd helped to carry up. Everything blurred as he toppled to the ground.

"Michael!" Kate shrieked. "Oh my God, are you okay?"

"I'm fine. I'm sorry I – I just need to go." He stood much faster than he should have. Tiny white stars exploded in front of his eyes and he'd definitely twisted an ankle, but all he wanted was to get out of that apartment.

"Well, thank you for all your help!" Kate called as Michael half hobbled, half sprinted out onto the landing. As soon as he closed the door behind him, the dizziness began to subside. He leaned against the wall and took several deep breaths.

That was close.

No. That wasn't close. That wasn't even remotely close. Close would have been making it out of the apartment *before* a malevolent spirit drained him to the point of semi-consciousness. No, what had just happened had been a near bona-fide disaster. Kate and Gavin must have thought he was a complete basket-case. He was just lucky that his ankle had been the only casualty of his undignified departure.

He didn't have to wonder why the ghost had drained him so quickly. He'd obviously been thriving off of Gavin's waning energy for months. So why didn't he take Kate's energy? From what Michael could tell, she was as healthy and energetic as anyone he'd ever met. Even ghosts with a vengeance usually didn't discriminate over whose energy they used. Maybe this one had a chivalrous streak.

It wasn't unusual for ghosts to attach themselves to a specific person, either, especially if they'd known that person in life, or if their unfinished business concerned that person. Whoever this guy was, he'd known Gavin. And judging by his hostility, it hadn't been a pleasant parting.

Out of all the ghosts Michael had met in the last twenty-seven years, only about a quarter of them were unaware of their passing. He had a few theories for this. Those who died of natural causes such as disease or old age usually had a fairly good idea that death was coming for them. That gave them time to prepare, to make peace with everything that might hold them to this realm or world or whatever, so that by the time they did die, they were able to pass from one life to the next without any sort of delay.

The ones who stuck around were usually the ones whom death had claimed unexpectedly. Brink, for example. One moment he was skateboarding around his high school parking lot, the next he was gone. Unfortunately, the ones who'd lost their lives in traumatic experiences, like Brink and his skateboarding accident, were the ones who looked death square in the eye. They knew what had happened. They couldn't forget. They couldn't move on. So, they stayed, until something - or someone – could bring them peace.

The remaining few seemed oblivious to their own demise. They were the ones Michael pitied the most; those who hadn't seen death coming at all. Perhaps death had come in the form of a heart attack or maybe they'd gone to bed one night and had simply left their body behind the next morning. Whatever the reason, they were left alone, confused, and in denial. Michael often cursed himself for ignoring them, for being such a coward. But he wouldn't, he *couldn't* do anything that might make history repeat itself.

With a heavy sigh, he walked back to his own apartment and flopped down onto the couch. Brink appeared almost instantly.

"Well you were gone a long time," he remarked as he took a seat, cross-legged, on the coffee-table.

"Yeah," Michael replied shortly. Eighteen-year-old Eugene Brinkley, otherwise known as "Brink," was the only ghost besides his grandmother with whom Michael willingly communicated. They'd met while Michael was still in high school. Of course, Brink was already dead by then. It had been too depressing for him to hang around his house, and since he'd vowed to keep an eye on his younger siblings, both of whom attended the same high school, he spent most of his time there. After they graduated, he'd somewhat moved in with Michael.

Brink had died in the early 90s, and his appearance reflected it. His blond hair fell in messy bangs across his forehead and he wore baggy jeans and an unbuttoned plaid shirt that hung loosely to reveal a white undershirt.

"So what are they like?" Brink asked.

"From what I can tell, cursed." Briefly, Michael told him all about Kate, Gavin, and their seemingly relentless streak of bad luck, including their ghostly visitor.

"Wow," Brink said. "For the first time, you're not going to be responsible for all the crap that happens in this building."

"*That's* what you got out of all of this?"

"What else is there? So they're haunted. Aren't a lot of people haunted?"

"Not like this. This guy looked like he wanted to *kill* Gavin."

"So what, do you think Gavin murdered him?"

15

Michael didn't want to go that far. Gavin didn't seem like the type to kill someone. Of course, that didn't necessarily mean he wasn't capable. In fact, Michael had learned in one of his psychology classes that psychopaths often taught themselves to mimic emotion and feign charisma in order to gain trust. But Michael had spent several hours with Gavin, and although he was sociable enough, he wasn't off-the-charts charismatic.

"Whatever he did, I don't think it was good," Michael finally answered.

"Maybe he did it in self-defense," Brink suggested.

"What do you mean?"

"I mean, you said this guy looked like bad news, right? What if he attacked Gavin first? Or Kate?"

It made sense, although the more Michael thought about it, the more he realized it was only one of countless possible scenarios. The guy could have been a stalker. He could have been a former friend. Maybe Gavin stole something from him, like a girlfriend. Maybe his death was accidental and Gavin had somehow been at fault.

And where did Kate fit in? She seemed to care immensely about her brother. She obviously worried about his health. Did she have any idea he was connected to this dark spirit? Would she recognize the man if she saw a picture of him? Would the ghost eventually hurt her to get to Gavin? It was all too much to figure out in one sitting.

"I don't know," Michael finally answered. "I guess anything's possible."

16

CHAPTER THREE

"So how do you like your new apartment?" Valerie asked as she and Kate carried an intricate, antique-styled rug into the house they were helping to renovate.

"I love it," Kate replied. It really was a great apartment. Along with being incredibly spacious, it included a fireplace, a washer and dryer, and a balcony that overlooked one of the nicest pools she'd ever seen in an apartment complex. "It's very light, very open, and I get a work out every time I run up or down the stairs."

"Like you need to work out." At only twenty-nine, Valerie Banks was one of the most popular interior decorators in the Dallas/Fort Worth metroplex. A bright, spunky black woman with a flair for both fashion and interior decorating, Valerie had the incredible gift of looking at a room once and knowing exactly what to do in order to make it beautiful, romantic, festive, or whatever her client had in mind. Of all the people who'd helped her after her accident, Val had been amongst the most supportive and understanding. "And how's Gavin liking it?"

"You know him. He never tells me how he feels about anything. But I think he's pretty happy with it."

Truthfully, Kate had no idea how Gavin felt about their new apartment. After they finally finished moving in, he went straight to bed and had slept away most of Sunday. He'd awakened in time to help her finish setting everything up, but that wore him out as well. After a quick dinner, he crashed again and was still unconscious by the time she left for work that morning.

This was ridiculous. There *had* to be something wrong with him. Maybe the doctors had screwed up his blood test, or gotten his results mixed up with someone else's. Maybe they

17

should seek a second opinion. If Gavin didn't get better within the next couple of weeks, Kate was going to consult a specialist.

"Have you met any of your neighbors?" Val asked as they situated the rug across the living room's fancy tigerwood floor.

"Just one. He helped us move."

"Ooh, how gallant! What's he like? Is he cute?"

Kate laughed. Although she'd pretended not to notice, Michael was really cute. He was tall and a little lanky, but his shoulders were broad and strong. Along with big dark eyes, dark wavy hair, and a great smile, he was definitely attractive.

"Yeah, I guess so."

"You guess so? Girl, you never guess about anything. Especially cute guys."

"Yes, he's cute," Kate grinned. "Really sweet too."

"So what are you waiting for? Go get him!" Unlike Gavin and her parents who worried dating might be too stressful for her after everything that had happened, Valerie was always encouraging her to be more social.

"We just met. Besides, the way my life's been going lately, he'll probably turn out to be a Gremlin or something."

"A Gremlin?"

"It was on ABC last night."

"You watch way too much television," Val said, rising to her feet.

"That's what Gavin always says…" Kate remarked lightly. It was true though. She was hooked on so many television shows, she couldn't keep up with them all. From *Once Upon a Time* to *Criminal Minds* to *The Big Bang Theory*, she had a different show for every night of the week. Monday night was *Cemetery Tours* night, which meant Gavin would not be watching with her. He mocked her relentlessly for her addiction to the popular paranormal investigation series which he called "the biggest load of bullshit to ever disgrace primetime," but Kate found it fascinating. She'd always believed in ghosts and a lot of the evidence they captured on the show was enough to send chills

18

down her spine. Not to mention Luke Rainer, the lead investigator, was one of the most beautiful men ever pixilated on a television screen.

But mostly, she watched it for the ghosts.

"Well I think you should give this guy a chance. When was the last time you had a real date?" Valerie had a point. Since her accident, Kate had only been on two dates, both of which were total disasters. The first guy, whom she'd met through mutual friends, loved to listen to himself talk so much that she barely got two words in. The second guy, Gavin's friend Alex, had thought it charming to spend a good portion of the night setting items in front of Kate and asking her what color they were. Fortunately, she'd managed to convince him that the tears of humiliation welling in her eyes were just allergies.

Come to think of it, she hadn't had much luck with guys even before her accident. She'd only had one real boyfriend, Jeff, whom she'd dated for nine months in college. Jeff was a sweet guy, but he was clingy. He made Kate feel more like a security blanket than a person. In the end, it was more than she could handle. None of the other guys she'd dated had been more than casual flings.

"If by 'real' you mean 'enjoyable,' oh, probably seventh grade when the cutest boy in my Spanish class took me out for a Blizzard at Dairy Queen."

"You really are that pathetic, aren't you?"

"Oh yeah."

Pulling into her driveway that evening, Kate noticed a familiar figure unloading groceries from his car. Thinking fast, she grabbed her lip gloss out of her purse and dabbed a little on her lips. Then, she ran her fingers through her hair and checked her reflection in the rear-view mirror before climbing out of her car.

"Hey," she called casually over to Michael. He glanced over his shoulder and smiled.

"Oh, hi," he replied. "How are you?"

"I'm great. How about you? Do you need some help?"

"I think I've got it. But thanks," he replied, slamming his car door shut with his free hand.

"No problem," she answered. It looked like he'd recovered from whatever was ailing him on Saturday. "Are you feeling better?"

"Yeah, lots. I think I was just dehydrated."

"Well, that'll do it."

"Yeah. I'm sorry I couldn't help you with the couch."

"Don't worry about it. It was a lot easier than I thought it would be," Kate assured him. Their conversation had carried them up the stairs and to Michael's front door, where they stopped.

"Still, I wish I could have helped," he said.

"You did help. You have no idea how much you helped." She could tell her praise embarrassed him, so she changed the subject. "Hey listen, Gavin's birthday is this weekend, and we were going to have a few people over on Saturday evening to celebrate and to show off the new apartment. Would you like to come?"

She could have sworn she saw a moment of hesitation flash in his eyes before he answered, "Yeah, that sounds like fun."

"Great. We'll probably be spending most of our time down at the pool, so uh, dress accordingly." Kate tucked a strand of hair behind her ear. It had been a while since she'd asked a guy out. Well, technically she wasn't *really* asking him out. She was asking her new neighbor to come to a party. As a friend. A cute friend who looked really good in the jeans he was wearing. But still, just a friend. "Party starts around seven. But I'm sure I'll see you before then, you know, because we're neighbors..."

Okay, time to shut up and leave before you awkward him to death.

"I'll be there," he smiled.

"Great. Well, I guess I'll see you around, then. And I'm really glad you're feeling better."

"Thanks, Kate. I'll see you later."

"Bye." And with a small wave, she walked across the landing and into her apartment.

Michael spent the rest of the week trying to think of a reason not to attend Kate and Gavin's party. It shouldn't have been that hard, really. Neither Kate nor Gavin knew very much about him. He could easily tell them that his cousin was in town, or that his mother had hoped to have dinner with him that evening. He could say that he had a friend who needed a favor. The more he thought about it, however, the feebler the excuses seemed. He could have always told them that he was sick. Then again, he wasn't sure how credible that would be given his "dehydration" the weekend prior. He could just not show up, claim that he'd forgotten or that he'd had a family emergency. Still, that seemed like a pretty weak cop out.

The real problem with all of those excuses, Michael realized, was that deep down, he actually wanted to go to the party. It was the perfect opportunity to mingle, to see what else he could find out about the Avery siblings' strange and rather unfortunate past. Maybe one of their friends could tell him something that would clue him into the identity of their spectral stalker.

He'd spent all Sunday browsing the Internet, trying to find anything he could on Gavin Avery. Aside from a few high school and college cross country records however, there wasn't much. Michael had also managed to track down both Kate and Gavin on Facebook (Kate added him as a friend later that evening), but even after scrolling through all of their photographs, he couldn't find a trace of the dark young man. He remembered Kate mentioning that Gavin had fallen ill around two months after her accident. That meant that whatever had happened occurred around late February, early March. Neither of their histories, however, revealed anything more than Kate had already told him.

Of all the questions Kate had left him with, she had been right about one thing; the break-in, the attack on their old apartment, had been personal, and it would likely happen again.

Or maybe something worse. And although Michael was about ninety-eight percent certain that the spirit's anger wasn't directed at Kate, he couldn't help but worry that she might still get caught in the crossfire between the ghost and his intended target.

Truth be told, Michael could count on one hand the number of people he'd met, or even heard of, who'd been critically injured by a spirit, so there really was no reason to worry about Kate.

Yet he did. He hadn't been in the room with the ghost for two minutes and already, he was turning out to be one of the most powerful spirits Michael had ever encountered. Only a handful could acquire and retain the amount of energy it took to trash an apartment, and he'd never met one that could drain energy so quickly and efficiently. Then of course, there was the rage; the intense hatred that had resulted in the destruction of a living space and that Michael had seen reflected all too clearly in the man's dark eyes. He'd met angry spirits before, but never of that caliber.

As much as he tried to convince himself the only reason he wanted to go to the party was to find out more about the ghost, he realized that wasn't quite true. Although he'd been hoping to avoid Kate, he couldn't deny the part of him that had been wanting to see her again. He knew that he would end up going to the party just because she'd invited him, and it was for that very reason he knew he should stay away.

He'd dated a few girls in the past and had even had one almost-serious girlfriend, Natalie, but he'd ended up hurting all of them. Not because he was some smooth heartbreaker. That would have been less insulting, at least according to Natalie. As she'd put it, Michael didn't trust her enough to open up to her. It was obvious that he was keeping something from her, remaining distant and aloof instead of being honest with her. That was a lot more offensive than a guy who simply couldn't commit. He didn't want to hurt Kate the way he'd hurt Natalie. Unfortunately, if he wanted to spend more time with her, the only alternative to eventually hurting her was telling her the truth.

He wasn't sure he'd ever be ready for that.

Kate woke with a start.

It was back. That horrible sense of unease. Those hairs standing straight up on the back of her neck. The feeling that someone was standing right outside her bedroom door, listening. Waiting.

Kate had prayed that with her new apartment would come a sense of security. She hadn't slept soundly in her old apartment since the break-in. There had been several nights that she'd crept into Gavin's room and spent the night curled up in his old sleeping bag. It wasn't the most comfortable accommodation, but it was better than being alone.

Now as she sat upright, dizzy and disoriented in the darkness of her new bedroom, she fought the urge to sprint across the hall into the sanctuary of her brother's room. She couldn't say for sure what had stirred her from a dreamless sleep, but she recognized the feeling almost immediately.

Someone, or something, was in her apartment.

Her therapist had told her that it was perfectly natural for victims of break-ins to experience insomnia, nightmares, even panic attacks. Kate knew she should trust her therapist, but she couldn't help but feel that her diagnosis wasn't entirely accurate. She had no trouble falling asleep and she usually had pleasant dreams. Her problem was what woke her up in the middle of the night; the sensation that she was being watched.

And now, it had followed her here.

Gavin had told her that it was all in her head, and that if she just kept reminding herself that, then the feeling would go away. "Mind over matter," he'd always say. Kate was no stranger to the concept. Over the years, she'd mastered the art of willing away premenstrual nausea.

She couldn't will this away. She tried as hard as she could to rationalize with herself. The apartment was locked. They were on the second floor. Gavin had been there all day. *There was no one in her apartment.*

So why couldn't she shake the dreadful feeling that she wasn't alone?

A quick glance at her cell phone told her that it was almost two in the morning. She had to wake up at six-thirty. Thank God it was a Friday.

With a sigh of resignation, she lay back down and pressed the heels of her hands against her eyes. She had to at least try to get some rest. Desperate, she tried to think of something, anything, that could keep her mind off of the unnerving presence. She thought of the movie she'd watched on Netflix earlier that day. She thought of the party that she and Gavin would be hosting on Saturday. She thought of all the friends they'd invited, and how they'd react to the new apartment. She thought of Michael.

As she conjured up an image of his face, a surprising wave of serenity washed over her. Again, she felt a sense of familiarity as she pictured him. The day he'd helped them move, she'd felt so comfortable around him that she'd shared things that she hadn't even been able to share with some of her closest friends. What was it about him that made her trust him so completely? She barely even knew him.

Whatever strange influence he held over her must have been powerful, because the next thing she knew, her alarm was ringing in her ear, and she was looking around her very empty sunlit room, wondering why she'd been so afraid a few short hours earlier.

CHAPTER FOUR

By the time Michael got to the party on Saturday evening, it seemed that most of the guests had already arrived. There weren't too many people, maybe a dozen or so, and most of them seemed too preoccupied with what Kate and Gavin had done with the apartment to notice the newcomer. The apartment really did look nice, he suspected all thanks to Kate and her flair for decorating.

Gavin came to greet him first. Michael shook his hand and wished him a happy birthday and Gavin thanked him for coming and again for all his help the week prior. Although he still wasn't a shining sample of perfect health, there seemed to be a little more life in Gavin's eyes.

Before he could think too much on it, Kate appeared, looking bright and lovely in a lime green summer dress and blue sandals.

"Michael," she smiled. "I'm so glad you came."

"Thanks for inviting me. The apartment looks great."

"Thank you," she beamed. "Can I get you anything to drink? We have more than water and Gatorade now."

"I'm okay," Michael grinned.

"Well, help yourself to anything. We have a bunch of snacks and a couple of our friends are already down by the pool. In fact, the rest of us will probably head down there in a few minutes. I really only wanted people to meet up here so they could see the new apartment, but now that everyone's seen it, I'm ready to swim."

Michael was relieved. He was beginning to feel kind of dorky in his tropical-themed swim trunks and orange polo shirt.

"Well, well, who is this?" A woman decked out in a bright magenta sundress covered with tiny sequined flowers and magenta heels to match appeared next to Kate. She brought with her a cloud of perfume so thick that Michael had to hold his breath to keep from coughing.

"Val, this is our new neighbor, Michael," Kate answered. "Michael, this is my boss and very good friend, Valerie."

"Nice to meet you," Michael shook her hand and tried his best not to inhale.

"Very nice indeed," Val grinned. To Kate, she muttered very indiscreetly, "You were right, Sweetie. He is cute."

Michael was sure his cheeks were blushing as vividly as Kate's as she chuckled nervously, "Okay Val, thank you." Valerie winked and flounced off to flirt with Gavin and his friends. "So that's Val..." Kate announced, still rather pink in the cheeks.

"She seems nice," Michael replied with a sheepish smile.

"Well, she's definitely not shy," Kate responded. "And on that note, I think I'm going to start herding everyone down to the pool."

"Before we go, would you mind if I used your bathroom?" Michael asked.

"Not at all. Just pretend that it's not messy. Gavin seems to think that shoving stuff to one side of the counter is the same thing as cleaning."

Knowing that the only bathroom in the apartment connected to Gavin's bedroom, Michael slipped inside and waited until the noise and chatter died down. Once he was certain the apartment was empty, he opened the door to Gavin's room and looked around. The room was dark, but the light from the bathroom spilled through the open door just enough to illuminate every corner.

No ghost.

"Looking for something?" The voice made Michael jump. He whirled around and found himself face to face with Gavin.

"Sorry I - " Michael wracked his brain for an excuse that would explain why he'd just been caught snooping around his neighbor's bedroom. "I thought I heard something in here."

Gavin shook his head. "You and Kate."

"What about her?"

"She's always hearing strange noises. Back in our old apartment, she was convinced she'd hear someone walking around late at night."

"But you never heard anything?"

"No," Gavin replied simply. "To be honest, I think the break-in traumatized her a lot more than she likes to let on. She's always had a crazy imagination. As a kid, she would actually make imaginary friends for herself out of poster board. She'd give them names, hometowns, back stories, birthdays… you name it, she thought of it. I think now, because she imagines things so vividly, she thinks too hard about the break-in and scares herself into believing she hears someone walking around our apartment. But what do I know? I'm not a shrink."

"It sounds plausible," Michael agreed, reeling from the revelation that Kate knew, or at least suspected, that someone other than Gavin was living with her in the apartment. The real challenge was going to be working that into a conversation without sounding, well, creepy.

"I don't know. I just hope she's okay. She's been through a lot more than I have this year."

"She seems happy," Michael told him.

"Yeah," Gavin replied listlessly. "Anyway, we should probably head on down to the pool before she sends a search and rescue squad to check on us."

Down by the pool, Michael and Gavin were greeted by the tantalizing aroma of cheese, pepperoni, and sausage pizza. The sun had almost set and the sky glowed a deep shade of violet. The lights inside the pool illuminated the entire area, and someone had brought an old 1990s boom box that filled the night air with a popular country song that Michael recognized but couldn't name.

"Ugh, this song is awful," Gavin complained loudly. "Someone change it to something good."

"Hey, I love this song," Kate, who was already shoulder-deep in the clear blue water, called. "Besides, it's summer. Summer time is country music time."

"Yeah, well, it's my birthday and I say it goes," Gavin argued.

Kate's face fell into a playful pout.

"You're no fun," she quipped before she slipped beneath the restless surface of the pool.

About thirty minutes later, everyone was lounging around the pool, eating, drinking, talking, and laughing. By that point, Michael had all but forgotten that he was supposed to be on a mission to find out all he could about the ghost. *But*, he reasoned with himself, *he wasn't there this time*. Maybe Michael had been wrong all along. Maybe the ghost hadn't been waging some crazy vendetta against Gavin. Maybe it was just a random haunting and he had left them for good. Unfortunately, the rational voice in the back of his mind told him that probably wasn't the case.

As the evening progressed, Michael found himself in a small group that consisted of a very chlorinated Kate (he tried to pretend he hadn't choked on his soda when she'd first climbed out of the pool in her dark blue bikini), a girl Gavin used to work with named Toni, her girlfriend Leah, and Gavin's friend Alex, who'd annoyed Michael from the moment he decided to grace them with his presence.

"Guys, watch this," he'd announced, grinning stupidly as he took a seat on the pavement next to Michael. "Hey, Kate, what color is the pool?"

"Hilarious, Alex," Kate remarked.

"I hope you don't wonder why you go home alone," Toni told Alex, who stared at her like a deer in the headlights. Michael decided then that he liked Toni.

"So Michael, how about you? Do you have a girlfriend? Or a boyfriend?" Leah asked.

"Um, no. I'm single." He glanced over at Kate, but only for a moment. Out of the corner of his eye, however, he could swear he saw her smile.

Later on that evening, everyone gathered around a platter full of cupcakes, throughout which were placed twenty-six candles, and sang "Happy Birthday" to Gavin.

"Did you make the cupcakes?" Michael asked Kate as Gavin blew out his candles.

"Actually, Toni and Leah made them. The last time I tried to bake something, half of my senior class ended up with food poisoning."

"Yikes."

"Yeah. It wasn't pretty. Fortunately for me, I didn't eat any of it," Kate grinned. She snatched up two cupcakes and handed one to Michael. He followed her to an isolated corner of the pool, where she sat down and dangled her feet in the water. He followed suit. "I don't want to jinx anything, but I'd say the party's going well. Wouldn't you?"

"Yeah, it's been great," Michael agreed. "Though I'm not sure how I feel about your friend Alex."

"Yeah, he's um... out there," Kate remarked, glancing over at Alex, who looked like he was trying to balance a beer bottle on his head. "He's one of Gavin's old college buddies, so I kind of had to invite him."

"You know, Gavin's looking a lot better than he did last week," Michael offered.

"You think so?" Kate looked hopeful, taking a large bite out of her cupcake.

"Yeah. Yeah, he really does."

"I hope he's getting better. I don't know what I'd do if anything happened to him."

"You know, I was talking to him up in the apartment. I think he worries about you just as much as you worry about him," Michael said.

"I know. I wish he wouldn't. He doesn't need to worry about me. It's just ever since the accident, my entire family has treated me like a china doll, like the slightest thing might break me. Then of course, with Gavin being sick and the break-in, I feel like they're just waiting for me to keel over," Kate explained. "I must sound like such a hypocrite to you after the way I fussed over Gavin."

"You've both had a hard couple of months."

"Yeah. To be honest, they had it a lot worse than I did. I don't even remember the accident."

"You don't?"

"Nope. But my parents and Gavin described it to me in such excruciatingly vivid detail that I might as well remember it."

"What happened?"

"I was driving a road I drive almost every day, hit a patch of black ice, and drove straight into a tree. Totaled my car and apparently wreaked some serious havoc on the poor tree. I'm just thankful that I drove into it and not oncoming traffic."

"That wouldn't have been good. Not that your accident was good but... it's good that no one else got hurt..." Michael rambled.

"Tell me about it. I definitely wouldn't want that on my conscience," she finished her cupcake and licked the remaining frosting off her fingers. "Well I don't know about you, but I'm getting back in the pool." With that, she hopped off the edge of the pool and into the water. Michael watched as she slipped beneath the pale blue waves, only to resurface a few seconds later. "Come on," she beckoned.

"Oh, I'm not much of a swimmer," he told her.

"You don't have to be a swimmer. This water is four feet deep."

"Yeah, but it's cold."

"If you don't get in, I'm going to splash you."

"No, you won't."

He shouldn't have tested her.

With a swift flip of her hand, Kate sent a shower of chlorine water raining down on Michael, who tried unsuccessfully to shield himself from the droplets.

"Oh, you asked for it." Michael tossed his shirt aside and heaved himself into the pool. Kate grinned and dove underwater. Before Michael knew it, she was halfway across the pool.

"I was a lifeguard in college," she explained upon seeing his stunned expression.

Before long, several others joined them in the pool. At one point, Gavin ran up to his apartment and reappeared with an old, beat-up volleyball. Michael had only played volleyball once or twice, and never in a pool. His lack of experience became apparent the first time the ball was lobbed to him. He'd leapt out of the way so quickly, a casual observer might have thought he was trying to dodge a bullet. Kate, who seemed wildly amused by his flagrant fear of being hit in the face, turned out to be a regular water-volleyball pro.

"Did you play in high school?" Michael asked her after a particularly powerful serve.

"Nah. I was too artsy to be any good at sports."

"You seem pretty good to me."

"It doesn't require a lot of skill to hit a ball over a net. No offense," she grinned playfully.

"Thanks."

"Head's up!" Someone on the other side of the pool called.

Michael looked up just in time to see the ball soaring through the air. Before he could react, the ball hit its target and Kate doubled over, clutching the left side of her face.

"Kate!" Gavin yelled and thrashed his way through the water, trying to get to her.

Michael placed a hand on her shoulder as blood dribbled down her face and into the pool.

"Come on. We need to get you out of here," he said.

She nodded in reply. Gently, he took her arm and guided her over to the steps.

"Kate, are you okay?" Gavin demanded as Michael wrapped a towel around her shoulders.

"Yeah, I'm fine," she replied, sounding like she couldn't breathe through her nose.

"Do I need to call an ambulance?" Gavin asked.

"No, it's just a little nosebleed. I'm fine," she insisted, looking up at her brother. The area around her left eye was red and swollen. "See? It's already stopped."

"It's not your nose I'm concerned about."

By that point, the rest of the party had climbed out of the pool. Toni, who'd hit the ball, was beside herself, apologizing profusely.

"Don't worry about it, Toni," Kate said. "You can't play volleyball without getting pummeled at least once."

"Kate, I think we need to get you to the E.R." Gavin told her again.

"Oh my God, I'm fine. If this had happened six months ago, you'd be telling me to suck it up and put some ice on it. Which is what I'm going to do now." Clutching the towel close, Kate turned on her heel and marched up to her apartment.

Gavin heaved a frustrated sigh and rubbed his forehead.

"I'll go with her," Michael told him.

"Thanks," Gavin muttered.

By the time Michael made it up to their apartment, Kate was already standing at the kitchen sink with a wash cloth full of ice pressed to her eye.

"Hey," Michael offered. "You okay?"

"Yep," Kate answered. "Though I might look like the Phantom of the Opera in the morning."

"I don't think that will happen," Michael told her. "I'm really sorry."

"Why? It wasn't your fault."

"But I feel like I should have pushed you out of the way. Or not been distracting you."

"Again, it wasn't your fault. It's just something that happens when you play volleyball with people who've been drinking all night," Kate grinned wryly. "Besides, if you'd pushed me out of the way, then you'd have been hit and all that work you put into avoiding it earlier would have been in vain."

"Not funny," Michael told her, but he laughed nevertheless.

"Sorry. I'm sure you have a lot of potential to become a great volleyball player."

"I'm not sensing a lot of sincerity in that sentiment."

"I'll have to work on that," Kate smirked, removing the wash cloth. The swelling around her eye had gone down, but the chill of the ice had left it even redder than before.

"So, and please don't get upset, but you're sure you don't need to see a doctor?"

"I'm not dizzy, I'm not seeing double, I don't even have a headache." He must not have looked very convinced, because Kate walked over to him and placed a comforting hand on his arm. "I promise, if I feel even the slightest bit lightheaded or woozy, I will go to the doctor straight away. Okay?"

"Okay," Michael echoed softly, suddenly realizing how very alone they were in the apartment. He cleared his throat, knowing that regardless of how much he liked her, it wouldn't be a good idea to let her get any closer. She must have sensed his reluctance, because she took a few steps back and tucked a stray lock of hair behind her ear.

"Well, I guess we should get back down to the party. That is, if Gavin hasn't sent everyone home."

"Yeah," Michael agreed, cursing his cowardice for the second time that night.

Kate turned from him and walked back into the kitchen to retrieve her makeshift ice pack. Michael ran a hand through his hair, wondering if she wanted him to wait for her.

His thoughts were interrupted by the dull *thump* of what sounded like a tennis ball bouncing off a wall. Acting on instinct, Michael's eyes flew to Gavin's bedroom, where a shadowy silhouette paced anxiously back and forth across the dark room.

He was back. Michael should have known his absence was too good to be true. Fortunately, he didn't seem to realize that they were there. Or if he did, their presence was of little concern to him.

Kate, meanwhile, stared at Michael from the kitchen.

"What was that?" she asked.

"Um... I'm not sure." He hoped she couldn't tell he was lying. "Maybe some kids are playing outside."

"No. It sounded like it came from in here." She breezed past him and looked around the living room.

"You know, maybe the building's foundation is shifting. I know that can cause some uh... unexplained noises."

"Yeah, maybe." Though she didn't sound entirely convinced. Michael knew this would be the perfect opportunity to press Kate for anything she may have seen or heard, but before he could, the front door swung open and Gavin appeared.

"Everyone's gone," he announced. "How are you feeling, Kate?"

"Fine."

"You don't think you have a concussion?"

Kate just sighed. Michael took that as his cue to leave.

"I guess I'd better go and let you get some rest," he announced.

"Thanks for coming," Kate said.

"Sure. I had a good time. Happy birthday, Gavin."

"Thanks, man. Good night," Gavin replied.

"Feel better, Kate. I mean, I know you don't feel bad but... you know."

"I know," she smiled, but it seemed oddly forced. "Thanks, Michael."

"Right. Well, good night."

And with that, he stepped out into night and walked across the short landing to his apartment, away from the restless, angry spirit.

And away from Kate.

CHAPTER FIVE

Kate couldn't sleep, and for the first time in ten weeks, it wasn't because she'd been startled awake by some unresolved fear of strangers breaking into her apartment. Tonight, she was just another girl, confused and frustrated over the irrational behavior of the cute boy next door.

First, he behaves like a total gentleman, helping them move, listening to her stories, and even showing up for their party. Then, he hangs out with her all night, exchanges a cute, nervous glance with her after admitting that he was single, and takes care of her after she was hit by the volleyball. She wasn't the kind to believe that every guy who did a nice thing for her was interested in her, but Michael had seemed, well, *interested*.

That is, until she'd gotten too close. Maybe he was like Trey, the cute guy from high school who would flirt and tease until a girl expressed genuine interest in him. After that, he'd be gone so fast, you'd think someone had lit his shoes on fire.

But Michael wasn't like that. He wasn't some shameless flirt. He seemed like a nice, down-to-Earth kind of guy. Maybe he just wasn't interested in her after all. They really hadn't known each other that long. He probably hadn't meant to lead her on. She'd just mistaken his acts of friendship for something more.

She tried to tell herself that it was probably for the best, and that whenever she'd jumped into a relationship in the past, it never ended well. So why did Michael's subtle rejection leave her feeling small, embarrassed, and a little sad?

Hoping to banish Michael Sinclair from her thoughts, she crept out to the dark living room and planted herself in front of the television. Nothing was on, so she began scrolling through Netflix and eventually decided on *Cemetery Tours*. Even though the show had just wrapped up its second season, Netflix only streamed the first. Kate had already seen every episode, some more than once, but she needed a distraction. And with his handsome, angular face, devil-may-care smile, and muscular physique, she couldn't ask for a better or more beautiful distraction than Luke Rainer.

Hours later, she was stirred to consciousness by the sound of someone pacing from the kitchen to the living room and back to the kitchen again. She was lying on the couch, facing the TV. The bright glow of the Netflix menu was almost blinding in the pitch darkness of the living room. She must have slept through the entire episode.

She could hear the footsteps returning to the living room now. She froze, listening intently, hoping to pinpoint their exact location.

"Gavin?" she whispered.

No answer.

The footsteps were much too close now. Just a few feet beyond the television. This time, when they reached the living room, they stopped. Kate felt her breath catch in her throat.

Why? she longed to cry out. *Why are you following me?*

Without a second thought, she flew off the couch, right through the spot where the footsteps had stopped, and into Gavin's room. Her brother, usually a heavy sleeper, woke with a startled gasp as Kate hastily shut the door behind her.

"Kate?" he hissed through the darkness. "Are you all right? Is your head bothering you?"

"Gavin, it's here," she whispered frantically.

"What?"

"It came back. That - that *thing*."

"Kate…" She could hear the aggravation in his voice as he climbed out of bed and shuffled across the room to comfort her. "Come on, we've talked about this - "

"Gavin, I know what you're going to say. You've told me a million times. But Gav, there is *something out there*," she insisted.

Gavin sighed.

"Okay." He opened the door and meandered out into the hallway. Kate followed slowly. Gavin flipped on the light switch and looked around the empty apartment. "Anyone here?" he called. "Didn't think so." He turned weary eyes on his sister.

"Something was standing right here." She directed him to the spot where the footsteps had stopped.

"Did you see it?"

"No, but I - I heard it. Footsteps. Someone was pacing," she told him.

Gavin wandered into the living room, where the Netflix menu still wondered whether or not she was going to select another episode of *Cemetery Tours*.

"Were you watching something?" he asked.

"I couldn't sleep," she explained.

"I wonder why," Gavin remarked, staring at the screen. "You know this is what happens when you watch this crap. It gets into your head and then you start imagining things - "

"But I wasn't imagining - "

"Kate, think about it. When did all of this start? After the break-in. Look, I know how much it scared you, but you've got to understand there is no one in this apartment but us."

"What if it's something else?" she demanded.

Gavin heaved an exasperated sigh and ran a hand through his disheveled hair.

"Kate, for the last time, there is no such thing as ghosts."

"I think there is."

"Where's the proof?"

"Watch an episode of *Cemetery Tours*."

"Are you kidding? That show is bogus. There is absolutely nothing scientific about what they do."

Actually, that wasn't quite accurate. The four investigators, Luke, Gail, Peter, and JT all used state of the art technology to record the voices of spirits, to detect changes in electromagnetic energy, and to capture images of shadow figures and apparitions that might otherwise have remained unseen.

"Come on, even you said you only watch it for that frat boy, Luke Snyder," Gavin continued.

"Rainer," Kate corrected him. "And he's the reason I *started* watching. I keep watching because of all the cool stuff they capture."

"That 'cool stuff' is called special effects and CGI. I promise you I could take a video camera into any old building, shoot an hour of footage, and replicate all of their so-called evidence in about three hours."

"But it's on the Discovery Channel!"

"What does that have to do with anything?"

"The channel that brings us *Shark Week* would never condone such fraudulence."

"How is it that you can spit out a mouthful like that but you can't even remember that the sky is blue?"

Kate couldn't have felt more stricken if he'd slapped her across the face.

Gavin's eyes widened as the full impact of what he'd just said came crashing down on him. "Kate, I am so sorry. I - I wasn't thinking."

"No, it's fine. I'm just being stupid." Kate turned away so he wouldn't see the tears pooling in her eyes.

"No, Kate - "

"You know, I'm really tired. I'm just going to go to bed. I'm sorry I woke you up."

And before Gavin could say another word, Kate disappeared into her bedroom, locking the door behind her.

For someone who had spent his entire life striving to blend in, shelving books at the public library was an ideal job. Although the hours could be long and the labor strenuous, the atmosphere was quiet and serene and Michael could easily go unnoticed amongst the rows of laminated covers and faded text. Best of all, he always had more than enough to distract him from the curious whispers of wayward spirits who, every so often, wandered through the aisles. Unfortunately, nothing seemed enough to stop his mind from drifting back to his neighbors across the landing.

He hadn't seen or heard from Kate or Gavin since Saturday night, and even though he realized that was probably for the best, it bothered him. Were they all right? Had their ghostly visitor wreaked any more havoc on their lives? He hadn't a clue and he wished with all his heart that he didn't care so much. He'd never worried about any of his other neighbors, and they'd all suffered the effects of hauntings from the ghosts who'd followed him home. Of course, this time, the haunting was not only personal, it was violent.

Michael grabbed a handful of books and stepped up onto the foot stool. He was so tall, he hardly needed it to reach the top shelf. Still, it kept him from having to strain his body by stretching to place books back in their proper places.

"Man, it's so quiet in here."

Michael was so startled, he dropped the books and had to grab ahold of the shelf to keep from toppling off the stool. He whirled around to see Brink, in all his plaid, 90s-style glory, lounging against a shelf and staring at the books as though they had been hand-crafted by aliens.

"Brink, what the hell?" Michael hissed.

"Michael?" One of his coworkers, a sweet, elderly woman named Barb, appeared at the end of the aisle. Barb worked at the help desk. She'd probably heard the racket he'd made when he dropped the books. "Are you all right, dear?"

"Fine. Just lost my balance," he explained. He saw Brink smirking out of the corner of his eye.

"You weren't dizzy, were you?" Barb asked.

"No, nothing like that. I just misstepped."

"Are you sure? You look a little pale. You are eating enough, aren't you?"

Barb's abundance of concern reminded Michael of Kate and the way she worried about Gavin. He hoped he wasn't scowling as he replied, "I'm okay, Barb. Thanks."

"That was smooth," Brink remarked once Barb had returned to her desk. Michael glared at him. "What?"

"How many times have I told you not to drop in on me like that? Especially when I'm at work?"

"Hey, you might want to keep your voice down. This is a library," Brink patronized in a hushed voice.

Michael felt like punching him. Unfortunately, his fist would fly right through Brink's smug grin and into the shelf behind it.

Turning his back on his friend, he stooped down to collect the fallen books and climbed back onto the stool.

"Wait a minute. Aren't you going to ask me why I'm here?" Brink asked. Michael ignored him. "Oh, that's nice. Pretend you don't hear me. Now I know how all the other ghosts feel." Michael cast him a sidelong glance. "That's a little better. At least it's a form of acknowledgement."

"*What* do you want?" Michael whispered.

"I wanted to talk to you. You've been so engrossed in your personal melodrama that you've barely said a word to me all week."

"My what?"

"Don't pretend like you don't know what I'm talking about."

"I *don't* know what you're talking about," Michael told him, stepping down off the stool, which he collected in one hand. With the other hand, he pushed the cart full of books to be shelved down the aisle.

"You. Being all mopey since you came home from that party the other night."

"Really? You're bringing this up now?"

"Well whenever I tried to talk to you at home, you'd shrug it off and tell me everything was fine."

"Everything *is* fine."

"Right. Because it's totally normal for you to spend your weekend binge-watching the *Pride and Prejudice* miniseries."

"When did I watch *Pride and Prejudice*?" Michael asked.

40

"Sunday morning and then again on Sunday evening because, God bless A&E, they decided to show it twice." Brink scowled at his friend, as though it was his fault he'd been forced to sit through twelve hours of Austenian television. Which, in hindsight, it kind of was. But still. "You were so distracted that you didn't even realize what was on. I wanted to change the channel but you know, kinda need a body for that."

"I thought you finally got the hang of that."

"It comes and goes. Don't change the subject. What's bothering you?"

"Nothing."

"I'm going to possess the librarian if you don't tell me."

"Go ahead. I'm sure a ghost who can't figure out how to work a television will have no problem with a full-blown possession."

"That hurts, bro. But seriously, does this have to do with Cute Neighbor Girl?"

"No," Michael lied, taking a stack of books and placing them back onto the shelf.

"So you had nothing to do with that gnarly black eye she's rocking?"

"How did you - oh no. Brink, please tell me - "

"Who's he talking to?" a small voice behind him whispered.

"I don't know."

Michael turned to see two small girls staring at him from one of the kiddie tables. He averted his gaze and pushed his cart around a corner and out of their line of vision.

"See? This is why I tell you not to bother me at work."

"Oh, like anyone will believe what those kids have to say."

"Brink. Did you spy on Kate and Gavin?"

"Yes," Brink answered shamelessly. "What's the big deal? I spy on all our neighbors."

"Well... don't."

"Why not? They can't see me. Besides, how is spying any worse than spending God knows how long Googling her?" He had a point. Not that Michael would ever admit it.

"That was different."

"Right," Brink deadpanned. "Well in that case, I guess I'll just go. I was going to tell you that she seems just as miserable as you are and maybe you should call her or something, but I'm sure you don't want to hear it. You know, since spying is so wrong and everything."

"Wait a minute." Michael turned to look at his friend.

"Yes?" Brink smirked.

Michael knew he was playing right into his hand, but for once, he didn't care.

"You think she's upset because of me?" he asked. Brink nodded. "Why?"

"Let's review, shall we? Cute girl next door invites you to a party. Although you don't want to admit it, you like this girl, so you go to the party like the sucker you are. There, you inevitably make a fool of yourself, accidentally give her a black eye, and knowing you, run off in order to avoid any sort of confrontation that might involve actual feelings. On top of all of that, you make no attempt whatsoever to contact her in the days that follow. That's a lot of mixed signals on your end, especially if she likes you too."

Brink had tried to offer Michael dating advice in the past, but it was usually something juvenile like, "Pretend you're not really into her. Chicks love that." He was also usually wrong. This time, however, he sort of made sense.

"You think I hurt her feelings?" Michael asked.

"I think you're afraid of getting close to people and because of that, yeah, you end up hurting them. Especially when they have no idea *why* you're pushing them away."

"But it's for the best," Michael argued.

"For them or for you?" Brink asked. "I think you underestimate people. I mean, yeah, if you'd come up to me while I was alive and told me you could talk to ghosts, I'd have thought you were a little crazy. But if you could prove it, man, I'd have thought that was just so cool."

"You still think that your cartilage piercing is cool," Michael countered.

"It's not my fault you can't appreciate my sublime fashion sense. I'm just trying to help you out. You know, you might not have the greatest people skills and your hair could use a trim, but you're a good guy. You deserve some happiness. You just need to learn to trust."

Michael was fully prepared to argue that trust wasn't the issue when Barb poked her head around the corner of the shelf.

"Michael dear, after you've finished, I need you to fetch a box or two from downstairs," she told him.

"Okay," Michael replied.

Barb smiled at him and shuffled back to the help desk.

Michael glanced back to where Brink had been standing, only to be met with shelves of dusty books. His friend was nowhere to be seen.

CHAPTER SIX

It was only Wednesday, but the way the week was dragging, Kate felt she should already be well into the following Monday. Work wasn't going well. Their most recent client, a woman who had hired Val and her team to decorate her house for an anniversary party, was an absolute pain. Her requests for her house had been very specific, but after Val, Kate, and a few other members of the team had spent a substantial amount of time and money meeting her numerous demands, she'd changed her mind and refused to pay Val extra for her troubles or the wasted materials.

On top of that, Gavin's health had been steadily declining ever since Friday night. Kate blamed herself. If the party hadn't been overexertion, then her waking him up in the middle of the night so he could investigate some imaginary presence had certainly done the trick. They'd spent Sunday afternoon with their parents, but Gavin had been so ill and exhausted that Kate hadn't seen much of him since.

With all of that on her plate, she shouldn't have had the time or energy to think about how Michael had made no attempt to contact her at all. She told herself that she was being irrational, that she had no reason to expect him to contact her. It wasn't like they were dating or anything, but she hoped he at least considered her a friend. And wouldn't a friend have texted her to ask how she was feeling after being pummeled by a volleyball?

Feeling drained and bitter, she pulled into her driveway and turned off her car. She probably should have gone to the grocery store, but she simply wasn't in the mood. Climbing out of her car, she was so wrapped up in her own thoughts that she almost missed the young woman storming out of the apartment directly below hers.

"I don't care, Billy! I'm telling you, I've had it with this apartment!" With that, she slammed the door behind her and began rummaging through her purse. She pulled out her sunglasses and turned her eyes forward. Only then, did she notice Kate. "Oh, hello."

"Hi," Kate replied, feeling awkward for having been caught eavesdropping.

"You don't look familiar. Did you just move in?"

"Yeah. About two weeks ago."

"Well, do yourself a favor and *don't* renew your lease. I've only lived here for four months and let me tell you, it's been a nightmare."

"What's wrong with it?"

"You haven't noticed?" Kate shook her head. "Well I guess you really haven't been here that long. I suppose you work during the day?"

"Yes. But my brother's taking some time off, so he's been here."

"Well, he must be pretty unobservant if he hasn't said anything to you. This building is cursed."

"Cursed? How so?"

"I have not lived here one day where something hasn't gone wrong. The lights flicker, the thermostat never works, I have problems with my television, and now, I'm getting absolutely no cell phone reception." Kate was surprised. She hadn't encountered any such problems.

"Have you reported all of this to management?"

"Of course, but every time they come by to inspect, they tell us that there's nothing wrong."

Sounds familiar, Kate mused. She may not have had the technical difficulties her new neighbor described, but something was definitely not right with Gavin. Of course, that had been going on since before they'd even discovered the Riverview Apartment Complex.

45

"What do you think it could be?"

"I told you. The building is cursed. Neighbors across the hall warned us before we moved in and we didn't listen. And you know, it's more than just the technical stuff."

"What do you mean?"

"Strange things happen here," the woman told her in a hushed voice, almost like she was trying to avoid being overheard. "Objects will disappear and turn up days later in places you'd never think to look. Just last week I thought I'd misplaced my curling iron. I found it inside our china cabinet. Or you'll hear noises, unexplained things like someone tapping on walls even though you're alone in the apartment, or footsteps pacing around an empty room." As she spoke, Kate felt shivers run down her spine. "You've heard them, haven't you?"

"I thought I was just imagining them," Kate confessed. "My brother thinks I'm crazy. We even had a fight about it."

"My husband has heard them, but he doesn't want to believe it. Men are kind of funny about things that can't be rationally explained. It makes their feeble little minds short circuit."

Kate laughed.

"I guess that's why Michael never said anything about the building being cursed."

"Who?" the woman asked.

"Michael Sinclair. He lives across the hall from me in 1723."

The woman's eyes widened with surprise. "You actually talked to him?"

"Yeah. He's a really nice guy."

"He didn't seem... *off* to you?"

Off? Kate wondered. Perhaps in the sense that one minute, he acted like he liked her and the next, he was out the door. But he'd never struck her as strange.

"No. Not at all," she replied. "Why do you ask?"

The woman shrugged.

"I don't know. He's always sort of kept to himself. And, well..."

"What?"

"Look, I know he's your friend, but there have been rumors about him."

Kate's mind spun with curiosity.

"Like what?" she asked.

"Like he may be behind the strange things that happen in this building."

"Michael?" Kate asked. "How? That's impossible."

"Well, according to Mrs. Riggs, out of all the tenants in this building, he's the only one who never reports anything suspicious."

"And because of that, she thinks he's the cause of it?"

"It's not just that. The building wasn't always cursed. Apparently, all of this started about five years ago, right after he moved in."

"It just doesn't make sense," Kate said, glancing upstairs at Michael's front door. "Michael's just a nice, normal guy. How could he be responsible for power failures?"

"I don't know. All I do know is that I am out of here as soon as our lease is up. And I'd encourage you to do the same, uh..."

"Kate." She held out her hand, feeling foolish for not introducing herself sooner.

"Elise," her neighbor replied, shaking her hand. "I'm sorry we didn't meet under more positive circumstances."

"That's all right. It fits right into the theme of how this week is going so far," Kate replied dryly.

Elise actually grinned.

"Well, I wish you luck. I'm off to gripe at management, yet again."

"In that case, good luck to you too."

"And listen, I'm not trying to ruin your friendship or tell you what to do, but be careful around that guy upstairs. He's probably nice and normal like you say, but better safe than sorry," Elise advised.

"Thanks. I'll keep that in mind," Kate answered half-heartedly as Elise turned her heel and walked briskly in the direction of the complex offices. Kate, on the other hand, began her trek upstairs to her apartment.

She didn't want to believe anything negative she'd heard about Michael. Then again, the more she thought about it, the more she realized how little she actually knew about him. He hadn't told her anything about his personal life, claiming that there wasn't much to tell. But even if he was a little socially awkward, how could he possibly be responsible for all the things Elise had mentioned? The mysterious footsteps for instance.

It was comforting to know that someone else had heard them too. It should have been even more comforting to know that whatever was up in her apartment had come with the building.

Except it hadn't. Not in their case, anyway. The building might have been cursed, but whatever was with them in that apartment had followed them there. And Kate had a horrible feeling that it intended to stay.

"So Kate, listen, I was wondering... Kate, hi. Your face looks a lot better... Hey, sorry I haven't called. It's been hectic at... the library..." As lame as the words sounded inside his head, it was nothing compared to how pathetic they all sounded out loud. Now, as Michael climbed the stairs to his and Kate's apartments, he had no idea what he was supposed to say. He still wasn't completely sold on the idea of speaking to her at all, really.

He had spent the whole of the afternoon thinking about what Brink had said and misplacing books on the shelves as a result. He'd had to go back and check to make sure they were all catalogued properly at least half a dozen times. It was true that he'd been a little distracted ever since the night of Gavin's birthday party. Well technically, ever since Kate and Gavin moved in across the hall, but he wouldn't say he'd been moping. The entire situation was more confusing to him than anything. Why couldn't he just get Kate Avery out of his head?

Because, Brink's voice answered inside his mind, *you like her. No matter how much you want to deny it.*

It was true. He'd love to be able to say he didn't have feelings for Kate, that she was just another neighbor to him, friendly in passing, but not much more. But he did, and she wasn't. She was bright, funny, understanding, and compassionate, if perhaps a little overprotective. It was hard to imagine anyone not liking her.

Maybe that's why the ghost has been hanging around them so long, he thought with a wry grin as he crossed the landing to her apartment.

Still unsure of what he was going to say, he took a deep breath and knocked on the door. He stood there for what seemed like a century, tapping his fingers nervously against his leg. Finally, he heard footsteps approaching the front door. Seconds later, the latch on the lock clicked and the door creaked open.

Maybe it was because he was nervous, or because he was finally willing to acknowledge his feelings, but somehow, Kate looked prettier than he remembered, even in spite of the slight bruising that lingered where the volleyball had struck her. Her hair was pulled up in a loose bun with a few stray strands falling into her eyes and she was dressed in a white blouse and yellow skirt. Her eyes, however, seemed more reserved than usual. Maybe she'd had a long week, too.

"Uh, hey," Michael offered. "How's it going?"

"Okay," she replied, sounding like she wondered if he'd really shown up just to make small talk. "How's it going with you?"

"Um, not bad. Life at the library is, you know, kind of hectic." *Stupid!* he scolded himself. Kate didn't seem to notice.

"Yeah, we've been pretty busy too." Her answer was casual enough, but Michael knew he wasn't imagining the distance in her voice. Maybe Brink was right. Maybe he had hurt her feelings.

"Well listen, if you're not doing anything, and um, if you want to, I was wondering if you wanted to go out tonight? Maybe get something to eat?" God, he *really* needed lessons on how to talk to girls.

"Oh, Michael, that sounds like fun, but I probably need to stay in tonight. Val has me perusing the Internet for some fancy antique candelabra for our newest client. Maybe some other time?"

Michael wasn't sure if she meant it or not. She sounded sincere, but he had dated enough to know that *maybe some other time* often translated to *thanks, but no thanks.*

"Yeah, absolutely," Michael told her, trying his best to sound nonchalant. "Well uh, good luck tonight."

"Thanks. I'll need it," Kate replied with a small smile. "Bye."

"Bye," Michael murmured as Kate shut the door. Feeling like a total idiot, he turned and walked back to his own apartment.

"Who was at the door?" Gavin asked, emerging from his bedroom with tousled hair and dark circles under his eyes.

"Michael," Kate replied without tearing her eyes away from her laptop. It was somewhat true what she'd told him. She really did plan on spending the rest of the evening doing research on the Internet. However, it had nothing to do with Valerie or their fickle client and her stupid antiques.

Meanwhile, Gavin meandered into the kitchen and pulled the milk out of the refrigerator.

"What did he want?" he asked, taking a long swig straight out of the carton.

"How many times have I asked you *not* to do that? It's disgusting," Kate griped. Gavin ignored her and took another drink. Kate rolled her eyes and turned her attention back to her computer.

"So, you're not gonna answer my question?" Gavin asked.

"What question?"

"What did Michael want?"

"Oh, that. He was just wondering how we were doing." It was, of course, just her luck that the guy she'd been thinking about all week would ask her out the day she discovers everyone else in the building believes he's somehow linked to all the creepy things that happen there.

If it had just been Elise, that would be one thing. Kate could easily overlook the suspicions of one person who, to be honest, had seemed a little frazzled. Even her hair, the same color as the Weasley kids' in the *Harry Potter* movies, stuck out in odd angles, like she'd run her hands through it one too many times. Probably out of frustration.

But it wasn't just Elise. Thirty minutes of Googling had disclosed dozens of reports and news articles about the "curse" of the Riverview Apartments' Building 17. Most of the reports were the articles only found on local news sites, the kind that are normally read by a grand total of ten people, if that. But they told her what she needed to know. Nearly everyone who had lived in the building had, at one point, complained of technical difficulties, unexplained noises, and even some mysterious ailments. Mrs. Riggs had been quoted in a few, each time disputing claims of a curse.

"There is not, nor has there ever been, anything malicious or dangerous about Building 17. Here at Riverview, we believe in putting our residents first and we'd never rent out an apartment that we believed to be anything less than suitable for comfortable habitation."

Reading her words, Kate couldn't help but recall the enthusiasm with which Mrs. Riggs had presented the apartment. She recalled thinking that the old woman had been a little overambitious in her attempt to convince them that apartment #1724 was the home they'd been searching for. She'd even offered them a discount on rent. It wasn't the nicest apartment they'd visited, but it was the best deal they could find. In the end, that was why they'd chosen Riverview. Now it all seemed incredibly suspicious.

51

"So what, you didn't invite him in or anything?" Gavin asked. "I thought you liked him."

"I do. But I'm busy and you've been sick so I figured it was best for everyone involved to just have a low-key kind of night."

"We have low-key kind of nights every night. And weren't you complaining just the other day about your lack of social life?"

"I wasn't complaining, I was commenting." That was bull. She'd totally been complaining. But at the time, it seemed justified. Most of her friends were either engaged or married and the ones who weren't worked more than she did. Yeah, she'd had fun at the party last week, but the one guy she'd really looked forward to getting to know had since decided to ignore her. Well, until today anyway.

"Right," Gavin remarked and sat down next to her on the couch. "Wait, the TV's not on? Are you feeling okay?" he asked and pressed a cold hand against her forehead.

She swatted him away.

"Stop."

"Is something bothering you, Kate?"

"Yeah, you."

"I'm serious. What's on your mind?"

Kate hesitated. She desperately wanted to talk to someone about her encounter with Elise and what she'd learned about the building's strange history. However, knowing how Gavin would react, she may have been better off keeping her thoughts and ponderings to herself.

"It's nothing really," she began, choosing her words slowly and carefully. "I was just talking to our downstairs neighbor earlier this afternoon. It turns out that she and a lot of other people who've lived here... think that this building is cursed."

Gavin stared at her for what seemed like a full minute.

I knew I shouldn't have told him.

"Cursed how?" he finally asked. She wished he could ask the question without sounding like he was humoring her.

"Well, for Elise, it's mostly been technical stuff and strange noises. But a lot of other people have had problems with things going missing, temperature fluctuations… One lady even said that they couldn't have friends over because every time she had a guest, they'd end up getting sick. But she never got sick."

"Kate, you're not seriously trying to tell me you believe in curses now."

"Everyone else who's lived here certainly seems to," Kate argued.

"So what, because a few people had problems with their lights, you actually believe there's a curse on this building?"

"I don't know what to think, Gavin!" Kate snapped, surprised by how irritated she suddenly felt. "All I know is that strange things have been happening for months now and I for one would love to know why! Maybe you don't care why you're sick all the time, but I do, and right now, I will take any explanation that I can get!" Kate closed her eyes and pressed the heel of her palm against her forehead.

"Kate, I'm sorry. Is your head okay?"

"My head is fine. I'm just frustrated," she muttered. "I want to know why you can't get better. I mean, even having a theory would be better than no clue at all."

"Yeah, but a theory that can't possibly be proven is just as useless as no clue at all. Come on, Kate, you're smart… ish. Smart enough to at least know that there is no such thing as curses."

Kate knew he was trying to lighten things up, but she wasn't in the mood to joke around. Instead, she ignored him and resumed her Internet browsing.

Gavin, realizing she wasn't going to meet him halfway, sighed and said, "I'm going to heat up that leftover Chinese for dinner. You want any?"

"No," Kate replied.

"Right, I forgot. You don't eat leftovers."

Kate glared at him as he stood and made his way into the kitchen.

An hour later, she was about ready to give up the search. She really wasn't finding anything that she hadn't already read. In fact, she was beginning to read the same articles over and over again. It was interesting, but unfortunately, she hadn't found any sort of answers or closure. If anything, she felt more confused.

As she was about to exit out of the browser, however, one of the page's recommended articles caught her eye.

Riverview Specter: Local Woman Reports Encounter with Full Bodied Apparition Residing Inside "Cursed" Apartment.

Kate could feel her curiosity spiking as she clicked on the link. It opened to reveal a short article a lot like the ones she'd read earlier.

Mrs. Marjorie Hampton of Dallas didn't believe in the supernatural before she moved to the Riverview Apartment Complex, located in North Dallas. However, a meeting with a ghostly entity quickly changed her mind.

"I was in the kitchen making dinner for my two boys when suddenly, I heard a noise, like someone banging on the wall, coming from my bedroom. At first, I thought it was the boys, but then I noticed that they were both in the living room, glued to the television. I heard the noise again, so I grabbed a steak knife from the kitchen and went to investigate. I flipped on the light in the bedroom and that's when I saw her. She was standing in the middle of the room, staring straight at me. She opened her mouth like she was going to say something, but then she just vanished."

Mrs. Hampton moved her family out of the apartment later that week, though she continued to pay rent up until her lease expired.

"I didn't want bad credit," she says.

Building 17 of the Riverview Apartment complex is notorious for the "curse" which residents claim is the cause of a variety of technical problems and unexplained illnesses associated with the building. However, the current tenants of Mrs. Hampton's old apartment have reported no such difficulties.

Kate's mind was reeling.

"I knew it," she spoke mostly to herself.

"Knew what?" Gavin asked, sounding remarkably uninterested.

"This! This article! Look. This lady said she saw an apparition here in this building." Kate leapt up off the couch and carried her laptop over to the kitchen table where Gavin sat with his own computer.

"A what?"

"You were right. It's not a curse. It's a haunting! I *told* you!"

"Kate, are you *serious*?" Gavin groaned. "I thought we talked about this."

"But it makes sense! On *Cemetery Tours*, they always talk about - "

"Please, do *not* start quoting that crap to me. If you want to convince me of anything, those clowns are the last people you should be referencing."

"But they talk about how ghosts use energy in order to manifest and to make noises and stuff. That would explain everything! It would even explain why you've been sick for so long."

"You think a ghost is making me sick?" Gavin deadpanned.

"Well, the doctors can't seem to come up with anything else."

"Kate. This is the last time I am going to have this conversation with you. There are no ghosts. There are no curses."

"You don't know that!"

"*Everyone* knows that!"

"Why are you getting so defensive?" Kate demanded. "You never used to get this upset before. And I came to you with some pretty ridiculous stuff."

"Because the last time you were this fixated on something, you were nine years old! You're an adult now, Kate."

"I know that."

"Well you sure as hell don't act like it."

For a split second, Kate wanted to hit him, but she knew that wouldn't do either of them any good. Gavin must have seen how angry he'd made her because he sighed and held his hands up in mock defense.

"Okay, you want to settle this?" He cupped his hands around his mouth and called out in a loud voice, "If there are any ghosts in this apartment, we are asking you to show yourself. Give us some sort of sign. Rattle the windows. Open the cupboards. Anything will do."

They stood in silence for a few seconds. Kate strained her ears for a creak, a footstep, anything. But there was nothing. Gavin rested his hands on his hips.

"Well, look at that. Guess there's no one here after all."

Unable to stomach the condescending smirk on her brother's face, Kate closed her laptop and retreated into the bathroom for a long, hot shower. Maybe if she was lucky, Gavin would get abducted by aliens before she finished drying her hair.

CHAPTER SEVEN

The next week was the Fourth of July. It fell on a Thursday, so Michael decided to take Wednesday and Friday off as well so he could spend the Fourth with his family. Every year, his mother and all his aunts, uncles, and cousins gathered at his grandmother's lake house up at Lake Texoma. His grandmother had passed away nearly ten years earlier, but per her request, they'd kept the lake house in the family. She'd told Michael about a year or so after her death that it was because she couldn't stand the thought of anyone else living there.

Wednesday morning, he woke up early, packed a small suitcase that would last him two nights, and then, after locking his apartment, made his way down the stairs. He tried not to look at Kate's door as he passed, but he still saw it out of the corner of his eye. He hadn't seen nor heard from her since he'd tried to ask her to dinner the week before. Brink had offered to spy on her again, but Michael had told him not to. Of course, that didn't necessarily mean that it hadn't happened.

As he loaded his bag into the back seat of his car, he heard a door slam from up above. He glanced around and was stunned to see Kate, capering down the stairs, wearing a yellow swimsuit coverup and carrying a towel, a bottle of water, and a book. She had her hair tied up in a ponytail that bounced against the back of her neck as she descended.

Before Michael had the chance to duck inside his car, she looked up and stopped dead in her tracks.

"Hey," Michael offered tentatively.

"Hey," she echoed and tucked a loose lock of hair behind her ear. "How are you?"

"Not bad."

"Are things at the library still hectic?" she grinned.

Michael smiled too. He was glad to have her teasing him again.

"Yeah, sort of," he replied. "How about you? How's your job?"

"As of right now, I don't really have one. The lady who had hired us for the next week decided on Monday that we were incompetent and we didn't have enough respect for her vision, so she let us go."

"She sounds like fun."

"Oh, you have no idea," Kate told him. "I guess it all worked out for the best. If she'd kept us, I would have had to work today and Friday. Now, I get the whole week off."

"Do you have any plans for the Fourth?"

"Just watching fireworks. We'll probably have hamburgers or something beforehand."

"Sounds good."

"How about you?"

"My family has a lake house up on Lake Texoma, so I'm going to spend today and tomorrow there. But I'll be home on Friday morning." As soon as the words were out of his mouth, he realized it sounded like he was assuring her that he'd be home soon, as though she were concerned that he wouldn't be. Why did he always have to sound like such an idiot?

Fortunately, she didn't seem to notice, or if she had, she politely overlooked it.

"I'm so jealous. I love lakes."

"I'm not a fan," Michael admitted without thinking. For reasons he didn't want to think about, lakes were usually crawling with restless spirits. The only ghost he didn't mind was his grandmother, who preferred to spend all of her time sitting on her old porch swing and watching the sun rise and set and rise again over the water.

"Really? But there's so much to do. Swimming and kayaking and fishing..."

Michael shrugged. "Lakes are dirty."

"Whatever," Kate said flippantly. "Hey listen, I'm sorry I was kind of distant last week. I've had a lot on my mind."

"Oh no, I completely understand. I've... had stuff on my mind too," he added lamely. "Everything's okay, isn't it? I mean, is Gavin all right?"

"I don't know," Kate sighed. "He says he's feeling better, and he does have days where he seems it, but he's basically been on a downward spiral since his birthday party. I'm not even sure he should go to see the fireworks, but I know how much he wants to. And he's been cooped up for so long. He really needs to get out."

Michael had never considered himself particularly astute, but he couldn't help but feel there was something she wasn't telling him.

"Are *you* okay? I mean, it sounds like you've been under a lot of stress."

Kate shrugged. "I'm worried about Gavin, but that's nothing new. I haven't really been sleeping well, but I think it's because I'm still getting used to the apartment."

"Are you still liking it here?"

"Yeah. The apartment's great." Again, her answer sounded vague.

"What is it?" Michael asked, hoping he wasn't pushing her too far.

She averted eye contact, like she was trying to decide whether or not to confide in him. Finally, she looked up.

"If I ask you something, will you promise not to think I'm crazy?"

"No - I mean yes! I - I mean," he fumbled pathetically, "I mean I'd never think you were crazy."

Smooth.

Thankfully, Kate didn't seem at all fazed by his less-than-stellar people skills as she looked him in the eye and asked, "Do you believe in ghosts?"

Michael had been anticipating a variety of strange questions, but for some reason, he hadn't been expecting that.

Rather than lie on the spot as he normally would have done, he froze up like a puddle in a snowstorm and felt all the blood drain from his face. While he wracked his brain for an appropriate response, a new voice, loud and irksome, broke the silence.

"Of course he believes in ghosts! Doesn't everybody?"

"Oh no..." Michael muttered as a man wearing dark denim jeans, a black T-shirt, and an arrogant smirk sauntered over to them. Everything about him screamed "obnoxious," from his preppy, dirty blond hair that made him look like he was getting ready for a seventh-grade dance to his stupid green Converse sneakers that were probably at least ten years old by now.

"How are you doing, Mikey?" he asked.

Before Michael could tell him to get lost, Kate made a strange noise that sounded like a small dog with an upset stomach and dropped everything she was holding.

"Oh my *God*, you're Luke Rainer!" she exclaimed, her voice about ten pitches higher than it normally was.

Michael stared at her in horror. Luke, on the other hand, heaved a sigh dripping with false modesty and self satisfaction.

"Guilty," he replied. Then, with a smug grin, he took her hand and kissed it. She squealed. Luke turned to Michael. "She's cute. I like her."

Michael scowled at him. Of all the times he could come barging back into his life, of course Luke Rainer would choose to show up *just* as he was trying to make things right with Kate.

"What do you want?" Michael asked.

"I'm back in town for the Fourth and I thought that while I was here, I'd drop in and say hi to my buddy," Luke answered.

"Super," Michael remarked lightly.

Kate, on the other hand, gaped at him with wide, starstruck eyes.

"You're friends with *Luke Rainer*?!"

"'Friends' is such a strong word..."

"How could you not tell me?!" she demanded.

"Because I didn't think you'd know or care who he was!"

"Oh Mikey, how you underestimate my extensive fan base," Luke said, clapping a hand onto his shoulder.

"Right, because ghost hunting shows are so mainstream, I should assume every pretty girl I meet has a secret shrine to you hidden away in her closet."

"Uh-oh, sounds like someone's a little jealous," Luke remarked in an irritating sing-song voice before turning his attention back to Kate. "So what's your name, Lovely?"

"Kate. Kate Avery. And I love your show. I watch it all the time. You are just so wonderful," she rambled, batting her eyelashes and gazing up at Luke like he was some sort of celestial being.

"Thank you, Sweetheart," Luke smiled, basking in her flattery. "It's all because of fans like you that we're able to do what we do."

Michael rolled his eyes. How did anyone take him seriously?

"You know, I actually died once," Kate told him, looking oddly proud.

That caught Michael's attention.

"Is that so?" Luke asked.

"You never told me that," Michael said.

"I didn't think it would impress *you*," she replied.

"Was it after your car accident?"

"Yep. Flatlined for four minutes before they revived me."

"And did you have an experience? With the afterlife?" Luke asked.

"I think I did, but it's pretty blurry," Kate said. "They pumped me full of so many drugs, I don't have too many solid memories. My brother's convinced my brain will never be the same."

"I don't know what he's talking about. Your brain seems just fine to me," Luke smiled.

Kate looked positively elated.

"This is just so cool. I can't believe you're here," she gushed. "Will you sign my book?"

"Oh God, you bought his *book*?" Michael groaned.

After the wild success of his stupid show, Luke Rainer had penned a memoir of his lifelong obsession with all things paranormal. Like the show, the book had been well-received by women between the ages of fifteen and fifty-five. By the critics, not so much.

"Of course I will. It'd be my pleasure," Luke responded with a cheeky grin. "You know Mikey, I'm proud of you. It's about time you found a girl. Especially one with such good taste."

"Well actually - "

"We're not dating," Kate interrupted him.

Luke raised an eyebrow.

"No?" he asked, eyeing her with renewed interest.

"No. I am very single," she replied emphatically.

Michael watched, incredulous. How could a smart, level-headed woman like Kate be reduced to a silly, fawning fangirl by an arrogant tool like Luke Rainer?

"Well lucky me," Luke winked.

Kate looked like she was about to faint.

"Okay, well, it's been fun, but you need to go," Michael blurted before he could stop himself.

"Going somewhere?" Luke asked, observing the suitcase in Michael's backseat and showing no intention of departing.

"As a matter of fact, yes, and I need to leave soon, so there's really no reason for you to stick around."

"*Au contraire*, I think I've found a perfectly good reason to stick around," Luke glanced back at Kate. "What do you say, Gorgeous? Are you doing anything today?"

"My schedule is completely open," she answered breathlessly.

"What do you say to dinner? I know a great Italian place downtown. Very expensive, of course."

Michael clenched his jaw. *Please say no, please say no, please say no.*

"I'd love to!" Kate beamed.

"Great. I'll swing by and get you around 7:30? Does that sound good?"

"It sounds perfect!"

"Excellent. Why don't I give you my number and you can text me yours? My phone is charging back at my folks' place."

Michael knew Luke had grown up in Dallas and that his parents still lived there, but he hadn't known that was where Luke stayed when he came back to visit. It made him feel slightly better about Kate's impending date with him… but not much.

"Sure! Let me run and get mine. I left it up in the apartment." Without bothering to collect her fallen towel, book, or water bottle, Kate dashed upstairs and across the landing, leaving Michael alone with Luke.

"She's something, isn't she?" Luke asked. "What was her name? Kaylee?"

Michael felt his usually mild temper flare.

"It's Kate," he snapped. "Why are you doing this?"

"She's a pretty girl. I haven't been on a date in a while. Plus, I know you want her so that's like a bonus." For the second time that morning, Michael was rendered speechless. This time, however, it was out of anger rather than surprise. "You really can't blame me. Knowing you, you probably haven't even asked her on a date. You can't take girls like her for granted. You've got to let them know you want them. Otherwise, someone else is going to swoop in."

Michael wanted to tell him that the last thing he wanted or needed was dating advice from a guy whose last girlfriend was Teresa Von Lock, the lead singer of the gothic rock band The Necromantics and known by her fans as The Queen of the Dead. However, a door slamming somewhere above them distracted him. Seconds later, Kate came bounding down the stairs.

"Here it is," she announced and handed her cell phone to Luke.

"Thank you, Sweetheart." Luke took the phone and punched his number in. "Text me."

"Oh, I will," she smiled.

"Well, I guess I'd better be off. Have a bit of editing to do for my new project. But I will definitely see you tonight," he promised Kate as he turned to leave. "Have a good trip, Mikey."

"Bite me," Michael muttered under his breath.

"Bye, Luke! See you tonight!" Kate waved. Once he'd disappeared, she turned to Michael. "Oh my God, I can't believe I just met Luke Rainer! How do you know him?"

"We met a few years ago. He came around wanting to film because... well..."

"Because of the curse?" Kate asked.

"You heard?"

"Our downstairs neighbor mentioned it to me. Do you believe in it?"

"Um, I'm not sure," Michael answered carefully. "Anyway, that's how I know him."

There was a little more to it than that. The truth was that Luke had shown up one day, about a year and a half before the Discovery Channel picked up his series, asking about the building. He'd heard all the stories about the "curse" of the Riverview Apartment Complex, and being the young, enthusiastic paranormal investigator that he was, he decided to check it out.

When he'd first come knocking on his door, Michael knew he couldn't turn down Luke's request to set up a night vision camera and three digital recorders without raising suspicion. The next morning should have been the last time Michael ever saw him. Unfortunately, Luke was so eager to set up his equipment downstairs where a woman had reported hearing mysterious voices singing in her bathroom that he'd forgotten one of his digital recorders. By the time he returned for it, it had already captured an extensive conversation between Michael and Brink. To the untrained ear, it almost sounded like Michael was talking to himself. Luke however, had been able to decipher Brink's voice through the static.

Michael held on to his claim that he was on the telephone and that any voice Luke may have heard must have been recorded through the earpiece, but Luke simply didn't buy it. He knew what he'd heard and he wouldn't rest until Michael admitted not only that he'd been talking to a ghost, but that the ghost was talking back, and Michael could hear every word he said.

The only person in the world to know Michael's secret, and it had to be Luke Rainer, ghost hunter, reality television star, and douchebag extraordinaire. He'd tried everything from begging to bribery to get Michael to join the *Cemetery Tours* team. Why? Michael hadn't a clue. Luke Rainer already had all the success, money, and star power he could ever ask for. He clearly didn't need Michael.

"This is just so cool," Kate repeated. "I've never met a celebrity before! You don't mind, do you? You know, that I go out with him tonight?"

Yes, he thought. Aloud, he said, "No, not at all. Go - " He paused to clear his throat. Why did his voice have to crack *now*? "Go have a good time."

"Thanks Michael." Much to his surprise, Kate threw her arms around his shoulders. "You're a good friend."

I'm an idiot, he thought drearily as he returned her embrace.

"Don't mention it."

CHAPTER EIGHT

"You've *got* to be kidding me."

Kate tried to ignore her brother as she applied her mascara, but it was difficult to do so with him hovering over her shoulder. Their bathroom was supposed to be big enough so that two people could stand comfortably in front of the mirror, but with Gavin practically breathing down her neck, they probably could have squeezed in a third.

"Well, I'm not. So get over it."

"You know, I can believe that he has friends here in Dallas. I can even believe he has friends in this complex. But honestly, *why* would he ask you on a date?"

"Gee, thanks, Gav. You want to tell me how ugly this dress makes me look, too?" Kate snapped. "It's not like it's a real date."

"So why are you going?"

"Hello, he's Luke Rainer!"

"Yeah, I got that," Gavin scowled. "How do you know this guy isn't up to anything?"

"Like what? You think he wants to kidnap me?"

"I'm just saying I don't think it's a good idea for you to be going out with some guy you don't know."

"Well technically - "

"No, stalking him on Twitter does *not* count."

"Fine," Kate huffed. "You know I spent more time with him than I would have if I'd met him speed-dating."

"Not making me feel better, Sis."

"Well, I tried," Kate shrugged as she dropped her back-up mascara and lipstick into her purse. Then, she pulled out her cell phone to check the time. 7:28. Luke would be there any minute.

She grabbed her favorite bottle of perfume and spritzed it onto her wrists and neck. Gavin took a few steps away from her to avoid any residual spray. He must have finally realized he wasn't going to talk her out of going, because he left shortly thereafter, but not before casting her one last look of blatant disapproval.

Knowing she didn't have much time, Kate took one last look at her reflection. She had to admit, she looked pretty good. She'd chosen a summer dress, and she'd tied her hair up with a few strands falling loosely into her eyes. With just an extra touch of smoky eye-shadow and a natural shade of lipstick, she finally felt worthy of a night with Luke Rainer.

As if on cue, someone knocked on the door, sending her heart into a frenzy.

"I'll get it!" she announced and scampered to the entry hall.

She pulled the door open to reveal Luke Rainer, looking more beautiful than he ever had on her television screen. He wore the same dark jeans from earlier, but he'd exchanged his T-shirt for a button-down collared shirt. She'd noticed earlier that he wasn't nearly as tall as he seemed on television, but with his rugged jaw line and big, forest-colored eyes, he was still the handsomest guy she'd ever seen.

He smiled as he greeted her with a cheerful, "Hello, Gorgeous."

"Hi," she squeaked.

Stop it, Kate! You're twenty-four, not fourteen! For Heaven's sake, he's just a person!

"Hello." Gavin suddenly appeared beside her, trying to look as important and intimidating as he could in his unkempt state.

"Is this the brother?" Luke asked Kate.

"Gavin. How you doing?" Gavin extended his hand. To anyone else, it might have seemed like a friendly gesture. Kate, however, knew her brother. He didn't really do "friendly."

"Great, thanks. I'm Luke."

"I know," Gavin frowned. "So why the sudden interest in my little sister?"

"*Gavin!*" Kate hissed. To Luke, she said, "You'll have to excuse him. He's not really a people person."

"No harm done," Luke assured her. "So, are you ready for the best night of your life?"

Kate laughed, but she could practically feel Gavin tense beside her.

"Absolutely. Let me grab my purse," she replied. She turned to her brother. "Don't talk," she ordered before sprinting off to retrieve her purse from her bedroom.

Once they'd finally made it out the door, Kate realized just how nervous she was. She was alone. With *Luke Rainer*. What was she supposed to say to him? Luke, however, was so outgoing and relaxed that she soon found herself talking to him as though he were one of her oldest friends.

Throughout the car ride there (he'd brought his more "modest" vehicle - a brand new Ferrari), he asked her about herself, where she'd gone to school, what she did for a living, what hobbies she enjoyed. She realized it was a little pointless to ask him such things after having read his book and seen every single episode of *Cemetery Tours*.

She already knew that he'd grown up in both Houston and Dallas and that he'd first become interested in the paranormal when, at the age of six, he saw the apparition of his grandfather standing in his living room. She knew he'd gone to a community college in the area for a few semesters before dropping out to pursue paranormal investigation full time, and that before he earned his time slot on the Discovery Channel, he'd made his living as a bartender in Deep Ellum. That's where he'd met Gail Marsh and JT Sawyer, two of his fellow investigators. Gail worked with him at the bar and JT was a patron who'd stop in every Friday after he'd finished his job as a busboy at one of downtown's most prestigious hotels. They began ghost hunting on weekends and by the time Peter Jamison, Gail's tech friend from college, had joined the team, they had already collected a handful of pretty spooky disembodied voices on their digital recorders.

Together they put together a compilation of their video evidence, which included a few shadow figures and one solid full bodied-apparition, and began showing it off to anyone who would watch. After receiving a lot of positive feedback, they decided to see if they could find an agent who would be willing to watch their video. That had eventually led to a contract with the Discovery Channel and the rest was history. The entire crew had been living out near Los Angeles ever since.

Instead of asking about his professional life, Kate asked, "So what do you like to do when you're not investigating?"

"More investigating," he grinned. "There's actually a place outside of Waxahachie I'm thinking of checking out while I'm here."

"Really?" Kate asked.

"Yeah. It's called the Old Bluebonnet Ranch. There's a cemetery right on the edge of the property where a lot of apparitions have been sighted. Think I'll go see if it lives up to all the hype."

"That sounds so cool. I've always wanted to go on a real ghost hunt."

"Why don't you come with me?" Luke offered.

"Are you serious?"

"Absolutely. I could always use an extra hand, especially since my crew isn't with me."

"Where are they?" Kate asked, her head still spinning at the thought of going on a real ghost hunt with Luke Rainer.

"Peter and JT are spending the week in New York and Gail is in Reno with her new boy toy."

"You're the only one who came home?" Kate asked.

Luke shrugged.

"I wanted to spend time with my folks. I really don't get to see them a lot." As he spoke, Kate realized that this was a side of Luke Rainer that most people never got to see. He always gave the impression that he was a hot-shot superstar paranormal investigator. She never expected he'd be the type to fly home to spend time with his parents while his friends partied it up in New York and Reno. "So how long have you and Mikey been friends?"

"Not very long," Kate replied. "How do you know him?" She remembered what Michael had told her, but he really hadn't gone into very much detail.

"Oh, you know, heard there was a cursed apartment complex. Thought it might be fun to investigate. My friends didn't think it was worth it, but I was curious, so I took my camera and a few digital recorders."

"Did you find anything?"

"That depends. How easily do you scare?" he asked.

Kate smiled.

"Don't worry, I already know my apartment is haunted," she assured him.

"In that case, there's definitely something there," Luke said. "I caught several disembodied voices, a couple unexplained mists, and even a few intelligent responses."

"Wow. So, it really is the whole building?"

"It really is the whole building. The question is... why?" He asked, sounding like a voice actor on a kid's Halloween program as he parallel-parked his beloved Ferrari alongside the busy downtown sidewalk.

Once they climbed out of the car, he offered her his arm and led her down the block to a fancy Italian restaurant called De Luca's. Two potted trees glittering with colorless Christmas lights stood on either side of the door, which a greeting host opened for them.

"*Buona serata.* Welcome to De Luca's."

"*Grazie,* my man," Luke grinned. "Reservation for Rainer?"

"For two?"

"Yes, sir."

"Right this way."

Kate knew she was ogling as they followed the host through the restaurant, but she couldn't help it. De Luca's was beautiful; full of classy artwork, ritzy furnishings, and crystal chandeliers. The lighting was dim, and the walls were the color of garnets and decorated with intricate designs the color of buried treasure. Passing by their fellow diners, elegant and sophisticated couples sipping wine by candlelight, Kate realized just how underdressed and out of place she was in her Target brand summer dress. Fortunately, no one paid her or Luke the slightest bit of attention.

Finally, the young greeting host directed them to a semi-secluded table near the window.

"Is this satisfactory?" he asked.

"Very. Thanks a lot," Luke replied.

"Anything else I can do for you, just let me know."

He disappeared, and before Kate had time to appreciate the smell of fresh marinara or the soft Italian mood music, a waiter arrived to take their drink orders.

"How about some wine?" Luke asked Kate.

"Great."

"Red or white?"

Kate bit the inside of her cheek as she felt the waiter's eyes drift from Luke to her. She had no idea which one she liked and she'd left her note cards at home.

"Whatever you prefer," she finally answered.

"How about a bottle of Cabernet?" Luke asked.

Kate wasn't sure she knew one wine from another any better than the names of colors. Still, she didn't want to seem naïve or childish by asking him to describe it.

"Sounds good."

They chatted casually about the restaurant, their favorite television shows (other than *Cemetery Tours*), and all the things they liked about Dallas while they waited for their drinks. The waiter returned quickly with two goblets of ice water and a dark bottle, which he uncorked and poured into their glasses. The wine was the same color as the walls, and Kate realized it wasn't the kind she was used to drinking.

"Cheers," Luke held up his glass. Kate raised her class and clinked it against his. Then, she took a sip and pulled back, grimacing. Luke laughed. "You okay?"

"It's a little bitter," she answered.

"If you don't like it, I can get you a bottle of Chardonnay. You might like that a little better."

"At the risk of sounding completely uncultured, what kind is Chardonnay?"

"White," Luke replied, grinning at her.

"Is that the lighter kind?" she asked.

Luke raised a confused eyebrow. Briefly, Kate filled him in on her Color Anomia.

"Interesting." Luke looked thoughtful once she'd finished. "You can't identify colors at all?"

"Not by their names," Kate replied. "It's weird. But the doctors told me that every brain injury is unique."

"Just like snowflakes." Luke sounded so profound that Kate burst into a fit of giggles.

"Exactly," she said and took a sip of water.

"Does it bother you to talk about it? Your accident, I mean."

"No."

"So what happened?"

Kate recounted the whole story to him; how she went for a drive in the snow and wound up with the entire front half of her car smashed up against a tree.

"And is that where you had your experience?" he asked, referring to her four minutes of death.

"No, I didn't flatline until they had me in the ambulance. Lucky for me, too. That's how they managed to revive me," she explained.

"Do you remember any of it?"

Kate tried to assemble the broken pieces of her memory before waking up in the hospital.

"This is going to sound bizarre, but I think I was in a Starbucks."

If Luke's face was any indication, he hadn't been expecting that.

"Really?" he asked.

"Yeah. Like I said, it's all pretty blurry. I didn't even start to remember it until a few weeks after I woke up. That's when it all started coming back in bits and flashes. But from what I can piece together, I opened my eyes and there was snow everywhere. I was literally in the middle of nowhere, just surrounded by snow. I had no idea where I was or where I was going. I'm not even sure I remembered my own name. Then, I was in a coffee house. I guess I just figured that was the place to be during a snowstorm." Now, Luke was smiling at her. "The part I remember vividly, though, was not being able to smell anything once I got there. That scared me. It must have been right before they got my heart going, because I began to panic. I think I even heard one of the paramedics' voices as they pulled me back. The next thing I knew, I was waking up in the hospital three weeks later."

"Wow," Luke said. "Forgive me if I seem creepy to you, but I love that you had that experience."

"You love that I died for four minutes?" Kate laughed.

"No. I love that you can say with certainty that after your body died, you continued to exist. You know, that's what we're trying to do on *Cemetery Tours*. Give people some reassurance that death isn't the end. That even if you've lost a loved one, even if the pain is still there, there's at least some peace knowing that you'll see them again."

"I like that too," Kate told him.

"You know, you said something else earlier that interested me," Luke told her.

"What's that?"

"You said you already knew that your apartment is haunted. Why did you say that?"

"It's more of a feeling than anything," Kate answered carefully. Before she knew it though, she'd told him about everything; the break-in, the footsteps, the sensation of being

73

watched, Gavin's illness, his steadfast refusal to believe in anything supernatural... It all came tumbling out before she could stop it. Luke listened intently, nodding every so often, and didn't speak until she'd finished her story.

"Well, I don't know about your brother, but that sounds like a Class-A haunting to me," he told her. "It is a little strange, though, that he's the only one that's been affected."

As he spoke, a memory from moving day suddenly surfaced, and Kate saw Michael stumbling to get out of Gavin's room as his health rapidly deteriorated.

"It did happen to one other person," she said and told him about Michael. That seemed to strike Luke's interest more than anything.

"So Mikey's been to your apartment?"

"Yeah."

"Did he say anything? Or have you said anything to him? About the haunting?"

"No. I didn't want him to think I was crazy," Kate explained, blushing slightly. Why? She was on a date with Luke Rainer. She shouldn't worry or care about what Michael Sinclair thought of her.

"Oh, I doubt he'd think you were crazy," Luke said with the air of one who knew more than he was letting on.

"Does Michael think his apartment is haunted too?"

"Oh, he knows it is. In fact, I captured my best EVPs in his living room." EVP, the technical term for a disembodied voice captured on a digital recorder, stood for electronic voice phenomena. Kate had learned that watching *Cemetery Tours*.

"Really?"

"Yeah. You should ask him about it."

"I will," Kate said.

"In the meantime, why don't you and I try a little experiment?"

"What kind of experiment?"

"I think after dinner, we should run back to my folks' place, grab some equipment, and conduct an EVP session with your ghost friend in your living room. It can be your indoctrination into the world of paranormal investigating. What do you say?"

CHAPTER NINE

Michael was not having the time of his life, so whoever was singing that song on the radio about hoping he was, well, he could take a hike.

Since he knew that being at the lake wouldn't do the trick, he'd hoped that being around his family, some of whom he hadn't seen in a long time, would cheer him up. That wasn't happening either.

It was mostly Uncle Carl's fault. Nosey Uncle Carl who asked him a multitude of questions about his personal life, and the answers to which all made him sound like a total loser.

Question: "So Michael, what are you doin' with your life, boy?"

Answer: "Shelving books at the library."

Question: "For money?"

Answer: "Yes."

Question: "Have any plans for something a little more prest-ee-gious?"

Answer: "No, I like it there."

Question: "Well enough about work. Didja find yourself a lady yet?"

Answer: "Not yet."

Question: "Well, you'd better get a move on that, boy! What are you now, thirty-five?"

Twenty-seven, but thanks for that additional kick in the gut, Michael thought miserably. He hated to be the mopey one at the party, but he just couldn't bring himself to have a good time. And it was all because he knew that right now, Kate was probably having a fantastic night out with *him*; stupid Luke Rainer and his stupid bad boy charisma.

Michael tried to at least put on a happy face for his mother, who arrived about an hour later than he did. As usual, she presented herself with natural warmth and grace, though Michael couldn't help but notice the new strands of gray amidst her dark brown curls as she greeted him with a long embrace.

"Oh, it's good to see you, Sweetheart," she told him.

"You too, Mom," Michael replied, breathing in the familiar scent of her floral perfume. It reminded him of joyful family gatherings from his childhood and he found comfort in the memories. Still, his mother could tell he had something heavy on his mind.

"You want to talk about it?" she asked.

"It's nothing," he assured her.

"I've heard that before," she sighed.

Michael knew it frustrated her that he rarely opened up about his personal life, but he wasn't sure she'd be any happier if he did. For that matter, he wasn't sure he would be either. How pathetic would it sound having to tell her that the girl he liked was out on a date with the Ghost Prince of Primetime? Even worse would be having to explain that he'd inadvertently introduced them. But worst of all would be confessing why he knew Luke Rainer in the first place and why, three years later, he was still coming around.

"How are *you*?" Michael asked her.

"Tired," she admitted. "I know I look it too."

"No, you look beautiful. Like always."

"Oh, I raised you so well," she smiled fondly as Uncle Carl came thundering across the yard toward her.

"There's my little sister! There's my little Dianne!" he bellowed as he threw his arms around her. She winced as he squeezed her against his beer belly, but returned his hug nevertheless.

Michael wasn't sure if it was characteristic of all mothers, but Dianne Sinclair had a gift, a natural way with people. She was able to see the good in anyone and everyone, and she never had one mean thing to say. She had a way of making everyone feel loved and respected, and everyone loved and respected her in return.

While the family congregated around Dianne, Michael meandered over to the shore. The sun was just beginning to set, pouring golden light through the trees, illuminating their silhouettes, and casting long shadows across the water. Although he preferred to avoid lakes, he couldn't deny that it was a peaceful atmosphere. Or it would have been were it not for all the drifting spirits.

Some of them, he recognized. Like the old man who wandered from boat to boat. Sometimes he seemed content to just sit and watch the water. Other times, he acted like he was searching for something. Maybe a favorite fishing rod or an old pocket watch. Then there was the young woman who haunted the dock across the lake. He'd seen her for years, pacing back and forth across the same dock. Was she waiting for someone? Or did she genuinely not know that she could leave that spot? Others were new, like the teenage girl screaming hysterically, begging for someone to help her find her lost dog. Michael knew he should have gone to talk to her. He was the only one that could.

And yet he didn't. No matter how guilty he felt, he couldn't bring himself to approach her. He tried to tell himself that it was for the best. The living weren't meant to get involved with the dead. When they did, they disrupted that delicate balance that kept the universe in order. That was his excuse, anyway.

Aside from the ghosts, however, the lake actually was a great place to be. The family's two-story lake house, wooden with white shutters and a swing hanging from the tree in the front yard, was as homey as ever. As usual, his grandmother watched her children, grandchildren, and great-grandchildren from the swing on the porch. She glanced over at Michael and smiled at him. She knew he would come see her once everyone else was asleep. Until then, he'd do his best to pretend he had nothing more on his mind than how pleasant an evening it had turned out to be.

On the list of places Kate had never expected to see with her own eyes, the inside of Luke Rainer's parents' house had fallen somewhere between Antarctica and the dark side of the moon. They'd stopped by after dinner to collect some of Luke's equipment to take back to her apartment. His parents, Dave and Susan, were as nice as could be. They lived in a modest house and Kate was surprised to learn that despite their son's success, Dave still worked his day job as a plumber. Susan had, however, quit her job and had since divided her free time between her two passions: quilting and blogging.

They welcomed Kate and offered her a drink while Luke rummaged through his bags for a digital recorder, a night vision camera, and a substantial supply of batteries. Once he had everything he needed, he wished his parents good night and promised he wouldn't be home too late, which Kate found adorable (and only slightly disappointing).

Back at her apartment, Kate wasn't surprised to find Gavin fast asleep on the couch. She shook his shoulder and whispered, "Gav, you can go to bed now. I'm home safe and sound."

"Huh?" he mumbled, only semi-conscious.

"I'm back. You can go to bed."

"Oh." He sat up, rubbed his eyes, and looked at her. When he noticed Luke standing over her shoulder, he frowned. "He's still here." Kate swatted his arm. "Ow," he moaned.

"Yes, he's still here. Be nice," she scolded. "We're going to do an EVP session in here, so get out."

"What the *hell* is an EVP session?"

"You know what it is! We're going to ask our ghost questions and listen to the responses on the digital recorder."

"Kate, how many times - you know what? Go ahead. Knock yourself out. I'm going to bed."

"Good. Good night." Kate took his seat on the couch as Luke began setting up his night vision camera.

Gavin gave one final shake of his head before disappearing into his room.

"All right, we're about ready. Do you want to hit the lights?" Luke asked.

Kate did as he asked, feeling excited, nervous, and, she hated to admit it, a little scared. What if they actually did make contact with whoever or whatever was inside their apartment? Would the nighttime anxiety become even worse than before? And what about Gavin?

Once all the lights were off, Kate began to have second thoughts. The room seemed much smaller in the dark, and far too quiet. Slowly, the tiny hairs on the back of her neck began to stand on end, and she scurried back to the couch.

"Are you sure this is a good idea?" she asked Luke.

"Whatever is in this apartment is already attached to you. There isn't a whole lot we could do to make things worse."

"What if we make it angry?"

Luke was silent for a few long moments before he finally answered, "I don't want to scare you, but I think it's already angry."

Kate shivered.

"How can you tell?" she asked.

"Working around spiritual energy for so long, you sort of develop a feel for it. You learn to detect different emotions. You can usually tell when something wants to beat the crap out of you."

"Is that what he wants?" she whispered, hoping he couldn't hear the newborn terror in her voice.

"I don't think so. I think he just wants someone to talk to," Luke replied. "And that's what we're going to give him." He handed her the digital recorder, a rectangular device about the same size as her iPod. "Would you like to do the honors?"

"I don't know how it works," she confessed.

"You just have to push this button," he showed her.

"I think you should just hold on to it. You're the expert." It really was for the best. Her fingers were so trembly that she would probably drop it, break it, and then the whole session would be over.

"Fine," he sighed playfully. "I know you've seen how we do this on TV, but just relax, talk, ask questions. After a few questions, we'll play it back and see if we hear anything."

"Right," she whispered.

"Okay, here we go." Although she couldn't see anything, she heard the faint *click* of a button being pressed. "Hello?" he began. "If you can hear me, my name is Luke. This is Kate. We just want to talk to you." He paused, waited a few seconds, and continued. "If you're here, can you make a noise? Or say something into our recorder? Anything to let us know you're here." Kate held her breath in anticipation, but they were met with silence. Luke pressed another button. "Let's just see if we got anything yet."

Kate could hear the recorder rewinding, and suddenly, her curiosity outweighed her apprehension. Luke hit the play button and his voice came through, sounding digitized and enhanced.

"Hello? If you can hear me, my name is Luke. This is Kate. We just want to talk to you... If you're here, can you make a noise? Or say something into our recorder? Anything to let us know you're here."

Kate strained her ears to hear anything through the static and noise behind Luke's voice, but there was nothing.

"Don't get discouraged. It takes a lot of energy for spirits to come through." Luke stopped the playback and resumed recording. "If you're here, we'd really like to talk to you, so if you have something to say, use my energy. Use my camera's energy." They sat in silence for a few more moments before Luke muttered, "Whoa."

"Are you okay?" Kate asked.

"Yeah, I just got dizzy," he replied. "Was that you draining my energy?"

Kate had seen almost the exact same phenomena on his show. She hated to admit it, but she'd always wondered if maybe he was exaggerating a little for the camera. Now, however, she wasn't sure.

Luke stopped the device again and played back what they'd just recorded. Again, his was the only voice they heard.

"You know, since he or she has been attached to you for so long, they might respond more to you," Luke told her. "Why don't you try?"

"Okay," Kate cleared her throat as Luke pressed the record button. "Hello? Is anyone there?" she asked. "My name is Kate. What's yours?"

Luke stopped and rewound again.

"Hello? Is anyone there?" Kate heard her own voice enhanced through the speaker. *"My name is Kate. What's yours?"*

"...Trevor..."

Kate gasped. The voice was rough, deep, and barely audible, but it was there. Luke was ecstatic.

"Yes! That's what I'm *talkin'* about!" he cheered exuberantly, the way a football fan might cheer for his favorite team at the Super Bowl. "'Trevor.' Did you hear it?"

"I heard it!" she exclaimed. "Oh my God..."

"Go on! Ask something else!" Luke pressed the button and handed her the recorder.

"Trevor. Who are you, Trevor?" She paused for a few seconds. "Is there anything you want to tell us?" She let the recorder run a little longer before handing it back to Luke. He rewound it. No response. He pressed record again.

"Trevor, what do you want with Kate and her brother? Are you following them?" Again, nothing. Luke passed the recorder back over to Kate.

"Why are you here?" Kate asked.

Rewind.

Play.

"Why are you here?"

"... Don't remember..."

"'Don't remember!'" Luke clapped his hands together. "Did you hear that? That is an intelligent response!"

Kate thought it was cute the way he still got so excited about capturing a spirit voice, even after five years.

"You don't remember why you're here?" she asked, pressing the record button. No response. "Is there anything we can do to help you?"

Again, nothing.

"Are you the one making Kate's brother sick?" Luke asked.

Rewind.

Play.

"Are you the one making Kate's brother sick?"

"...Maybe..."

The voice was the same, but it was much harsher than before; violent, menacing. Luke had been right. He was angry.

"Why?" Kate asked.

Rewind.

Play.

"Why?"

"...Won't tell you..."

Kate felt chills run down her spine again for the second time that night. She could see how a skeptic might pass off any voices they'd heard up until that point as static, a faulty connection to a radio, or even a glitch in the recording. That, however, was a direct response to a question she'd asked. It even sounded like it was mocking her.

Luke, however, was absolutely giddy.

"Oh, so that's the way you're gonna play, huh Trevor? You wanna be a smart ass?" he asked.

Kate stared at him, horrified.

"Don't make him mad! I still have to live here!"

Luke ignored her. "Talk to us! Come on, use my energy! Use it all!"

CRASH!

Kate screamed. Luke leapt almost a foot off the couch.

"Get the light," he told her.

But Kate was shaking too hard to move. Somewhere down the hall, a door opened with a loud bang.

"What the hell was that?!" Gavin demanded.

Kate could barely make out his shadowy figure stumbling around in the darkness. He switched on the overhead light and Kate had to blink several times before her eyes adjusted.

"Shit," Luke muttered.

Kate looked over his shoulder to see his night vision camera, or what remained of it anyway, leaning up against the wall, still attached to the tripod. It had hit the wall with such force that bits and pieces had gone flying. It was only upon closer inspection that Kate noticed the damage done to the wall itself.

"What the hell did you *do*?" Gavin demanded, staring at the hole in the wall. "Do you have any idea how much it's going to cost to fix that?"

"Gav, it wasn't us - "

"Kate, I don't want to hear it," Gavin snapped. "I have had enough of this. You need to *grow up*," he hissed. To Luke, he said, "And *you* need to leave."

"But we - " Luke started to protest, but Gavin cut him off.

"Get out." Gavin wasn't as muscular as Luke, but he was much taller, and he could certainly be tough when he wanted to be.

Luke, obviously not wanting to cause any trouble, grabbed his tripod and camera and stuffed them into his backpack.

"I'll pay for the wall," he muttered to Kate.

"We don't need your help. Get out," Gavin ordered.

"Sorry about your camera," Kate told Luke. He shrugged.

"Wasn't one of my good ones." Kate couldn't tell if he was lying or not. She handed him his digital recorder. "Thanks for tonight," he told her and kissed her on the cheek. Gavin must have made a threatening move behind her back, because Luke took two steps backwards and threw his hands up, "Hey, I'm going. See? I'm going." Seconds later, he was out the door.

Kate and Gavin stood in a tense silence, neither seeming to want to look at the other.

Finally, Kate said, "It wasn't his fault."

"Kate, just stop talking."

"We didn't do that, Gavin. Something else did."

Gavin had clearly had enough, because without another word, without even acknowledging her, he turned and stormed back to his room. She knew she should just let him go, but she didn't want him to think he'd won.

"Don't you want to know what we caught?" she called after him.

Gavin turned and glared at her.

"*Stop. Talking,*" he snarled through gritted teeth.

Stunned by the furious look on his face, Kate froze in her tracks. Gavin disappeared into his bedroom, slamming the door in the process. Kate winced. If Trevor really was there, she hoped that he would keep his haunting to a minimum once the lights went out, because she had a feeling she wouldn't be welcome in her brother's room, no matter how scared she felt.

CHAPTER TEN

The next morning, Michael was exhausted. Part of it was his fault. He had stayed up visiting with Gram until almost 4 A.M. He wouldn't have gotten such a late start, however, had it not been for his little cousins, all of whom had stayed up until almost one in the morning, jumping, screaming, eating junk food, and playing on the new Wii that Uncle Carl had brought up for the holiday.

Furthermore, his Great Aunt Martha, who drew up the room assignments, just couldn't seem to get it through her head that he was any older than twelve, because every year, she stuck him in the kiddie room. His mother tried to make him feel better by telling him that she probably thought the room needed a chaperone. That theory was debunked, however, when he'd asked Aunt Martha if someone else could chaperone the kids' room and she'd responded with, "What are you talking about? You never have a chaperone."

So he had an uncle who thought he was five years from forty and a great aunt who thought he was prepubescent. He couldn't decide which one he found less flattering.

It was the Fourth of July, and although Michael knew he had a fun day ahead of him, he was seriously considering driving back home as soon as the fireworks were over. He wanted to spend the day with his family, but he'd be leaving first thing in the morning anyway. If he drove back tonight, he'd be able to sleep in his own bed.

After lunch, the family headed out onto the lake for swimming, kayaking, and fishing. Michael opted for fishing, the most relaxing option, even though he'd never caught a fish in his life. A few of his cousins fished with him for a while, but soon the allure of the cool lake won out over the summer heat, leaving Michael alone on the dock.

While he sat there, watching his cousins splash around in the murky water of Lake Texoma, he let his thoughts drift back to Kate. How had her night with Luke gone? Had they made plans to see each other again? And what if they had? Would their one night evolve into something more? He didn't know Luke to be all that big on commitment. Then again, Luke had probably never dated a girl like Kate; smart, funny, normal...

Footsteps behind him snapped him out of his stupor. He glanced around to see his mother, dressed in a navy sundress and sunglasses, smiling down at him.

"Hey," she said, taking a seat next to him and dangling her feet into the water. "Catch anything yet?"

"Nope," Michael replied.

"You know, I remember when you were little and we'd come out here. You were so determined to catch a fish. You would sit out here for hours, just waiting for a bite."

"And I haven't caught one yet," Michael quipped matter-of-factly. His mother laughed. Michael grinned too. "Kinda pathetic, huh?"

"I was just thinking you were the opposite. More than twenty years later and you haven't given up. That's something I admire about you, Michael. You're so strong-willed." It wasn't a phrase Michael would have used to describe himself, but he supposed his mother was a little biased. He was her son, after all. She was supposed to think the world of him.

"I'm not as strong as you," Michael told her. It was true. From his older brother Jonathan being diagnosed with depression and bipolar disorder at an early age, to his father walking out on the family after Jonathan's disease became too much for him to handle, to Michael's accidental arrest at seventeen, Dianne Sinclair had endured more than anyone's fair share of turmoil in the past three decades.

"I'm not strong. I just do what I have to do to make it through each day."

If that wasn't strength, Michael didn't know what was.

"Trust me Mom, you're the strongest person I know."

His mother smiled and wrapped her arm around his shoulder.

"I'm glad you came. Even if you're still in the kiddie room," she teased.

Michael chuckled.

"I'm glad too."

"But you still don't want to talk about what's bothering you?"

"How can you tell something's bothering me?" He was genuinely curious.

"Mothers always know," she replied. "So tell me. Is it about work?"

"No. Work's fine."

"Is it about one of your friends?"

Michael wasn't sure what friends she was talking about. Most of his college buddies were married and in different states. But he simply replied, "No."

"So then it must be about a girl." When Michael didn't respond, his mother groaned. "I swear Michael, there will be a snowstorm in July before I get any sort of straight answer out of you."

"Good. It's hot," he grinned.

"Don't be a smart aleck. Talk to me. What's her name?"

Michael sighed. She wasn't going to let it go, so what was the point in denying it? Maybe she could offer him some advice.

"Kate."

"How'd you meet her?"

"She's my new neighbor." He proceeded to tell her everything, except of course, the parts about the ghost and about her date being television's hottest paranormal investigator. His mother had no idea that he'd even met Luke Rainer (not that she'd know who he was because he wasn't *that* famous), and he certainly wasn't going to brag about it.

"Well, I'm pretty sure I already know the answer, but have you told her how you feel?"

"Not really, but - "

"No 'buts.' You didn't call. You didn't tell her. You can't blame her for saying, 'Yes' to someone who did."

It was nothing Michael hadn't expected to hear, but he felt like she could have sugarcoated it a little.

"So what do I do?"

"Be her friend, and if the time seems right, be honest with her. Don't pressure her or anything, just lay it on the line. And most importantly, be yourself. Any girl who doesn't love you for you isn't worth it." She smiled at him. "Now was that so hard?"

"No," he grinned. She kissed his forehead.

"I love you."

"Love you too."

"Well, I think I'm going to go help Aunt Martha with dinner," she announced, rising to her feet. "Are you going to stay out here a little longer?"

"Yeah. Who knows? I might catch something."

As Dianne walked away, Michael turned his attention back out to the shimmering surface of the lake, to his cousins kayaking and laughing, and to the great blue heron that watched from the neighboring shore. Talking to his mother really had made him feel better, even though she hadn't told him anything that deep down, he didn't already know. It must be a mom thing.

Just then, something tugged on his line. Acting instinctively, he leapt to his feet and began to reel in his catch. After what seemed like much longer than a few seconds, the silver hook appeared, glinting in the sunlight and stripped clean.

The fish had eaten his bait.

Kate sat in the passenger seat of Gavin's truck, pretending to text and wishing she'd had the sense of mind to bring her own car. Gavin had turned the radio on high and stared straight ahead at the road, barely acknowledging his sister. They hadn't spoken much since the night before, and the few words exchanged had been uncomfortable. Kate knew Gavin still hadn't forgiven her for the hole in the wall, and she was pretty sure that Gavin knew she hadn't given up on the ghost thing.

"So, are we going to act all grouchy and awkward around Mom and Dad?" Kate finally asked.

"Guess so," Gavin grunted as he pulled out a bottle of Super-B Energy, which he downed in one gulp.

Kate tried not to scowl as he tossed the empty bottle into the backseat. She knew that he was trying to irritate her with that nasty stuff, but she wasn't about to give him the satisfaction of knowing that it was working.

"Don't you think they'll ask what's wrong?" Kate asked, keeping her voice calm and her tone smooth. "You know they're more paranoid than I am. Especially Mom."

"They'll be fine, Kate."

"Okay," Kate replied in a patronizing tone that she knew would get on Gavin's already frazzled nerves. Sure enough, he clenched his jaw and tightened his grip on the steering wheel. "You know, we really did talk to someone last night," she told him, well aware that she was egging him on. He ignored her. "Gav, what happened to you? You always used to listen to me when we were kids."

Gavin sighed.

"Fine. What did your ghost friend say?"

She knew he was humoring her, but she didn't care.

"He said that he didn't remember why he was there, but he admitted that he was the one that was making you sick. The cool thing is that they were all intelligent responses. You know, actual answers to the questions we asked? He even told us that his name is Trevor and - "

Suddenly, Kate felt herself flying sideways. Pain shot through her right arm as her shoulder collided with the window and a passing car blared its horn as Gavin swerved quickly back into his own lane.

"Gav, what the hell?!" she cried.

"Sorry!" he gasped; his face even paler than usual. "I thought there was something in the road."

"Well, be careful. Do you need me to drive?"

"No. I'm fine," he said.

"Well anyway, that's all we got. Oh no, wait! He started talking back to us, so Luke started provoking him and that's when he kicked the camera into the wall. Trevor, I mean. Not Luke."

Without warning, Gavin pulled over to the side of the road and parked the car.

"What are you doing?" Kate asked. "Is everything okay?"

"Kate, I need you to listen to me." Gavin looked her straight in the eye. "I don't want you mentioning any of this to Mom and Dad."

"What? Why not?" Kate wasn't sure that was even possible. There were very few things she didn't share with her mother. She couldn't *not* tell her that she'd met Luke Rainer, let alone had a date with him!

"It's complicated." Gavin rubbed his forehead.

"You want to elaborate?"

"I just don't want them worrying about you any more than they already do," he said. "You know if Mom had her way, you'd be living with them in some sort of cushioned room to make sure you didn't get hurt again. I think that if you told them all that stuff about... Trevor... it would just be too much for her."

"I guess you have a point," Kate conceded, although it really didn't make a lot of sense to her. "Can I at least tell her I met Luke Rainer?"

Gavin thought about it.

"Yeah, that's fine," he said, though she could tell by his tone that he'd rather she didn't.

They didn't speak again until they'd reached their parents' house. It was an older house, built by their grandparents back in the sixties. Although there were several things that could have been spruced up and modernized, Kate loved her childhood home, and couldn't imagine anyone other than her family ever living there. Before they'd even made it to the front porch, their mother, Terri, a vivacious woman with fading fiery hair and loads of freckles, opened the door and ran out to greet them.

"Hey!" she squealed, engulfing them in one big group hug. "Happy Fourth of July! How was the drive?"

"It was fine."

"Uneventful," Kate and Gavin answered simultaneously.

"Excellent! Well, come in, come in! Your dad's out back, finishing up with the burgers." She ushered her children into the house, which smelled like freshly cooked beans, rolls, and even a hint of potato salad.

"Good, I'm starving," Gavin said.

"How are you guys?" Kate asked her mom, kicking her shoes off and taking a seat at the kitchen table.

"Better than we were last week. Your father picked up a flu bug at work and I caught it the next day."

"That's a pretty short incubation period," Kate noted.

"Uh-oh! Sounds like the family nurse is here," her dad teased, appearing in the kitchen with a plate full of grilled hamburger patties. Rex Avery looked the same as he always did; casual clothes, big nerd glasses, and a baseball cap to cover his shiny, bald head. Kate grinned and rose to give him a hug. "How you doing, Pumpkin?"

"Good. Are you feeling better?"

"Much. Not sure what I had last week, but it was miserable."

"Glad you're over it," Gavin said.

"Speaking of, how are you feeling, son?"

"I'm all right," Gavin replied.

"Have you gotten *any* better?" Terri asked.

"I think so."

That was bull, but Kate didn't feel like calling him out on it. They seemed to be back on neutral ground after their discussion in the car, and since she still had to live with him, Kate wanted to keep it that way. Besides, though she'd never tell him to his face, she really did love him and she hated knowing that he was upset or stressed out because of something she'd said or done.

As a family, they filled their plates and sat down at the dinner table. Once they were settled, Terri asked, "So what's new with you two?"

When Gavin didn't volunteer an answer, Kate spoke up.

"Well, I had a date with Luke Rainer last night."

"That name sounds so familiar," Rex muttered through a mouthful of potato salad.

"He's that cute boy from *Cemetery Tours*," Terri reminded him.

At first, Kate was confused by her nonchalant tone. Then she realized that her mother must have thought that when she said she'd had a date with him, she meant she'd spent an entire night in front of the television, staring at his face and eating ice cream straight out of the tub.

"Oh right. The loud one," her father remarked.

"No, I mean I actually had a date with him. Like, the dinner-at-a-fancy-restaurant kind of date," she told them.

Her parents didn't seem to comprehend.

"You mean you actually met him?" her mother asked. She was, if possible, an even bigger television fanatic than Kate. And, although she'd never admit it to her husband, Terri Avery had a huge cougar crush on Luke Rainer. "How?!"

"He's friends with our neighbor."

"Oh Kate, that's so exciting! You've got to tell me all about it!"

While Kate regaled her night with Luke (excluding the bits about Trevor, as per her promise to Gavin), Gavin and Rex continued eating, neither attempting to hide their complete and utter disinterest.

When Kate finished, Terri sighed. "Oh, he sounds like an absolute dream! Are you going to see him again?"

"I'm not sure," Kate replied honestly. She hadn't heard from him, and although he'd offered to take her ghost hunting, she didn't know if he'd really follow through. She liked to think he was a man of his word, but after the abrupt end to their evening, she wasn't holding her breath.

It was probably for the best. Even if she did get to see him again, she knew any sort of relationship forming between them was unlikely. He would go back to Los Angeles soon to begin filming the next season of *Cemetery Tours* and she would stay in Dallas, decorating houses for people with a lot of money. And oddly enough, she was okay with that. As exciting as the night before had been, there hadn't really been anything romantic about it. In fact, there were moments when Kate felt more like Luke's long-lost buddy than a girl he'd asked on a date.

"Will you be disappointed if you don't?" Terri asked.

"A little, but I really didn't expect anything long-lasting," Kate answered. It would be really cool to go on a real ghost hunt though.

As soon as they'd finished eating, they loaded the dirty plates and utensils into the dishwasher and left for the fireworks show. The big fireworks display had been in Addison the night before, but Rex and Terri were friends with a man who worked at one of the local country clubs, and they always put on a show for the actual Fourth. It was the same show the Averys had been attending every year since Kate was little, probably because it was a lot less crowded than the one in Addison.

Once they arrived, Gavin and Rex sauntered off to talk with a few of their buddies, leaving Terri and Kate alone in the lawn chairs that they'd brought. It was the perfect moment for a mother-daughter chat, and although Kate knew she'd promised Gavin not to talk about her EVP session, she was sorely tempted to bring it up. She wasn't accustomed to keeping secrets from her mother. Besides, Terri was a *Cemetery Tours* fan herself. She'd think it was cool.

Kate couldn't resist.

"So I think our apartment is haunted," she began.

"Oh really? Why do you think that?" her mother grinned.

"Strange noises. Creepy feelings. But mostly because Luke brought a digital recorder and we actually talked to him."

"You talked to... a ghost?" Terri's eyes lit up. Kate knew then that had been right. "What did he say?"

"Not a lot. Just that his name is Trevor and he doesn't remember why he's still hanging around. But isn't that neat? I *actually* conducted an EVP session with Luke Rainer and we..." Suddenly, Kate realized that her mother didn't look so delighted anymore. Her eyes were wide and all the color had drained from her face. "Mom? What's the matter?"

Terri gave a tiny shake of her head, as though willing herself to snap out of an unpleasant spell.

"Nothing, nothing. Go on, Sweetie."

"That's really it," Kate replied. "Are you sure you're all right? Do I need to go get you a Coke or something?"

"No, I'm fine. Really."

Somehow, Kate wasn't convinced.

CHAPTER ELEVEN

Despite his family's insistence that driving from Lake Texoma to Dallas late at night on the Fourth of July was nothing short of idiotic, Michael made the ninety-minute commute back to his apartment once the last firework had exploded over the lake. About halfway there, however, he was beginning to suspect that they were right. He'd never seen so many fender benders or drunken drivers swaying back and forth across lanes. Fortunately, he made it back home in one piece.

He was so tired that he fell into bed without even taking off his sneakers and slept clear until he was woken the next morning by someone pounding loudly on his door. He moaned and, rubbing a hand through his unruly hair, staggered over to the door.

"Hey there, Mikey." Luke Rainer flashed him an obnoxiously cheerful smile. "You look like you had a rough night. What's wrong? Have more than two sips of beer at the fireworks show?"

"What do you want?" Michael asked. He was in no mood for Luke Rainer or his cheeky grin.

"Just stopping by to see Kate. I told her I'd take her out to Waxahachie for a ghost hunt and I wanted to see if she was available tonight."

"So why didn't you just text her?"

"Oh, where's the fun in that?" Luke grinned. "You know, you could always join us."

"No, thank you." Watching the girl he liked fawn over Luke Rainer once was more than enough. Besides, they'd had this same conversation a million times. Nothing Michael said could convince Luke that he hadn't overheard him openly communicating with a spirit on his digital recorder.

"Oh, come on. Why not? I bet Kate wouldn't mind."

"I've told you, I'm just not into this stuff," Michael insisted.

Luke heaved a condescending sigh.

"Whatever you say, Mikey."

Kate woke up after a restless night of strange dreams. First, she dreamed that she'd been swimming when, all of a sudden, Gavin came running out of the apartment, warning her that a massive snowstorm was on its way, and that she needed to get out of the pool.

Her second dream had been about Luke. They were on their way to investigate an old cemetery in Europe. The people buried there were the world's worst criminals, some of whom were even believed to be demons in human form. As Kate followed Luke around the centuries-old graveyard, she noticed that some of the graves were empty. The woman guiding them explained that they didn't know how it happened, but that at times, the graves opened up and the dead disappeared. The woman then led them underground to a mausoleum, where gossamer blood-colored curtains hid the coffins in the walls. Finally, they arrived at the end of a long hallway, where the same curtains concealed a bright, misty light. Kate reached out to pull back the curtain, but Luke grabbed her arm and held her back. Only, it wasn't Luke. It was a tall man she'd never seen before, dark and muscular with intense eyes and an angular face. She tried to pull away from him, but he held her wrist in a firm grip. She looked back at the curtains, where a figure had appeared behind the curtain.

It was Michael. Kate opened her mouth to ask what he was doing there, but she woke up before she got the chance.

Thinking back, it was one of the coolest dreams she'd ever had, and it served as a much-needed distraction. She'd been feeling guilty ever since she'd told her mother about the EVP session. Gavin had been right. It *had* upset her.

Kate tried not to dwell on it as she cruised through her morning routine. She brushed her hair and changed into jeans and a tank top. For breakfast, she made herself a plate of scrambled eggs and toast and washed it down with a glass of milk. She was in the process of rinsing off her dirty dishes in the sink when someone rapped on the front door.

She answered it and was pleasantly surprised to see Luke Rainer smiling back at her.

"Hey, Gorgeous," he greeted her.

"Hi," she replied with a grin. "I wasn't sure I'd get to see you again."

"I promised to take you ghost hunting, didn't I?" he asked. "Luke Rainer is a man of his word. You still want to go, don't you?"

"Uh... yeah!" As if he needed to ask.

"Great! I was thinking we might head out tonight around 7:30 or so. It will take about an hour to get to the Old Bluebonnet Ranch and by the time we get there, the sun will almost be set, but we'll still have enough daylight to get set up."

"Sounds good to me," Kate told him. Somehow, she was more excited about searching for ghosts than she had been about the fancy Italian dinner.

"And listen, I know your brother would probably kick my ass if he knew I'd been back here, but I wanted to give you this." He handed her an envelope. Inside were five crisp, new twenty-dollar bills. "It's for the wall."

"That's sweet of you, but you really don't need to do this. I looked it up and it won't be that expensive to fix."

"For collateral damage then," he replied.

"Luke, I can't accept this."

"Sure you can. I'm rich. Now just say, 'Thank you and I'll see you tonight.'"

Kate grinned.

"Thank you, Luke. And I'll see you tonight."

"Yes, you will," he replied. "Do me a favor though and don't tell Mikey. He's always wanted go on a ghost hunt and I don't want him to get jealous or anything, you know, that I'm taking you and not him."

"Well, why don't we invite him?" Kate asked.

Luke thought about it.

"I suppose we could..." he replied. "Would you be okay with that?"

"Yeah, absolutely," she answered truthfully.

"All right. Would you mind telling him about it? I'd ask him myself, but I've got to be somewhere in about half an hour."

"Sure. I'll head over there in a few minutes," Kate told him.

"Thanks, Beautiful," Luke winked. "I'll see you at 7:30."

"See you then," Kate replied, closing the door after him.

Then, she ran into the bathroom, brushed her teeth, and applied a light layer of makeup before walking across the landing to apartment #1723. She knocked on the door. No answer.

She knocked again. Still nothing. He was probably still with his family. Or maybe he was on his way back. Either way, Kate decided to text him to find out when he would be home.

Michael emerged from the shower and changed into a comfortable pair of jeans and a t-shirt. He meandered into the kitchen to make himself some lunch when Brink appeared.

"You had a visitor," he announced, taking a seat on the kitchen counter.

"If it was Luke Rainer again - "

"It wasn't. It was Cute Neighbor Girl."

"Kate?" Michael asked. "What did she want?"

"I don't know. Living girls don't tell me much." Oh, duh. "I think your phone went off though."

Michael bolted out of the kitchen and scrambled around his bedside table, where he'd dropped his phone the night before.

He had a new message from Kate.

Hey! Are you coming home soon?

The message had been sent about thirty minutes earlier. Instead of texting back, Michael pulled on his old sneakers and walked over to Kate's apartment with Brink following a few steps behind. Gavin answered the door, looking tired, pale, and slightly irritated. His expression softened, however, when he saw Michael.

"Oh good, it's you. I was afraid it might be that tool from the ghost show."

"Fun guy, isn't he?" Michael remarked. Gavin clenched his jaw in response. "So uh, is Kate around?"

"Yeah, I think she went down to the pool," Gavin answered.

"Ooh." Brink sounded positively gleeful.

Michael wanted to tell him to get lost, but that wasn't about to happen with Gavin watching.

"Okay, thanks."

"Think she's in a bikini?" Brink asked once Gavin had shut the door.

"Is there anything I can say that will convince you *not* to follow me?" Michael asked.

"I think we both know the answer to that," Brink replied matter-of-factly.

Michael groaned and tried to ignore the ghost trailing him as he trudged down the stairs and across the complex to the pool.

At first glance, the water looked empty. But then, Michael noticed a pale figure gliding across the bottom of the pool. She surfaced and pulled her hair back off her face. She must have sensed him watching her, because she looked over to where he was standing, squinting in the sunlight.

"Hey." She smiled in recognition once she'd blinked the chlorine away. "You're back."

"Yeah. I've actually been back. I was in the shower when - you texted me." He tried to refrain from breathing a sigh of relief. He'd almost said, "*When you stopped by.*" Fortunately, he realized that he'd have no way of knowing she'd stopped by if

100

he'd been in the shower. Or if he didn't have a ghost friend who told him everything that happened when he wasn't around.

"Oh, I can tell. Your hair looks lovely." Kate grinned up at him as she swam over to the edge.

"My God, she is hot," Brink muttered.

Before he could help it, Michael threw him a murderous glare. Brink was too distracted by the beautiful woman in the pool to notice. Unfortunately, Kate *did* notice.

"You okay?" she asked.

"Yeah. Just thought I heard something," Michael answered lamely, turning his attention back to her. "So uh, how was your Fourth of July?"

"You know, you could sit down," Brink told him. "Do you have any idea how awkward you look?"

At the same time, Kate answered, "It was fun. Gav and I went to see our parents. We watched some fireworks. You know, very patriotic and whatnot. Did you get to see fireworks at the lake?"

"Yeah," Michael replied. "It was actually pretty cool. There were about six parties, including ours, setting them off all around the lake, so the sky was full of exploding color."

"Wow. I would have loved to see that," Kate sighed.

"Maybe next summer you can." The words were out of his mouth before he could stop them. Had he just accidentally invited her to go with him next summer? He didn't know a lot about girls, but he knew that coming on too strong was rarely the right move. A guy would have to be a lot more charismatic than he was to be able to pull it off. "I mean uh, maybe you and Gavin could drive up and see them. You know, with your family."

If he'd made her uncomfortable, she didn't show it. She simply smiled and said, "Yeah, I think we should." She floated there for a few moments, allowing the water to toy with her long blonde hair before she asked, "So are you doing anything tonight?"

"No..." Michael answered curiously as he took a seat, cross-legged, on the edge of the pool. Was it possible she was asking him out? Did that mean that she'd turned down a night in the country with Luke Rainer?

"Well, I know it's kind of last minute, but Luke and I are driving out to Waxahachie for a ghost hunt and I was wondering, do you want to go with us?"

Of course. How had he not seen that coming? He wondered what Luke had told her, how he'd been able to convince her to invite him on their little haunted rendezvous.

"Say yes," Brink quipped.

Michael ignored him.

"Thanks, Kate, but I think I'm going to pass."

"Aw, how come?" Kate asked.

"I don't want to crash your date."

"It's not a date," she told him.

Wait. What did that mean? Was that code for something?

"It's not?" Michael asked, suddenly feeling far less annoyed by Luke Rainer than he ever had in his life. "So uh, you and he aren't like, a thing after the other night?"

"Oh no," Kate said. "Don't get me wrong, going out with him was a lot of fun, but there was nothing romantic about it."

"Really?" Michael couldn't believe what he was hearing. He'd seen the way Kate had reacted to Luke and his obnoxious advances. She'd been pretty quick to tell him how "very single" she was. Now she was acting like he was just another guy. Had she really been so disenchanted by one evening? Or was that just a girl thing?

"Really," Kate assured him.

"But you were so excited to meet him."

"Well yeah, he's Luke Rainer."

"But you don't want to date him?"

Kate raised a curious eyebrow. Michael knew instantly that he'd gone too far.

"Michael, were you jealous?" she asked, her face breaking into a playful grin.

"No," he answered a little too quickly. "I mean, not technically - well - I - maybe a little... I mean - "

Before he could utter another unintelligible syllable, something (or Brink) shoved him forcefully in the back. Caught completely off guard, Michael could do nothing but flail as he flew face forward into the water. He surfaced seconds later, coughing and sputtering.

"Are you all right?" Kate laughed.

"Yeah, just lost my balance," he replied, wiping the water out of his eyes. Behind him, he could hear Brink howling with obnoxious laughter. "Guess I'll have to take another shower."

"Yeah. Can't go ghost hunting smelling like chlorine," Kate said with a quick grin.

Michael sighed.

"Do you really want me to go?"

"I really do. I think it will be fun. Besides, Luke told me how much you'd always wanted to."

Oh, that Luke. Always thinking of others. Now he really didn't have a valid excuse not to go.

Well, unless he wanted to tell her the truth.

"So, will you go?" Kate asked.

He knew he should say no. Agreeing to accompany them would be reckless, stupid. It could potentially throw a huge monkey wrench into his lifelong quest to remain completely anonymous. But just like with Gavin's birthday party, he knew he would end up going with them. Just because she'd asked him to.

"Sure. Count me in."

CHAPTER TWELVE

"Well, look who's finally going ghost hunting," Luke grinned as Michael climbed into the backseat of the Lexus that he'd bought his parents for their anniversary. "You excited, Mikey?"

"Oh, I'm having fun already," Michael remarked. They hadn't even pulled out of the apartment complex and already, Michael was thinking he should have backed out when he'd had the chance.

"Where's the Ferrari?" Kate asked from the front seat.

"Couldn't fit all the equipment in the trunk," Luke explained, turning the stereo up. The theme from *Ghostbusters* blared through the speakers. Luke began bobbing his head to the beat.

"Are you serious?" Michael asked.

"What? It's a classic," Luke said. Michael rolled his eyes. Kate just laughed. "So Kate, did you tell Mikey about our friend, Trevor?"

"Who's Trevor?" Michael asked.

"Trevor's our ghost!" Kate explained, twisting around in her seat so that she was facing Michael.

"How do you know his name?" Michael asked stupidly before realizing that the more *normal* response would have been, "You have a ghost?"

"We conducted an EVP session in my living room."

"You should have been there, Mikey. Maybe you could have told us what he looked like," Luke remarked.

Michael felt his blood freeze in his veins. He stared at Luke like a deer in the headlights.

"What do you mean?" Kate asked.

"I'm just joshin' with him. Right, Mikey?" Luke glanced back at Michael through the rear-view mirror and grinned.

Michael made a feeble attempt to laugh it off, but inside, he was fuming. Why did Luke have to say stuff like that? Why couldn't he get it through his thick head that if Michael wanted the world to know about the ghost thing, he would have opened up about it a long time ago?

Right before they reached downtown, Luke pulled into a QuikTrip convenience store to stock up on snacks and batteries.

"You never know when a ghost is going to drain your energy or your camera's energy, so you have to be prepared for everything," he explained, leading Kate and Michael through the aisles loaded with candy, chips, and an abundance of other snacks.

"I've always loved these roadside stores," Kate said, checking out the price on a bag of Trail Mix.

"How come?" Michael asked.

"Well for one thing, they're full of cheap junk food," she grinned, grabbing a bag of beef jerky and tossing it into their ever-growing pile of snacks. "For another thing, whenever you stop at them, you're on a road trip or about to go spend the day somewhere fun and exciting. I remember in high school, we took a day trip to Waco to visit the Dr. Pepper Museum - "

"Seriously?" Michael asked. He wished his high school had been that cool.

"Yeah, it was awesome. But my favorite part of that trip was stopping at the gas station right before we left and splurging on chips and candy." She added a bag of M&M's to their smorgasbord. "The free Dr. Pepper was good too."

They paid for their food and 32-ounce cups of soda (or in Luke's case, tea), and were about to head out the door when Kate told them that she was going to run to the restroom before they hit the road again. Michael offered to take her drink and her snacks to the car.

"So are you going to tell her?" Luke asked once they were outside. "That you like her, I mean. Not that you talk to dead

105

people. Though if you want to ask her out, you're going to have to tell her eventually. That's not the kind of thing you can just keep to yourself - "

"Do you *ever* stop talking?" Michael growled under his breath.

"Well, I do host a television show for a living, so you tell me," Luke said. "Pretty clever, getting her to ask you to come tonight, right? I knew you wouldn't say no to her. I guess you're just kind of pathetic that way. Of course, I wouldn't want *my* girl alone with a guy like me, either."

"She's *not* my girl."

"Right. Hate to break it to you Mikey, but you're a lot easier to read than you think you are. Speaking of, way to be subtle in the car. You know, when I mentioned you being able to tell us what Trevor looked like? If I didn't already know you could see ghosts, that reaction would have given you away in a heartbeat. Word to the wise, next time, act like you don't know what I'm talking about. Or at least remain neutral. Anything's better than acting like I just spilled your deepest, darkest secret to the girl of your dreams. Which I guess technically, I did, but - "

"All right boys, let's hit the road!" Kate interrupted, striding over to them. "Where're the Cheeto Puffs?"

Thirty minutes and a dozen bad 1980s power ballads later, they'd made it through downtown (and about half the snacks) and were headed south to Waxahachie.

"So, what's the plan for tonight?" Kate asked Luke once the latest 80s classic had faded out.

"I was thinking of putting you in charge of the digital recorder since you mastered the art the other night. I brought the SB7 also, but I usually don't use it unless we're getting absolutely nothing on the digital recorder."

"What's the difference?" Michael asked.

"Kate? Would you like to explain it to him?" Luke asked.

"The SB7 is a frequency scanner. It scans radio waves and emits static that ghosts can speak through. It's also called The

Spirit Box. With the digital recorder, you have stop and rewind to hear responses, but with the SB7, you can hear them directly."

Luke grinned.

"Is she not delightful?" he asked Michael. To Kate, he said, "I should take you on as my protégé."

Kate beamed.

"So why don't you just use that all the time?" Michael asked, trying to pretend he wasn't jealous of how easily Luke could make Kate smile. He reminded himself that she'd smiled for him on several occasions, but it was hard to stay optimistic when you were up against a guy who'd been featured in *People Magazine*'s "Sexiest Man Alive" edition.

"Because it's loud and annoying," Luke replied. "I also brought two night vision cameras and a digital point-and-shoot. One of the night visions is a little less advanced, so I thought I'd leave that one with you and let Kate handle the point-and-shoot."

"Awesome," Kate grinned.

"Wait a minute. You want me to carry around one of your cameras?" Michael had thought they were just going to be poking around a cemetery. No one had said anything about fancy video cameras that probably cost more than he made in a year.

"Well yeah, unless you don't think you can handle it. In which case, I'll pass the heavy stuff over to Kate - she's probably stronger than you anyway - and put you in charge of the recorder and the point-and-shoot," Luke replied with a smarmy smirk.

"Gee, thanks."

They reached the cemetery at about a quarter to nine. The sun had already set, but enough dim daylight remained for Kate to be able to distinguish the layout of the graveyard.

It really was a beautiful area. After exiting the main highway, they'd driven through a few smaller towns, then turned onto a long dirt road that led seemingly out into the middle of nowhere. With only Luke's GPS to guide them, they passed a stretch of farmland and a wide meadow bright with sunflowers before turning left onto an off-road that ran through a forest. The trees were so close together that Kate couldn't see the sky, or anything really, through their thick leaves and heavy branches. She wondered how many people had gotten lost hiking through those woods. Unwillingly, she imagined herself trapped beneath the lush, wooded canopy, unable to escape, not knowing what could be lurking just beyond the brush. The thought made her shiver.

Finally, they'd emerged from the woods and found themselves in a wide, open clearing. Thin, wispy clouds streaked across the sky and fireflies began to dance around the edges of the forest. Crickets chirped and a cool breeze toyed with the strands of hair that had fallen loose from Kate's ponytail. It reminded her of a scene out of a Western or a romance novel; not at all the setting for a good ghost story.

Or it wouldn't have been, were it not for the cemetery. Sealed off by a rusty old gate, it seemed the picture-perfect old Texas graveyard with large concrete headstones and metallic words above the gate that read *Blue on et Cemet ry*.

"It's so beautiful," Kate murmured to Michael, who was staring intently into the graveyard.

"Yeah," he agreed halfheartedly.

Kate wondered what he was thinking about. Luke, on the other hand, automatically switched into professional mode.

"All right. Kate, I want you to grab that backpack out of the trunk. It has the point-and-shoot and the recorder, so if you would, take those out and add the batteries and grab whatever snacks you want. Mikey, come here. I'm gonna teach you how to work the night vision camera."

Kate did as she was told and ten minutes later, she found herself armed with cameras, recorders, and an EMF Detector, a device that Luke used to measure electromagnetic energy and monitor changes in temperature, both of which, he explained, could indicate the presence of a spirit.

"That's why the EMF is so important to our investigations. It's easy for us to believe we're in the presence of a spirit, but for those who aren't there to actually experience it, it's nice to have some scientific evidence that yes, something is happening around us. This is the proof," he said.

"Sounds like a little kid at Christmas, doesn't he?" Kate asked Michael.

"Something like that," Michael remarked.

Luke didn't even hear them.

"Okay. This is what we're going to do. Kate, as soon as we start rolling, I want you to turn on the digital recorder. You can carry it around if you want, but I recommend sticking it in that little strap on your backpack since I also want you snapping pictures. Take as many as you want, totally at random. Just like the name, point and shoot. Don't even look."

"Right," Kate said.

"Mikey, your job is easy. You just film. You see anything strange, any movement, or if you hear something, you try to capture it on camera. Got it?"

"I think I can handle it," Michael told him.

"Guess we're ready then," Luke announced, heaving his own camera onto his shoulder. "Before we start, I usually like to say a few words, let the spirits know who we are, why we're here, so I'll do that now. Kate, would you mind switching on the recorder?" Kate pressed the button as Luke cleared his throat. "We're here at the old Bluebonnet Cemetery in Waxahachie, Texas. Just a little background information. This historic cemetery dates back to the mid-1800s, and a lot of pioneers and cotton barons are said to be buried here." Then, he addressed the ghosts. "To anyone who might be listening, hello, my name is Luke. These are my friends, Kate and Mikey. We're just here to talk to you."

A heavy silence descended on the graveyard. Kate glanced over at Michael. His brow was furrowed and his eyes scanned the entire cemetery. It almost seemed like he was looking for something.

"Do you guys want to add anything?" Luke asked.

Michael remained silent, so Kate spoke up.

"Hi, everyone. If you're here, please let us know. I'd love to see you." She hoped she didn't sound too foolish speaking to the wind.

The investigation began as soon as what remained of the soft glow of daylight began to fade from the sky. In the darkness, the ethereal beauty of the scenery surrounding the graveyard gave way to an eerie stillness; one that caused the hairs on the back of Kate's neck to stand on end. Illuminated only by the light of the waning moon, the headstones of the graveyard seemed far more sinister and ominous. If she didn't know better, she'd have sworn that the eyes of the angels perched atop several graves were following them as they made their way to the center of the cemetery.

"Okay, I'm not really picking anything up on the EMF Detector. Kate, I think I'm going to ask a few questions to see if we get any responses on the digital recorder. Mikey, you just keep an eye out for anything... unusual." Luke cleared his throat. "Hello? Is anyone there?" He paused for a few seconds. "Who are you? How did you die?"

Somewhere, just beyond the perimeter of the cemetery, something rustled through the tall grass. Kate gasped and, thinking it might be something paranormal, whirled around and snapped a picture.

Eager to see if she'd captured anything, she pressed the "play" button on the camera and reviewed the photograph; lots of dry grass, the iron gate, a headstone or two, and the startled eyes and long ears of a wild Texas jackrabbit.

No ghost.

"Anything?" Luke asked Kate after she'd taken the picture.

"No," she sounded disappointed.

"Mikey? You see anything?"

"Nope," Michael replied without tearing his eyes away from the camera's screen. As long as he kept his eyes glued to the screen, he knew he wouldn't see anything. It wasn't impossible to catch a spirit on camera. Luke and his crew had proven that enough to land them their own television show. But more often than not, they barely had the energy to manifest themselves to the general public. It took a lot more than that to be able to allow themselves to appear on video or in a photograph. For example, he could take one hundred pictures of Brink and chances were he wouldn't appear in any of them.

"Do you hear anything?" Luke asked.

"Just crickets."

It was true. The only ghost he'd seen all night had been hanging around the entrance to the forest. He'd been sitting at the base of a tree, looking lost and forlorn. The cemetery, however, was as still and silent as a church on a Monday. It was possible that it was haunted and they'd just hit it on an off night. It was more likely, however, that those who'd made the claims of ghostly noises and apparitions had just let their imaginations and fear get the better of them. Michael had found that was often the case with cemeteries. People expected them to be haunted, so they took every little noise or movement caught out of the corner of their eye as a sign from the other side. In his experience, however, he'd found most cemeteries to be far less spiritually active than other more public places.

Brink's theory as to why that was was that no one wanted to hang around a cemetery all day. Ghosts were still the people they'd been in life. Unless they just really liked hanging around at graveyards or thought it was the "ghostly" thing to do, they were far more likely spend their time around loved ones or places that brought them joy and comfort. The ones who did haunt cemeteries, he guessed, were the ones that were either bitter about their passings or still so attached to their lost lives that they wanted to remain as close to their earthly bodies as possible.

"Well, the night is still young," Luke observed. "Kate, why don't you try snapping a few more pictures?"

She did. When she went to review the pictures, Luke and Michael leaned in over her shoulders. Most pictures showed nothing out of the ordinary. However, they did come across one with a tiny ball of light floating in front of one of the headstones.

"Look! An orb!" Kate exclaimed. "Do you think it's a spirit?"

Michael could have told her that it wasn't, but seeing the delighted look on her face was reason enough for him to keep his mouth shut. Luke, however, didn't seem to have the same reservations.

"It could be, but more often than not, these orbs are debunked as light anomalies or bugs."

"Oh," was all Kate said before they were all caught off guard by the blinding beam of an LED flashlight.

"Who's there?" the rough and deeply Southern voice of an older man called through the darkness. Trying to avoid staring directly into the light, Michael was able to make out a man's broad silhouette marching toward them. "You kids aren't supposed to be out here. No one's permitted after dark."

"I'm sorry, sir, we didn't know." Luke stood and held out his hand. "I'm Luke Rainer. You might recognize me from the Discovery Channel?"

"I don't get cable. What are you doing out here?"

Michael's eyes finally adjusted enough to make out the man's features. He looked to be in his mid-fifties, but he was so weathered that he may have actually been younger. His light brown hair was graying and frazzled, and he wore an old red plaid shirt and tattered jeans.

"Well you see, I'm a paranormal investigator. Actually, a *famous* paranormal investigator. Have my own show and everything," Luke explained, brimming with pride.

The man wasn't impressed. "If you're so famous, what are you doin' filmin' out here?"

Luke's face fell. Michael tried not to smirk.

"We heard your cemetery was haunted and we thought it might be fun to check it out," Kate explained. "We're sorry we disturbed you. We didn't know there was a curfew."

The man finally seemed to understand.

"Oh, so you're one of them ghost hunters. I get it," he said to Luke. "Well, I'm afraid you're not gonna find much out here.

Worked here for almost twenty years now and I've never seen hide nor hair of any sorta specter."

"Dammit," Luke sighed, looking defeated.

"However," the man continued. "I hear lots of reports of a girl hauntin' the old bridal barn a few miles that way." He pointed west.

"Bridal barn?" Luke asked.

"Oh yeah. Few years back, the Chapel at Bluebonnet Trail was one of the most popular spots for weddings in the county, and all the brides were allowed to stay and get ready in the bridal barn. Then one evenin', a girl was found stabbed to death in her weddin' dress, just moments before the ceremony."

"Oh my God," Kate whispered.

"Yeah, it was a real shame. The fella that did it wound up killin' himself, too. Jealous groomsman. Always had a thing for her. Anyway, they tried to open it up a few months later, but almost every bride after her ended up reportin' really strange things happenin' in the barn. A few even saw her. It got so bad that they decided to shut it down, but the barn is still there. And if talk is to be believed, so is she."

Luke looked at Kate and Michael.

"What do you think, guys? Want to check it out?" he asked.

"Do whatever you want. Just get out off this property," the older man ordered before he turned and disappeared into the darkness.

"Well?" Luke prodded.

"I'm down," Kate said. "Besides, we came all this way. Might as well make the most of it while we're here."

They both looked at Michael. He knew he was outnumbered.

"Sure. Let's go."

CHAPTER THIRTEEN

Once they were back in the car, Luke handed his iPhone to Kate and asked her to get online and see what she could find out about the haunting. She typed, "Bridal Barn Murder, Waxahachie, Texas" into the search engine and clicked on the first link that appeared.

"*What was supposed to be a joyous occasion quickly turned into a family's worst nightmare when Grace Bledsoe, a Waxahachie native and bride-to-be, was found slaughtered in her wedding dress. She was 24 years old,*" Kate read. "*Her body was discovered by her bridesmaids, who went searching for her after she failed to show up for a photo shoot.*" Kate read on silently. "It says that they found her fiancé's best man, Daniel Ford, with a self-inflicted gunshot wound to the head after someone reported seeing him leaving the barn. His fingerprints were discovered at the scene and they found a knife covered in Grace's blood on his person."

"Well, they definitely weren't lacking evidence," Luke remarked. "When did all this happen?"

"About two years ago."

"What was her fiancé's name?" Luke asked.

"Jim Loveday. Neither he nor his family made any sort of statement."

"That's okay. At least now we've got something to go on."

"How long ago did they shut it down?" Michael asked.

"Only a few months. It says that the people who own it are hoping to reopen it again sometime, but after what happened, they just can't find anyone interested in having a wedding there."

A few minutes later, they came upon a weathered sign that read *Chapel at Bluebonnet Trail*. Luke turned into the driveway. They drove through pitch darkness for another thirty seconds or so before a building appeared off to the right. Most of its windows were boarded up, but Kate could still make out the circle of stained glass just below the steeple. Luke parked a few meters away.

"If the chapel's here, the barn can't be much further," he reasoned.

Again, they clamored out of the car and began to assemble their equipment. This time, however, the world around them was so dark that they each needed their own individual flashlight to see a few feet in front of them.

Kate wasn't sure what it was, but as they trekked along the graveled pathway that Luke guessed would lead them to the barn, the familiar feeling that they were being watched by some unseen presence returned. She shone her flashlight into the surrounding woods, expecting to see a flash of eyes, or maybe even a shadowy figure darting through the trees, trying to evade her glance.

"Are you okay?" Michael asked.

"Yeah," she replied. "It's just creepy out here."

"Don't you love it?" Luke asked. Kate couldn't see his face, but she was pretty sure he was grinning. "If I could visit locations like this and get paid for it - oh wait, I do!"

"I would so love to hit you right now," Michael told him.

"I've told you before, Mikey. You want to be on the show, you just say the word."

"Thanks," Michael muttered.

"He's offered you a spot on the show?" Kate asked Michael. That was new information. "Why don't you take it? You'd have so much fun! You'd get to see a bunch of new places and you'd be on television!"

"See, Mikey? *She* has a brain," Luke remarked.

"It's just not my thing," Michael told them.

"Whatever you say," Luke sighed as a broad and very neglected building came into view. Unlike the chapel, no one had bothered to board up the windows, all of which were cracked, shattered, or non-existent. The brick-colored paint was chipping away to reveal the wooden planks beneath it.

Glancing up to the second story, Kate began to feel the world closing in around her. Something was watching them from that window. She couldn't see it, but it was there.

Suddenly, that barn was the last place on Earth Kate wanted to be. She wanted to run, to climb back into the car, and get as far away from that horrible place as quickly as possible.

Luke and Michael took a few steps toward the pathway leading up to the porch. Kate remained frozen on the spot.

"You coming?" Luke asked her.

"I don't know if we should do this," she told them.

"What?" Luke asked. "Why not?"

"I just feel like whatever's in there really doesn't want us disturbing it."

"Kate, if you were murdered, wouldn't you want to be able to tell the world what happened to you?"

"Well yeah, but - "

"If you'd stayed dead after your car accident, wouldn't you have wanted to talk to someone?"

"Hey, knock it off," Michael snapped. "If she doesn't want to go, then she doesn't have to. You don't have to bring up stuff like that."

"What? She's not sensitive about it. Are you?" Luke asked Kate.

"No, but - "

"See? No problems." Kate was still hesitant. "Kate, I promise. Nothing bad will happen. I do this all the time and under a lot nastier circumstances. Did you see the episode where we investigated the witch's house where they used to perform Satanic rituals? Or what about the music hall with all those demonic entities?"

As a matter of fact, she had seen those episodes, and if memory served, Luke and his crew had spent the next weeks being haunted and scratched and God knew what else by those spirits that had decided to latch onto them. A more skeptical person may have laughed over the idea of an invisible figure following them home from a haunted location, but she already had a ghost. She didn't want another one.

Still, they had come all this way. And she'd been the one who'd said she wanted to make the most of a ghost hunt with Luke Rainer. She couldn't back out now.

"Okay," she agreed.

"That a girl," Luke grinned.

They followed the porch around the side of the barn until they finally found the front door, which had been chained and shackled shut by a large, rusted padlock.

"That looks locked," Michael remarked.

"Never fear, Mikey. Where there's a will, there's a way," Luke assured him, gently setting his camera on the ground. "Kate, may I see the backpack, please?"

She passed it to him. He rummaged around in it for a few seconds before he pulled out a pen and a large paperclip.

"Are you going to pick it?" Kate asked.

"Yep."

"Wait, what?" Michael demanded. "We're going to break in?"

"How do you think this business works, Mikey? As a professional, yes, I prefer to call ahead and get permission, but back when I was first starting out and no one wanted me inside their decrepit old buildings, I had to learn to pick a few locks."

"Are you crazy? We'll get caught!"

"By who, a possum? There's no one out here."

Michael exchanged a wary look with Kate before the soft *click* of the lock turned their attention back to Luke.

"We're in," he announced, pulling the chains off from around the handles.

"But - "

"Don't worry, Mikey. I'll put it back just the way we found it," Luke patronized, pulling the door open with a loud *creak*.

Although the air inside of the barn was much cooler than the humid summer night outside, it was still stuffy and musty from months of being locked up and undisturbed. While Kate and Luke shone their flashlights around, taking in the dusty decor, the brown leather couches, the old-fashioned fireplace, the western-themed tapestry that hung on the wall, and the narrow, winding staircase, Michael's eyes drifted up to the second story, where the shadowy figure of a woman in a flowing gown watched them from the railing.

"Kate, turn on the recorder," Luke whispered.

"Got it," she replied. Luke cleared his throat.

"Hello? Grace? Are you here?"

A swift movement out of the corner of Michael's eye almost caused him to jump back. He turned his camera in her general direction and shifted his eyes just above the flip screen, praying silently that she wouldn't notice him staring. She now stood in front of the staircase; her pretty face screwed up in what could only be called contempt for her intruders.

"What do you want?" she hissed.

"Luke," Kate said, unaware of the girl's presence. "The recorder just died."

Luke's face lit up.

"She's here. I just put fresh batteries in that thing," he said. "Did you just drain all the energy from this recorder?"

Michael's eyes shifted back to the girl, who looked confused and irritated. The way she stared at Luke reminded Michael of the way a girl might stare at someone who'd just used a really terrible pick-up line.

"Do you want me to change the batteries?" Kate asked.

"Actually, I was thinking we could try the Spirit Box," Luke answered.

"I thought you said it was loud and annoying," Michael said.

"It is, but it will spare us the trouble of having to go back and rewind to hear what she has to say," Luke explained, setting his night vision camera onto a ledge.

It made sense, Michael acknowledged, as Luke pulled a rectangular, black device out of the backpack. It looked a lot like a larger version of the digital recorder.

And Luke was right. It was loud and annoying. It was more than static, as Kate had described. It was like static slowed down so that you could almost make out certain sounds and it was ten times as loud.

"How are you supposed to hear her through this?" Michael had to yell to be heard above the racket coming out of the SB7.

"Trust me, you'll be able to," Luke replied. "Grace?" he called out. "Are you here Grace?"

Michael glanced back at their spectral visitor. She was a beautiful girl with wavy dark brown hair and big dark eyes, dressed in an elegant yet simple lace wedding gown. She'd clasped her hands over her ears, clearly just as put off by the device as they were.

"Turn that thing off!" she screamed. At the same time, her voice broke through the static of the Spirit Box.

"*Off!*"

Michael stared at the device.

"It actually works!"

"Told ya." Luke grinned. "Do you like this Grace?"

"What is that?" Grace asked.

"*What?*" the Spirit Box relayed. Grace eyed it curiously.

"What is it? This is a Spirit Box. You can talk through it," Luke explained.

"I don't want to talk to you," she snapped.

"*Don't want to.*"

"Why does it only pick up fragments of sentences?" Michael asked, still competing with the disruptive volume of the Spirit Box. Both Luke and Kate looked at him. Michael instantly regretted asking the question. How would he know that a ghost was actually saying more than what the box conveyed? Quickly, he tried to cover for himself. "I mean, no one actually talks like that."

119

"Maybe it has to do with energy," Kate suggested.

"I think it has to do with that and with the device itself," Luke replied. "Grace, why don't you want to talk to us?" Michael glanced back to the spot where Grace had been standing. She wasn't there. Michael looked around the room, wondering just how he'd missed her. "Grace?" Luke called again.

"Stop," Kate yelled, grabbing Luke's shoulder. "Did you hear that?"

"Hear what?" Luke asked.

But Michael had heard it too. Above the roar of the Spirit Box, it was almost inaudible, but it was there; the screech of a wooden chair being dragged across the floor above them.

"Turn that off," Kate said, indicating the SB7. "Listen."

With the sudden absence of the irritating static, the silence was almost deafening. It didn't stay so for long. Footsteps, soft but distinguishable, paced anxiously back and forth across the floor above them.

"Come on, Grace. We just want to talk to you," Luke called up to her. Seconds later, a small, hard object bounced off the ground near their feet. Kate shrieked and leapt back. Luke wasn't as easily shaken. "What the hell was that, Gracie? You throwin' rocks at us?"

Grace appeared once again at the foot of the stairs, glowering fiercely at Luke.

"*Don't* call me Gracie!" But without the Spirit Box, her harsh voice fell on (mostly) deaf ears.

"I'm going to turn the Spirit Box back on, okay, Gracie?" He pressed a button and again, the irritating static broke the silence of the barn.

"Who are you?" she asked. This time, the Spirit Box conveyed the entire phrase.

"*Who are you?*"

"'Who are you!' Did you hear that?" Luke asked his companions. "My name is Luke. This is Kate and Michael. Do you have anything you want to tell us?"

"No. Get out!"

"Get out!"

Kate exchanged an apprehensive glance with Michael, but Luke pressed on. "Why don't you want to talk to us?"

By now, Grace was seething. The temperature in the barn dropped even further, and as she growled in frustration, Michael felt the all too familiar rush of dizziness as she drained away his energy. Kate seemed to feel it too. She pressed a hand to her forehead, like she was trying to ward off a headache, and squeezed her eyes shut.

"Kate," Michael tried calling out to her before another wave of dizziness nearly knocked him off his feet. He slumped against a wall and took a few deeps breaths.

Luke remained focused on the investigation.

"Come on, Grace. You don't have anything to say?"

As his vertigo subsided, Michael glanced up just in time to see Grace summon every ounce of newly acquired energy and send something, probably a small vase, toppling off of the coffee table next to the couch. It hit the ground with a loud *crash*, heard even above the Spirit Box.

Kate screamed. Luke jumped back.

"Whoa!" he cried. "Did you *see* that? Mikey, did you get that on tape?" Luke turned and looked at Michael.

He didn't respond. He was frozen, staring into the virulent eyes of Grace Bledsoe.

Turn! Look away! Blink! Do something! a voice in the back of his mind screamed at him. His body didn't obey. He'd seen her and she knew it. He could avert his eyes as much as he wanted, but it wouldn't do him any good.

"Mikey!" Luke's voice finally tore him away from Grace's hostile gaze. "What's going on?" he asked.

But before Michael could reply, Grace's voice once again rang loud and clear, not only through his ears, but through the cold, loathsome speaker of the Spirit Box.

"He can see me."

CHAPTER FOURTEEN

Three things happened almost simultaneously.

First, the screens on both night vision cameras flickered before going completely blank.

Second, the Spirit Box short circuited with a loud *pop* and began emitting a penetrating, high-pitched squeal that continued even after Luke tried to turn it off.

Finally, a bright light, the color of a firetruck began to flash around the room, rekindling the headache that Kate had been fighting since before the vase flew off the table.

"What *is* that?!" she yelled as a new loud buzzing noise began to pulsate through the already shrill atmosphere.

"It's the fire alarm! She must have set it off!" Luke yelled back, frantically gathering all the equipment and stuffing as much as he could into the backpack, which he quickly passed off to Kate in order to grab his camera.

"I thought they would have taken the batteries out of it!" Michael shouted.

"They probably did!" Luke responded. "Come on, we've gotta get out of here!"

Neither Kate nor Michael argued with him. Less than a minute later, they'd abandoned the chaotic barn and were sprinting blindly through the darkness. It was difficult to see more than a few feet in front of her. Kate had to listen to make sure she didn't get separated from the guys. She couldn't help but notice they weren't on the gravel pathway anymore, and she hoped and prayed that Luke had a better sense of direction than she did.

"Come on, I think the car is this way!" Luke yelled from somewhere up ahead.

As Kate looked around, trying with all her might to pinpoint his location in the dark, she tripped over something and tumbled to the ground with a loud "Oomph!"

"Kate!" Michael called.

"Give me the camera," she heard Luke say.

Seconds later, Michael was standing beside her. He knelt down next to her, took her hand, and pulled her to her feet. A nasty jolt of pain shot from her knee down the front of her leg and she grimaced.

"You okay?" Luke asked.

"Fine," Kate managed, hobbling along as fast as she could.

"Here, give me the backpack." Michael took the backpack from her and slung it over his left shoulder. He then took her arm and wrapped it around his back, supporting her with the right side of his body. Together, they followed Luke back to the car.

By the time they got there, Luke had already loaded the two video cameras into the trunk and was waiting to take the backpack. Michael helped Kate into the backseat of the Lexus so she could prop up her leg while Luke finished loading the trunk. Both Michael and Luke had just climbed into the front of the car when the distant wail of a siren filled the air.

"Okay, we're going." Luke turned on the ignition and sped off into the night.

"How's your knee?" Michael asked, turning around to look at Kate.

"It's fine," she replied. Truth be told, it didn't feel as bad as it could. She was pretty sure she'd scraped it and she knew there'd be a nasty bruise there tomorrow, but nothing felt broken.

"We're still going to put some ice on it as soon as we hit a gas station," Luke told her. Kate didn't object. "Guess you were right about something not wanting us there."

"What happened back there?" she asked.

"Grace went ballistic. Not the first time it's happened to me, but that was pretty violent. Not to mention it was totally unprovoked - "

"No, before that. She said something. She said... you could see her.'" She turned to Michael. Everything had started happening so quickly after the EVP was captured that she hadn't had time to dwell on it, but now she was curious. "Could you?" she asked.

"Yeah," he replied shortly, without meeting her eye.

"Oh my God! What did she look like? Was she in a wedding dress?"

"She looked angry," Michael answered. "And yeah, she was in her dress."

"Wow! I wish you'd said something!"

"Trust me Kate, it's a miracle you're getting this much out of him," Luke remarked from the driver's seat.

"What do you mean?"

"Luke..." Michael cast him a warning glare.

"Mikey can see ghosts. He's been seeing them his entire life, but this is the first time he's willingly broached the subject. Around me, anyway."

"What are you talking about?" Kate asked. Did Luke really expect her to believe that Michael was some sort of medium or something?

"Nothing," Michael insisted, but Kate got the feeling that he was talking more to Luke than to her.

"You know Mikey, I think you're full of it. I think that if you didn't want her to know, you'd have tried a little harder to stop me. Hell, if you *really* didn't want her to know, you wouldn't have agreed to come along tonight. But I can't blame you. It must be a real nuisance trying to keep something like a sixth sense a secret for twenty-seven years. I bet you even feel a little relieved right now, even though you'll never admit it."

"You can't be serious." Kate said.

Michael turned to look at her, almost like he'd forgotten she was there.

"Why?" Luke asked.

"Because it's - "

"What? Impossible?" Luke interrupted. "This coming from the girl with the ghost smashing cameras in her living room?"

He had her there. Still, she wasn't quite convinced. She'd had a friend in high school who had sworn up and down that she could see and communicate with spirits, but in the end, she'd been all talk. But then, Michael had never said anything at all. He would have had to say something if all he wanted was attention. She looked back to Michael.

"Can you?" she asked. He looked like the last thing he wanted was to answer her question. That was enough. "How?"

"I don't know," Michael replied. "They've just always been there."

"Do you talk to them? Are you like those mediums on TV who stop people on the street to tell them that their dead aunt has a message for them?"

"I'm pretty sure some of those shows are scripted," Luke commented.

"Is that how you guys became friends?" Kate asked. "You found out about the ghosts?"

"Not exactly. But it is the reason I've been trying to get him on the show for the past two years," Luke replied.

"That's what I don't understand. You don't need me on your show. It's already what, the second highest-rated ghost show on television?" Michael asked.

"It has nothing to do with ratings, Mikey. Don't you get it? If all I cared about was ratings, I wouldn't be giving you the time of day. I'd be off celebrating my success, partying it up on the west coast with a bunch of Victoria's Secret models."

"What do you care about?" Kate asked.

"Credibility," Luke answered. "When we first started investigating haunted locations, we weren't trying to get rich or famous. We were trying to prove that life does not end with death, that there are still things that we can't explain. That's all we've ever wanted. Now with the show, some people watch and believe and that's great. But if you read reviews, most critics out

125

there believe it's all a hoax. They think we're just a bunch of dumb kids playing it up for the camera."

"They're critics. Isn't that their job?" Michael asked.

"If it was just them, then it wouldn't bother me. But no one outside of our fan base takes us seriously. Hell, half the people who like the show don't take us seriously. Have you read some of the articles written about me? *Luke Rainer: Television's Fallen Angel. Luke Rainer: The Spectral Sex Symbol.* They've made me out to be a caricature of myself. Instead of a legitimate paranormal investigator, I've become some sort of weird fetish."

Listening to him made Kate realize just how much she'd objectified him. Yeah, she enjoyed watching *Cemetery Tours* for the ghosts, but a huge part of its appeal was its sexy lead investigator.

"That's why I've been trying so hard to get you on the show," Luke continued. "I thought it might make people see us a little differently. Don't get me wrong, I'm not complaining about the success we've had. It's more than I could have ever hoped for and I thank God for it every day. It's just frustrating when you realize that your passion is regarded by so many as nothing but cheap entertainment."

For a moment, neither Kate nor Michael spoke. Kate never would have guessed he felt that way. She'd seen every episode of *Cemetery Tours*. Luke always seemed to be having the time of his life, but he never struck her as anything less than professional. He could be a little goofy at times, but to her, that made the show worth watching. She'd tried watching other ghost hunting shows and the way they took themselves so seriously just made the whole thing seem boring. Luke and his friends always seemed so into what they were doing, and that drew viewers in as well. At least, that was how she'd always felt.

"I'm sorry, Luke," she said.

"Don't be sorry. The last thing I want is for any of my fans to think I don't appreciate them. Especially any fans I consider friends." He flashed a quick grin back at her. "I do probably owe you an apology though."

"Why?"

"I sort of took advantage of you. I knew that Mikey liked you and that he wouldn't be able to say no if you asked him to come tonight."

Kate blushed as she glanced over at Michael, who looked like he couldn't believe the words that were tumbling out of Luke's mouth.

"You know, anytime you want to shut up would be great." He tried to sound like he was making light of the situation, but to Kate, he seemed about ready to jump out of the car and hitchhike his way home.

"Fine, I'm done," Luke conceded. "But for the record, as of December, we are the *highest*-rated paranormal show on television."

An awkward forty-five minutes later, they pulled into the Riverview Apartment Complex, where Luke dropped Kate and Michael off in front of Building 17. It wasn't until after they'd watched his taillights disappear into the darkness that Kate finally spoke.

"Interesting night, huh?" she asked as they climbed the flight of stairs up to their apartments. Kate moved a little slower than usual due to her injured knee.

"That's one word for it," Michael agreed. Once they reached the top, he pulled his keys out of his pocket, preparing to make a mad dash for his front door. "So uh, I guess I'll see you around."

"Hold up," Kate grabbed his arm. "Did you really think you were getting off the hook that easily?"

"I was sort of hoping," Michael admitted.

Kate shook her head.

"Not a chance."

Michael sighed. He knew he owed it to her. Besides, thanks to Luke, he really had nothing left to hide.

"Would you like to come in?" he asked.

Kate glanced around at his front door.

"Is there a ghost in there?"

"Yeah. But he's friendly."

"What's his name?"

"Brink."

"Brink?"

"His real name is Eugene Brinkley but he'll throw a temper tantrum if you call him that," Michael told her as he unlocked his door. Glancing around the apartment, he wished he'd taken the time to tidy up. It wasn't as horrible as it could have been, but with the laundry basket full of clean clothes waiting to be folded, the shoes kicked aimlessly to the side, and his laptop still sitting on the couch where he'd left it, it could have been a lot better. "Sorry it's so messy in here," he apologized.

"Whoa!" Brink appeared suddenly, gawking at Kate. "There's a girl here!"

"Michael, I live with my brother. My apartment is always messy," Kate reminded him.

"What is she doing here? Are you hooking up?"

"What? No!" Michael cried.

Kate looked alarmed.

"No what?" she asked.

"Sorry, not you." Michael apologized.

Brink was visibly confused.

"Wait, did you tell her?"

"Oh, Brink?" Kate asked at the same time.

Brink stared at Kate like she'd just sprouted a second head.

"She knows my name? How did this happen? Did you mean to tell her? How did she react?"

"Yeah, he's here," Michael told Kate. "But he just said that he would clear out to give us some *privacy*."

"Yeah, yeah, get lost. I get it. But she's really okay with it? Does that mean you guys are dating? Is she gong to be here a lot now? Did you tell her about that guy in her apartment yet?"

"Brink..." Michael cast him a warning glance.

128

"One more thing. Can you ask her to say my name again? It's been so long since I've heard a cute girl say it - "

"No. Get out," Michael cut him off.

"You know, I'm still going to listen in - "

"Out!"

Brink heaved a dramatic sigh, but finally disappeared. Meanwhile, Michael could feel Kate's curious eyes watching him. He looked at her and was relieved to see she was smiling.

"Sorry."

"No, it's fine," she said.

"Not weird?"

"It's a little weird," Kate acknowledged, taking a seat on the couch. "I mean, of all the things that guys don't tell you in the beginning, having a ghost for a roommate is one you really don't expect." Michael grinned, thankful that she was trying her best to act nonchalant. He sat down next to her. "Do they scare you?"

"No," Michael replied. "They startle me from time to time, but they're not at all the way horror films would have you believe."

"So is that the reason this building is cursed? Because you have all these ghosts following you around?"

"Pretty much."

"Why don't you talk to them? Try to help them move on?"

Michael took a deep breath.

"That's... a really long story," he told her.

"I've got time if you do."

Michael remained silent for a moment, trying to organize his thoughts. Although Brink had heard bits and pieces over the years, Michael had never told anyone the whole tale. Truth be told, he wasn't quite sure where to begin.

"There are a lot of reasons I don't talk to them anymore, and most of them are the same reasons I've never told anyone that I see them. The first and I guess the most obvious reason is that I didn't think people would believe me. Or worse, they'd think I was crazy, or making it all up to get attention. I didn't want any of that. I wanted people to think that I was normal, that I was just like everybody else."

"That's funny," Kate remarked, looking pensive.

"Why?"

"Well, most people would say that they don't want to be normal. They want to stand out. So the fact that you wanted to be like everyone else, in a strange way, kind of sets you apart."

"Huh. Never really thought of that," Michael murmured.

"Don't worry, it's a good thing," Kate smiled.

"Maybe. But when you're a kid, you'll do pretty much anything to be accepted, or at least to not have people look at you like a freak."

"Is that what happened to you?"

"Not as much as you'd think. Mostly, they just avoided me. It was like they knew there was something weird about me, but they couldn't quite put their finger on it," he explained. "The second reason, the personal one, was my brother, Jonathan."

"I didn't know you had a brother," Kate said.

"He was a few years older than me, but he had a lot of problems; depression, bipolar disorder, you name it. By the time I was old enough to realize that no one else could see all the extra people living in our house, my dad had already left. I saw what Jonathan's illness did to my family. I tried so hard to be normal for my mother, to give her some sense of stability. She didn't need another son hearing voices that no one else could hear."

Kate's expression grew somber while she waited silently for him to continue.

"Against my better judgment, I did try to help some of the spirits I encountered. There was one who wanted me to deliver a message to her five-year-old daughter. Another wanted me to tell his wife where she'd be able to find the pearl earrings he'd been planning on giving her for her birthday.

"Then, during my senior year of high school, a guy followed me home from school. He'd been murdered in the alley behind his house and he told me that he was going to terrorize my family unless I helped him. So I started investigating. I stopped by the library almost every day after school to research it. He told me it wasn't enough. Finally, I decided to take a trip to the neighborhood where he'd been killed. Dumbest thing I've ever done."

"What happened?"

"It turned out that he wasn't the only guy killed in that neighborhood, so the local police had asked for FBI assistance in the case. They'd profiled that the suspect would return to the scene to try to relive his crime. When they caught me sneaking around in the dead of night..."

"They thought it was you," Kate concluded.

"That was the absolute worst night of my life. The look on my mother's face when she arrived at the station to take me home... I'll never forget it. She looked so tired and confused. To this day, I've never felt as guilty as I did on that night."

"Did that guy finally leave you alone after that?"

"Not until they caught the real killer about a week later."

"My God..." Kate breathed. "I can't even imagine. That must have been so hard for you."

"It wasn't fun," Michael admitted.

"But you never thought that telling someone may have made things easier? What about your mother?"

"There were times I got really close to telling her, but something always held me back. Then, the summer after my freshmen year of college, Jonathan got a lot worse. He started neglecting his meds and he cut off all contact with us."

Kate seemed to know where the story was going.

"Oh no..." she muttered.

"We got the phone call right before I began my sophomore year. My mother was devastated. And of course, she blamed herself for everything. She should have gotten him better help, she should have tried harder, she should never have let him out of her sight..."

"Oh Michael, I'm sorry," Kate whispered, tears pooling in her pretty eyes. "I'm so sorry you had to go through all of that."

"I am too. But sometimes things happen. You can't really control it."

"Can I ask you something else?"

"Sure."

"After all that happened, why didn't you tell your mother then? Maybe it would have brought her some peace."

Michael shook his head.

"It would have done the exact opposite."

"Why?"

"Because I never saw him. After he died, my mother was terrified that because he'd committed suicide, his soul might not be saved. If I'd told her then that I could see the spirit of everyone she'd ever loved except for her son... I just don't know what that would have done to her."

"You don't believe that, do you? That he would be damned because he killed himself?"

"No. I think the reason he moved on so quickly is because he chose to die. It was what he wanted. He had nothing left on Earth to stick around for, no unfinished business."

"I think that makes a lot of sense," Kate told him. Just then, the clock on the wall chimed three times, marking a quarter till two. Kate sighed. "I hope Gavin didn't wait up for me. He'll be pitching a fit wondering where the hell I've been." Her face suddenly broke into a wry grin. "At least he trusts you more than Luke."

"I'll walk you back," Michael offered.

They walked the few meters to Kate's door in a comfortable silence. When they reached her apartment, she stopped and looked at him.

"You know Michael, I'm really glad you told me," Kate said.

"I am too," Michael replied. And he was. As much as he hated to admit that Luke had been right about something, he did feel that a huge weight had just been lifted off his shoulders.

"I do have one more question though."

"Okay."

"Do you want to go out with me? Maybe tomorrow around lunch time?"

For a moment, Michael's mind went blank. The next thing he knew, he was tripping over his words, trying and failing to come up with a simple "Sure, I'd love to," or "That sounds great."

But Kate seemed to understand what he was trying to say. With a coy smile, she took a step toward him, rose up on her tiptoes, and kissed him swiftly on the mouth.

"I'll take that as a yes."

Then, with one last grin, she opened the door and disappeared into her apartment.

CHAPTER FIFTEEN

There was music playing. Kate knew she'd heard the song before, but for some reason, she couldn't name the title or the artist. It was a catchy tune, lively and upbeat, exactly the kind of song she enjoyed listening to while she drove.

Then suddenly, the music stopped. Everything stopped. With a flash of light and the screech of skidding tires, Kate felt the very air being sucked away from her lungs as her head struck something cold and metallic.

The next thing she knew, she was standing on the side of a road, watching snow fall in flurries around her. In the distance, she saw the flashing lights of a firetruck, or maybe an ambulance, gathered around a tall tree. She was too far away to make out what was happening, but she knew from the approaching wail of yet another siren, it wasn't good.

Where was she, exactly? Wherever it was, it was very bright. And very cold.

Or at least, it should have been cold. With nothing but snow as far as the eye could see, she should have been freezing. But she wasn't. She wasn't warm either. She simply felt... nothing.

Only slightly worried, she wracked her memory, desperately trying to remember where she was supposed to be. Where would she usually go in a snowstorm?

An instant later, she was standing in the middle of a very busy Starbucks. She scanned the room for a familiar face. Was she supposed to meet someone here? She didn't see anyone she recognized. Maybe they hadn't arrived yet.

Out of the corner of her eye, she noticed a large man walking directly toward her. She expected him to maneuver his way around her, but when he didn't alter his course, she had to dive out of the way in order to avoid a collision.

"Hey!" she cried.

He ignored her. As if almost running her over wasn't rude enough. She hoped he spilled coffee all over his extra-large T-shirt.

That is, if he even ordered coffee. From the lack of smell in the usually potent coffee house, everyone in the entire room had ordered odorless tea.

"Latte for Dennis!" the barista called.

Kate looked around the room. Everybody in the shop seemed to be sipping at a steaming cup of hot coffee. The place should have been reeking of coffee. And yet, she couldn't smell it. Why? She wasn't congested. In fact, her nose felt as clear as it had ever felt.

So why couldn't she smell anything?

And why hadn't she felt the cold?

And why, for the life of her, could she not remember where she was supposed to be?

Something wasn't right.

What had happened? Before she'd found herself standing beside that barren winter road, she must have had sort of destination.

So why wasn't she there now?

Something definitely *wasn't right.*

Suddenly, the building felt like it was beginning to close in on her. She looked frantically around the room, desperate for any sort of explanation, or even the simplest form of recognition, but she found none.

Just then, she was struck by a powerful jolt across her upper body. It felt like someone had hit the center of her chest with a baseball bat. She inhaled sharply and clasped a hand over her heart.

"Are you all right?" The young man's voice was full of concern. She turned to see who'd addressed her and found herself staring into familiar dark eyes.

"Michael?" she whispered, and reached out to touch his face.

Then she woke up.

Kate somehow managed to fall back asleep before she climbed out of bed a few hours later, but her mind was still reeling. Eager to see Michael again, she showered quickly and changed into a skirt and tank top before bounding into the living room and greeting Gavin with a cheerful, "Good morning."

"Morning? It's almost noon. I thought I was having a stroke when I woke up and realized that I was actually up before you."

"Had a late night."

"Oh God, Kate, if you were with that Luke person - "

"Relax, I was with Michael."

"Oh." Gavin sounded a lot more okay with that. Meanwhile, Kate slipped her shoes on and grabbed her keys and wallet off the coffee table next to the sofa. "Going somewhere?"

"Yeah, I have a lunch date," she replied. "See you later!"

"Hey, wait - "

But Kate was already out the door and practically sprinting across the landing to Michael's apartment. She rapped quickly and a little more loudly than she'd intended on the door. He answered within a few seconds.

"Hey. How are - "

"You were there," she interrupted.

"What?"

"The day of the accident. You were there at the coffee shop. That's why I recognized you the first time we met," she explained breathlessly. "You saw me."

She watched the expression on his face shift as the memory dawned on him.

"That was you?" he asked.

Kate grinned.

"Yeah. You talked to me. You asked me if I was okay."

"I thought you were having a panic attack," he explained. "I didn't realize you weren't..."

"Alive?" Kate asked.

Michael shook his head.

"I only saw your face for a moment before you disappeared. Then I realized that I'd broken my own personal vow of never speaking to a ghost in public."

136

"Well, since I didn't stay a ghost, we can say your record is still clean," Kate grinned. "So, are you ready?"

"Yeah. Yeah, let's go," Michael replied.

Kate stared up at him, almost like she was seeing him for the first time. Which, in a way, she guessed she kind of was. Everything he'd told her last night had been unbelievable, and although she had believed him, she hadn't really appreciated how miraculous it was until she remembered looking into his eyes for that brief moment before her heart began to beat again.

"Everything okay?" Michael asked.

Kate smiled.

"Everything's fine," she assured him. Then, she leaned in and kissed him as she had the night before. When she pulled back, she could see the blush creeping up his neck and settling in his cheeks. She grinned nervously, her own heart beating erratically. "Shall we?" she asked.

He nodded, looking like he was still trying to process what had just happened. Kate laughed and took his hand.

They decided on Chili's for lunch, which turned out to be both a poor decision and good decision. It was a poor decision because Chili's was quite literally packed to its full capacity at lunchtime. It was a good decision because with so many people talking, they were far less likely to be overheard. And since Kate had about a million and a half questions to ask, she preferred a room full of loud chatter to a calm, quiet cafe.

"What can I get you to drink?" their waiter asked once they were seated.

Michael looked at Kate. She ordered a Sprite and a water. He ordered a Dr. Pepper.

"Do you know what you're going to get?" Michael asked, as they perused the menu.

"I might get some fajitas," Kate answered. "How about you?"

"Everything looks good. I haven't eaten since the car ride last night."

"Same. And we've done a lot of running since then," Kate remarked, closing the menu. "So, are there any in here?"

"You mean ghosts?" Michael asked. She nodded. "Only two that I've noticed so far. One's standing behind that guy over there." He indicated a boy who looked to be in his early teens. He was sitting with a group of friends, but he didn't look particularly cheerful. "And the other is over at the bar."

"And they just look like regular people?"

"Yeah."

"Then how can you tell?"

"Sometimes it's hard. Like when I saw you. I really had no idea that you were a spirit. But most of the time, it's pretty obvious. Their behavior gives them away. For example, the way they'll stand in a place where no one would usually stand. Odd stuff like that usually wouldn't go unnoticed."

"That was something that really scared me that day; that no one knew I was there. Then I heard your voice. Knowing you saw me brought me so much peace, even if just for a moment. I think that's why I felt so comfortable around you when we first met." As she spoke, Michael's eyes shifted down to his napkin. "What's wrong?"

"I feel so guilty," he admitted.

"Why?" she asked.

"Because if I had figured out that you were dead, I would have gone out of my way to ignore you, just like I do all the other ghosts. I wouldn't have said a word to you. I wouldn't have even looked you in the eye. I'd have just gone about my business, pretending you didn't exist."

"You're trying to protect your family. There's no shame in that."

"But there is. My grandmother has always told me that there's a reason for everything. She even believes that there are reasons that people get sick or lose their jobs or have their houses broken into. She's always said that there's a reason that I can still talk to her. She thinks it's such a wonderful gift and I... it's completely wasted on me."

"I wouldn't say that," Kate said, crossing her arms on the edge of the table. "I think that if you've used your gift even if only to help one person, then it's not a waste. And who knows? Maybe the time will come when you will find a reason for it. Maybe you'll find it on *Cemetery Tours*," she teased.

"Ha, funny," Michael rolled his eyes, but grinned nevertheless.

"So you *really* wouldn't want to be on the show? Even if Luke said you could keep your secret?"

"I really wouldn't."

"Why not?"

"You mean the fact that I would have to work with Luke Rainer isn't enough?"

"Come on, he's not a bad guy."

"He's obnoxious."

"He's enthusiastic."

"Which is a polite word for 'obnoxious,'" Michael quipped. Kate laughed. "I guess the real reason I don't want to be on the show is because I couldn't handle the lifestyle. You're talking to a guy who has spent his entire life trying to live below the radar. Being on a television show... it just sounds like a nightmare."

"I don't know," Kate grinned. "I still think it would be kind of fun. But then, you're talking to a girl who has spent a good portion of her life in front of a television screen."

"So that's why you're so okay with the ghost thing. All those hours of TV fried your brain. It all makes sense now," Michael said.

"Cute," Kate remarked as their waiter returned with their drinks and asked if they were ready to order. Once he'd disappeared again, Kate asked, "So what was the worst experience you've ever had with a ghost? After the one that got you arrested. I'm guessing that one sort of takes the cake."

"Yeah, pretty much. There really weren't too many other *horrible* experiences. Though there was this one lady. She was huge, and I'm not saying that to be mean, I'm saying that because she was this rock-solid tower of a woman. And she was terrifying. She had really stringy hair, a puffy face, and these beady little eyes. When she first appeared, I thought she was going to hit me."

"Can they do that?"

"Oh yeah. Remember when I fell in the pool yesterday? That was Brink. Shoving me in."

"Are you serious?"

"Unfortunately," Michael said. "Anyway, this lady comes up to me, I don't even remember where I was, but she starts yelling and screaming something about her son and this girl and she kept telling me, 'You've got to get it back! She doesn't deserve it! It's mine! You've got to get it back!' It turned out her son had given her favorite necklace to his girlfriend, and she *hated* his girlfriend."

"Snap," Kate remarked.

"Snap?" Michael laughed.

"Yeah, snap," she grinned. "Okay, so is there anything you like about what you can do?"

Michael thought about it.

"I like that I can still talk to my grandma. I like having a roommate, even though he doesn't help with the rent and makes talking to girls I like really difficult," Michael said. Kate grinned. "I like that death has never been much of a mystery. I was four years old when my grandmother died, and a lot of people commented on how well I was taking it. A few of them worried that I was taking it a little too well. But she was sitting right next to me at her funeral. I didn't understand that no one else could see her. I didn't know that I was supposed to be sad. And although I don't know where people go once they pass on, I at least know that life doesn't end when your heart stops beating."

"You know, Luke said almost the exact same thing after I told him about my accident," Kate said, taking a sip of water. "I think you and he are more alike than you think."

"That's not nice," Michael said.

140

"I'm serious. I don't know how much you've actually talked to him about this stuff, but I think together, you guys could make a pretty big impact."

"Is he paying you to say this?"

"No. I'm just saying it." Kate assured him. "So what about animals?"

"What about them?"

"Can you see them too?"

"Oh, yeah. My dog, Lollie, still lives with my mom."

"Lollie?"

"Yeah. Like a lollipop."

"That's adorable," Kate said.

After lunch, neither of them was ready to call it a day, so they decided to head over to the adjoining shopping center. There wasn't much to look at; a few trees planted along the sidewalk, a bench here and there, and a lot of stores that held no real appeal for Kate but were still fun to explore.

"So how many ghosts have you actually talked to in your life? And how often do they realize that you can see them?" Kate asked. They strolled along the sidewalk, sort of window shopping, but mostly enjoying the weather, the scenery, and each other's company.

"You know, we've been talking about me a lot this afternoon. I want to know more about you," Michael said.

"Oh, but I'm so boring," Kate groaned.

"Not true. I don't know many other girls who would be so cool in this... situation."

"See, when you put it that way, it makes me feel like Bella from *Twilight*."

Michael laughed. "Sorry."

Kate looked up at him. "So what do you want to know?"

"Well, I guess for starters I've got to know, did you actually read *Twilight*?"

"Oh yeah. All four of them," Kate answered matter-of-factly.

"Seriously?"

"In less than a week."

"That's kind of sad."

"No, the sad part is that I reread them. Twice," Kate admitted. "Next question."

"Okay. What's your favorite holiday?"

"Tie between Halloween and Christmas. How about you?"

"I like Christmas."

"Too many ghosts around Halloween?" Kate teased.

"Too many weird people in masks," Michael shuddered.

Kate raised an eyebrow.

"Really? You see ghosts on a daily basis and you think masks are creepy?"

"Ghosts are just normal people. Some of those masks have eyeballs hanging out of the sockets."

"That's twisted," Kate told him.

"Okay, so what are you afraid of?"

"Bugs, Yoda, germs, and guys who wear socks with their sandals."

"Not ghosts?" Michael asked.

Kate thought about it.

"There's only one who really scares me," she confessed.

"Trevor."

"Have you seen him?" Kate asked.

"Yeah. I saw him the day you moved in."

Although there was no doubt in her mind that Trevor existed, Michael's confirmation made her shiver.

"What does he look like?"

"He's tall. He's got an army haircut, dark eyes. He sort of looks like a biker."

"And um... do you think he's angry at us?"

"I think he's angry at Gavin," Michael answered slowly.

"Why?"

"You know him better than I do."

"I can't think of anything. Gavin's never been in trouble a day in his life. Growing up, he was the golden child. Straight A's, athletic, multiple scholarships... I was the one who would get in trouble for staying out late or getting a tattoo or - "

"Wait, you have a tattoo?"

"Maybe," Kate grinned. "The point is whatever problem this guy has with Gavin, it wasn't Gavin's fault. I don't even know where he would have met a guy like that."

Michael's brow furrowed, like he was doing some serious considering.

"We could always ask him."

"Oh no. Gavin made it very clear that he doesn't want to hear anymore 'ghost talk.'"

"I meant Trevor." Michael stopped and turned to face her.

It took Kate a moment to process what he was proposing. After everything he'd told her the night before, she understood that this wasn't just a simple favor between friends. She wanted to say that she couldn't ask that of him, that he'd already helped them so much. But maybe, just maybe, if they could find out why Trevor was there, they would be able to help Gavin.

"You'd do that?" she asked.

"It's something I should have done the day I met you," Michael told her.

Kate wrapped her arms around his shoulders.

"You will never know how much this means to me."

"Then let's go talk to him." He turned to walk back toward the car, but Kate stopped him.

"One more thing," she said.

Then she took his arm and pulled him down into another kiss. This time, he kissed her back.

CHAPTER SIXTEEN

Throughout the ten-minute car ride back to their apartment complex, Michael tried not to show how anxious he was about talking to Trevor. That he hadn't willingly spoken to a ghost who wasn't Brink or his grandmother in ten years would have made him nervous enough, but the fact that he was going to talk to the guy who'd been making Kate and Gavin's life a living hell...

He'd rather be off chasing a bunch of pioneers with Luke Rainer.

As nervous as he felt, however, Kate seemed ten times worse. While he was more the kind to remain silent in the face of a nerve-wracking situation, Kate dealt with her anxiety by listing every single worst-case scenario that she could possibly imagine. Surprisingly, it wasn't making Michael feel any better.

"Okay, so say this guy does have a problem with Gavin. You don't think we're going to make it worse by talking to him, do you? Or what if he hurts you? You said ghosts can do that, right? Maybe we shouldn't do this. But if we don't and it gets worse, then I'll never forgive myself for not helping Gavin when we had the chance. But if we make him angrier and things get worse, we might have to call an exorcist. Do you know if there's a Cathedral around here?"

"If you don't want to talk to him, we don't have to," Michael told her, halfway hoping she took the out. And by *halfway*, he meant *desperately*.

"No, I know we need to. I'm just nervous."

"Me too," Michael admitted.

"I mean, what if Gavin did do something? I'm sure he didn't, but still. What if it was a hit and run? Or what if Gavin owed him money and he died and Gavin never paid him the money and now he thinks it should go to his family, but Gavin thinks that since he's dead, he doesn't need to pay but his family is starving and their only hope for money is the money that Gavin owes him?"

"Your brain seems like a stressful place," Michael remarked.

"It can be."

Much sooner than Michael would have preferred, they pulled into the apartment complex. He parked the car in his driveway and together, he and Kate climbed up the stairs.

Kate was still rambling.

"We're going to have to figure out how to get Gavin out of the apartment, or at least out of earshot. Or maybe if we can't get him out, we can ask Trevor to follow us back to your place and we can talk to him there. Or we might be able to - "

"Hey." He stopped her and took her hand. She looked up at him with wide eyes. "Everything is going to be okay. I promise."

She grinned wryly, but Michael could tell she was still nervous. He was, too.

"Thanks," she said. Then she took a deep breath and pulled her keys out of her purse. "All right, let's do this."

Four people were waiting for them in the living room. Gavin sat with an older couple, probably his and Kate's parents, on the couch, while Trevor paced angrily back and forth across the room. He was clearly agitated. Every so often, he'd run a hand over his short hair. All four of them looked up when Kate and Michael appeared.

"Hey, what are you doing here?" Kate asked her parents.

"Well, if you bothered to check your phone, you would have known that they called last night to tell us that they were stopping by for a visit this afternoon," Gavin told her.

"Why didn't you tell me this morning?"

"I tried, but you were out the door before I could say anything."

"Oh."

"Kate?" their mother said. "Aren't you going to introduce us?"

"Oh, I'm sorry. Mom, Dad, this is my friend Michael. He lives across the hall. Michael, these are our parents, Terri and Rex."

"Hi." Michael gave a nervous wave.

"It's nice to meet you." Mrs. Avery nodded.

"You too."

"So, what's going on?" Kate asked.

"Actually, we wanted to talk to you," Rex replied.

"Okay."

"Maybe we should speak in private," Terri suggested, lightly implying that she would rather Michael not be there for what they needed to say.

"Why? Is something wrong?" Kate asked.

"No, of course not. We just want to talk to you."

"Then why would we need privacy?"

"It's all right. He can stay," Rex said. "Why don't you kids sit down?"

Together, Kate and Michael retrieved a few chairs from the dining room table and dragged them into the living room so that they were facing the couch. They exchanged curious glances as they sat down.

"Kate, your father and I have been talking," Terri began. "And we think it would be best - "

"For everyone," Rex interjected.

"- if maybe you moved back in with us for a while." Terri pursed her lips as she waited for her daughter's reaction.

"What?" Kate asked, looking as though she wasn't sure she'd heard them correctly.

"Back when you and Gavin decided to become roommates, we all agreed to give it a trial period, remember?"

"So why are you saying this now? Why not back before I put my name on the lease for a new apartment?"

Neither parent seemed to know how to answer.

"We wanted to give you every opportunity to make things work on your own," Terri finally said. "But with Gavin still being sick, we just think it would be better for you to - "

"Wait a minute. If this is about Gavin being sick, then why don't you make *him* move back in with you?" Kate demanded.

Michael glanced over at Gavin, who was looking terribly pale and uncomfortable. His eyes were locked on a spot on the floor and he was clutching the arm rest on the sofa so tightly that his knuckles were turning white.

"He's older. He's lived on his own a lot longer than you have," Terri tried to explain.

"You mean he didn't bust his head open in a car wreck," Kate translated.

"Kate, I know you think we're being overprotective, but I still don't think you understand just how critically injured you were."

"I was in a coma for three weeks. Trust me, I get it. What I *don't* understand is why you think I need this. Every single doctor I've seen has told me I couldn't be healthier."

"Yes, but sometimes things happen," Terri insisted.

"What could *possibly* happen?"

"We just don't want you overexerting yourself," Rex said.

Kate narrowed her eyes.

"What does that mean?"

"You've just seemed so stressed since the break-in - " Terri began.

"Oh, here we go," Kate murmured.

"- and the doctors said we needed to be vigilant of your mental recovery as much as your physical recovery."

"Mental recovery?" Michael asked before he could help himself.

"Mom, please..." Kate begged.

"Kate has retrograde amnesia. She lost two and a half years of memories after the crash and if she ever wants to get them back, the last thing she needs is to be stressed out over nothing," Terri told him.

147

Michael looked at Kate.

"You didn't tell me that," he said.

"I didn't want you feeling sorry for me," Kate explained. "Besides, they all filled me in on what I'm missing. They showed me a bunch of pictures and videos and Facebook posts, so I sort of remember everything."

"Pumpkin, it's nothing to be ashamed of," Rex told her.

"I'm not ashamed of it! I don't particularly enjoy *talking* about it..."

She may not have been ashamed, but Michael could tell that thinking about all the time she'd lost upset her.

"Then we won't talk about it," Terri said. "Kate, if you start packing now, we can have a few bags of your things back at the house tonight and - "

"Mom, I am *not* moving back in with you. I'm happy here. Besides, Gavin needs someone here with him. As long as Trevor's around - "

"Kate, don't you understand?" Terri pleaded. "There is no Trevor. *That's* why we're so worried about you. You're getting yourself so worked up over something that isn't there. Honey, that's not healthy."

In that moment, it was all Michael could do to not drop to his knees and beg Mrs. Avery to take that back. On the far side of the room, Trevor had stopped his anxious pacing and had turned dark, furious eyes on the woman sitting across from Kate. Gavin, meanwhile, pressed a hand to his forehead and closed his eyes.

Even from across the room, Michael could sense Trevor's anger escalating. He wasn't sure what he would do or what he was capable of, but he really didn't want to find out.

"Trevor is real," Michael blurted. All four Averys looked at him, expecting him to elaborate. Trevor, on the other hand, looked stunned, then suspicious. Michael tried to ignore his dark stare as he cleared his throat and fibbed, "We uh... had a paranormal investigator come through a few years ago. This building is notorious for being haunted, and Trevor was one of the names that they caught during their uh..."

"EVP session?" Kate supplied.

"Yeah, that."

"Interesting," Rex murmured, not sounding all that convinced.

"Well regardless, I still think it would be in Kate's best interest if she moved back home with us," Terri announced.

"Oh, so now we're talking about me like I'm not here. Super," Kate remarked, rising up off the chair and onto her feet.

"Kate, we're only trying to help."

"Well you know what, Mom? I don't need your help. Come on, Michael, let's go." And with that, Kate stormed out of the apartment.

"Um, it was nice meeting you," Michael offered awkwardly before following her out the door.

Kate was already halfway down the stairs. Michael sprinted after her. Kate whirled around and looked at him.

"Let's just get out of here."

"Okay," Michael agreed. "Where do you want to go?"

"Anywhere."

They ended up at the movie theater. After catching the latest superhero summer blockbuster, they went out for a light dinner. Then Kate announced that she knew a cool independent coffee house not too far from downtown. They decided to grab a quick cup of coffee and spend the rest of the evening at the neighboring White Rock Lake. Although he was more than happy to spend time with Kate, Michael was worried about her. She hadn't said a word all afternoon about her parents, their request, or their concerns about her memory. He didn't want to pester her by asking about it, but he wished he knew that she was all right.

He didn't have to wonder long. During their sunset walk around the lake, Kate's phone buzzed, revealing a text message from Gavin.

Hey are you okay?

Kate stared at the phone, evidently trying to decide whether or not she wanted to ignore her brother, before punching in the message, **Yeah, I'm fine**, and pressing **Send**.

"So, have you ever seen the Lady of the Lake?" she asked Michael as she stuffed her phone back into her purse.

"From the Arthurian legend?" Michael asked.

"You've never heard of the Lady of the Lake?" She looked stunned. He simply shook his head. "She's the ghost of a woman who's said to haunt this area. According to the legend, she died sometime during the 1920's. Some say it was a car accident, some say she killed herself. But over the years, several people driving around the lake late at night have reported seeing a young woman, dressed in a wet gown, stopping drivers and asking them for a ride home. Then, once she's inside the car, she vanishes and leaves a puddle on the seat."

"That sounds annoying," Michael quipped. "So, is that why you suggested coffee out here? You wanted to find out if the lake is really haunted?"

"No, I brought you out here because I like lakes. And because that coffee was delicious."

"It was pretty good," Michael acknowledged. And though he still wasn't as keen on lakes as Kate, he had to admit it was a beautiful place. The peaceful, mirrored surface of the water reflected the warm colors of the evening sky. Not to mention for an area supposedly so haunted, he had yet to see a single ghost. That was definitely a plus.

"Listen, I'm sorry about the way I acted around my parents earlier. I should've handled it better," Kate said.

"You don't have to apologize to me."

"Still, I feel like I owe you some sort of explanation."

"You've told me before that you think your parents worry about you too much."

"*That's* the understatement of the new millennium," Kate remarked. "Still, I should have told you about the memory thing, especially after you answered all zillion of my questions. It's just that after everyone found out that I had amnesia, they began

150

treating me different, like I was broken. They'd walk on eggshells around me, afraid they might say something that would upset me.

"Then I had friends that I'd made in the past two years that I didn't remember. One of them doesn't talk to me anymore. It hurt her feelings that I couldn't remember her, and even though we both knew that it wasn't personal, it was just too hard for her."

"I'm sorry," Michael muttered.

"It's not your fault. And you know, for the most part, everyone has been really supportive. Val, for instance. When I woke up, I had no idea who she was. But in spite of everything, she was willing to take me back. It still depresses me though, losing two and a half years of my life. I mean, I don't remember the trip I took to Europe. I don't remember my last year of college or my graduation. I don't remember any of the Christmases or birthdays. All I have are pictures. And it's so frustrating because I try so hard to remember..." Kate trailed off and wiped a few stray tears off her cheeks. Michael wasn't sure what to say, so instead, he dug a tissue out of his pocket and handed it to her. "Thanks," Kate took it and dried her eyes.

By the time they finally walked back to the car, dusk had fallen and stars were beginning to appear in the sky. Soft mist danced across the glassy surface of the water. And perhaps his mind was still reeling from the legend Kate had told him earlier, but Michael could have sworn he saw a woman dressed in white climbing out of the water on the other side of the lake.

Kate didn't need to know that.

Once they were inside the car, Michael began to fasten his seatbelt, but Kate reached over, stroked his face with her fingertips, and pulled him into a kiss.

"Thanks for this afternoon," she whispered.

"Any time." Michael replied, leaning in to kiss her again, when suddenly, she pulled away. "Are you okay?" he asked.

"Yeah, I just... I don't know," Kate murmured as she glanced around. "Something feels... off..."

Before Michael could ask Kate what she meant, he saw it; the figure standing about fifty feet away, illuminated by the glow of a neighboring streetlight. Michael couldn't make out a face, but he knew that whoever he was, he'd seen them.

"Kate, don't move," Michael whispered.

"Why?"

"There's someone out there."

Kate drew in a shaky breath.

"Is it an alive someone?" she asked.

"No," Michael muttered with certainty. From a distance, it might have been hard to tell, but Michael could see no shadow at the stranger's feet, where, given his position under the streetlight, it should have been.

"Do you recognize him?"

Michael didn't respond. The man was walking silently and steadily toward the car with obvious intent. Under normal circumstances, Michael wouldn't have panicked. He would have simply ignored the man, who was now so close that Michael could see the whites of his eyes, and driven off, seemingly blissfully unaware. Even if the man decided to crawl into the backseat, as others had done in the past, Michael would have been able to handle it.

But these were not normal circumstances. This wasn't a ghost with whom Michael had accidentally made eye contact or whose unheard question he'd happened to answer. This guy had found *him*. Michael realized, as the man came to a stop just outside of Kate's window, that he'd probably been following them. The man peered through the window directly at Michael, who stared (stupidly) back.

"Michael, what's happening?" Kate whispered.

Michael didn't know how to respond. The man didn't look particularly threatening. He was of average height and build, with blue eyes and light brown hair. He was probably around his mid-to-late twenties and although his expression was somber, he didn't look angry or out for revenge. Then again, the way he'd chosen to spy and sneak up on them didn't exactly register as "not creepy."

The stranger raised a fist and knocked on the window. It wasn't very loud, but it was just audible enough for Kate to gasp and whirl around so that she was staring out the window and, unknowingly, into the face of their ghostly visitor. Michael didn't want to acknowledge him, but he also didn't want him letting himself into the car, especially with Kate there. She already had her own ghost to deal with.

"Kate, stay in the car," Michael instructed.

"What are you going to do?" she asked.

In response, Michael opened his door, climbed out, and faced the ghost from across the top of the car.

"Can I help you?" he asked.

The guy smiled.

"So, it's true," he said as he strolled around the car to meet with Michael.

"What is?" Michael asked.

"You can see us."

"Who told you?"

The man shrugged.

"Word gets around," he replied. "Can your girlfriend see us too?"

"No, but she knows you're here."

"She must be pretty understanding," he remarked. Michael didn't respond. "You know, I've heard about people like you. Mediums and such. Didn't think you actually existed."

"Some people would say the same about you," Michael retorted.

"Yeah, I used to be one of them."

"So, who are you?"

"Gracie didn't tell you?" he asked, his blue eyes suddenly solemn.

"Gracie?" Michael asked. "You mean Grace Bledsoe?"

"She's the one. Or she was," the ghost replied sadly.

"Oh! Are you, um..." Michael was ashamed to admit that he couldn't remember the guy's name. The guy who had been in love with Grace even though she was engaged to his best friend.

The guy who'd stabbed her to death just hours before her wedding.

Crap.

"Daniel Ford. And judging by the look on your face, you've heard all about me."

"A little..." Michael could feel the blood draining from his face. Why did he have to get out of the car? Why did he think this was anything other than a very dumb idea? Why did he *never* learn that by talking to ghosts, he was basically asking for bad things to happen?

"Well, whatever you heard, it wasn't true. I don't know who killed Gracie, or me for that matter. But whoever it was, I can guarantee you, is still out there."

CHAPTER SEVENTEEN

Kate barely noticed the world passing by outside her window as she tried to sort through everything Michael had just told her.

The ghost outside her window had been Daniel Ford, the man who was supposed to have murdered his best friend's bride and then turned a gun on himself. Only as it turned out, he hadn't killed anyone. At least, that's what he claimed.

He didn't deny his feelings for Grace. He even admitted to engaging in a seven-month-long affair with her. That was why his fingerprints had been discovered at the scene. He *had* been there, but not with any intention of killing her.

He also admitted to getting drunk after they'd said their last goodbyes, but he hadn't even known that she'd been killed until after he'd opened his eyes and found himself staring down at his own body, blood flowing from a single bullet wound in his skull. A gun had been set near his right hand in an attempt to make it look like he had taken his own life.

He'd been so stricken, seeing his body lying lifeless on the distant riverbank that he didn't catch a glimpse of his murderer, who had darted back through the tall grass and into the forest. He'd wandered the area ever since, waiting for whatever it was that kept him there to finally relinquish its hold on him.

After admitting all of this to Michael, Daniel had asked him one favor; that he find his parents and tell them that their son was innocent. He didn't need them to know that he hadn't killed himself, and he didn't want them knowing about the affair, but they had to know that he was no murderer. He'd advised Michael not to seek them out at their Waxahachie home, because they rarely answered the door unless they knew someone was going to

155

stop by. Even if they were given a heads up, he felt they'd be less inclined to listen to a stranger who happened to know their address. Instead, Daniel had suggested that Michael seek them out at their church, Calvary Hill. Michael had neither agreed nor disagreed.

"So, what are you going to do?" Kate asked once he finished recounting everything the ghost had told him.

"I don't know," Michael admitted, without tearing his eyes away from the road. "The problem is I know what I *should* do, but unfortunately, it's the same thing I've been trying to avoid for the past ten years. What do you do in that situation?"

"You know, back in college, I had a friend who'd dated this one guy for like, five years. She'd been with him since high school. Now, all of us could tell she wasn't happy in the relationship, but she stayed with him because she felt like she had to. Everyone they knew from high school told them how perfect they were for each other, and she felt like she had to put everyone else's happiness before her own. Well, she finally worked up the nerve to break up with him near the end of our junior year and for the first time since I'd met her, she seemed truly happy."

"No offense, but I really have no idea where you're going with this," Michael told her.

"The point is she spent so much time trying to do what she thought everyone else wanted her to do, just like you've spent so much time trying to be the person you think everyone wants you to be. But like it or not, that's not who you are. You're not normal and you never will be. And I don't want to tell you what to do, but I do think that until you accept the fact that you're not like everyone else, you can never *really* be happy. You said you spent the last ten years avoiding situations like this, but you really spent the last ten years trying to hide a huge part of what makes you who you are. And when you think about it, that's really no life at all."

"Kate, I know you're trying to help. But this isn't some little personality quirk that people will embrace with open arms. I am a scientific - no - I am a *spiritual* abnormality. This isn't the kind of thing where people pat you on the back and say that it's okay to be different. This is the kind of thing that gets people committed."

"I believe you," Kate reminded him.

"You're different," Michael said.

"Luke believes you."

"Luke is insane."

"You know, I'm not sure how much you want to hear this, but he might be able to help you."

"How?"

"Well, he does communicate with ghosts for a living. Maybe he has some advice."

"You know, sometimes I wonder why he wasn't the one born with Ghost-Vision. He's the one who wants to see them."

"Because then it wouldn't be exciting for him. It'd be a boring, everyday thing. I know you think it's a nuisance, but for most of us, the afterlife is this huge mystery. You're lucky in the sense that you've never had to wonder what happens after we die, but at the same time, you'll never feel that fascination when a vase goes toppling off a table with no explanation. For you, it's someone pushing a vase off a table. For the rest of us, it's something that can't be explained. It's proof that there isn't always a rational answer. And that's really cool to a lot of people." Michael pulled up to a red light and looked at Kate. She could tell he didn't know what to say, but she was pretty sure she'd gotten through to him. "I've probably put way too much thought into this," she laughed nervously.

"I'm glad you did," Michael told her. Then, with a sigh of resignation, he said, "Call Luke."

An hour later, they were all three gathered at Michael's apartment. Luke and Kate sat silently on the couch while Michael paced back and forth and relayed his encounter with Daniel Ford.

"That's interesting. In between reviewing our footage and working on some new stuff for the show, I've actually been researching Grace and the murder. Almost every article I read mentioned something about Daniel being in love with her, but there was nothing about it being a mutual thing," Luke said.

"Do you think that's why she was so violent the other night?" Kate asked.

"Probably. She didn't want anyone, including us, finding out about her affair. She'd rather have the world, especially her fiancé, believe she died an honorable, faithful woman than you know, a two-timing harlot," Luke said, leaning back and propping one foot up on the coffee table.

"Charming," Kate remarked.

"So, what do we do?" Michael asked.

"Well, first we need to make sure these people are actually still in the area," Luke said.

"The way Daniel was talking made it sound like they still lived in Waxahachie. I mean, he told me what church they go to," Michael told him.

"Yeah, but hasn't he been hanging out in the woods for the last two years? How would he know if his parents still go there?"

"He probably goes to check up on them. Brink still visits his brother and sister."

"Really?" Luke asked. "So, ghosts can travel?"

"You didn't know that?" Michael asked.

"I wasn't sure," Luke confessed. "I always figured they had the ability, but considering several of the locations the *Cemetery Tours* crew visits have been haunted by the same ghosts for decades, some centuries, I couldn't be one hundred percent positive."

"So, if ghosts are mobile, I guess that means Trevor did follow us here," Kate said.

"Has he been around since before you moved?" Luke asked.

"I think so, but at the time, I didn't realize we were being haunted. I thought it was my imagination."

"I think a lot of sensitives think they're just imagining things. At least at first."

"I wouldn't say I'm a 'sensitive.' I just think that Trevor makes his presence known because he wants us to acknowledge that he's there."

"I don't know. You seem pretty in tune to me," Luke told her.

"Not as much as you guys."

"Well, no one is as in tune as Mikey. But I really had to work at it. You know, seeing my grandfather as a kid was kind of a freak thing. Even after that happened, I could never tell when a ghost was around. But when I started investigating and really immersing myself in that world, I began to recognize the feelings, the subtle changes in the atmosphere... You feel that, don't you?"

"I guess." She remembered the night before, the creepy sensation she'd felt standing outside the barn. She'd known that whoever was in there hadn't wanted them there, and she'd been right. Then earlier that evening, she'd been able to tell that something was off just as Daniel Ford showed up. "But it's all new for me. I mean, I never noticed anything until the break-in."

"You know why I think that is? I think it scared you."

"Of course it scared me. Someone broke into my home."

"No, I mean it scared you so bad that you suddenly became hyper-sensitive to everything going on around you. It's a defense mechanism. I once dated a girl who had a bad experience with roaches when she was a kid, and ever since then, she'd had this super-sensitive hearing. If there was a roach around, she could hear it from across the room."

"It must be so odd being you," Michael remarked.

Luke shrugged. Kate decided to try to steer the conversation back on track.

"So, let's say we actually go to this church tomorrow. Then what?" she asked.

"Well, I'm assuming that even though Mikey told you about his little talent and the world didn't explode - "

"*You* told her," Michael interjected.

" - he still doesn't want anyone else to know, which means that we can't just walk up to them and say, 'Hey listen, our friend

159

here sees ghosts and he has a message from your son.' So the real question is, 'How do we make them believe we have a message from their son without telling them about Mikey?' Fortunately for you, I have the answer."

"We tell them that he came to you instead," Kate said.

"No wonder we get along so well." Luke grinned at her.

"Wait, I don't understand. What makes that so believable?" Michael asked.

Luke and Kate both looked at him.

"Hello, world famous ghost hunter? Host of *Cemetery Tours*? Ringing any bells?" Luke asked.

"What if they don't watch the show?"

"Hey, I'm offering to do you a favor here, Mikey. If they have any doubts about who I am or why they should trust me, I've got more than enough to convince them that I'm someone they should be listening to. And of course, you two will be there to back me up."

"Okay, so what's our story?" Kate asked.

"No story. We tell them the truth. I'll introduce myself, tell them about the show, how the new season will be on the Discovery Channel in September, every Monday night at 8. Then I'll say that we were investigating that old cemetery and we came into contact with Daniel and he asked us to deliver a message. It's as good as gold."

To Kate, it sounded like a reasonable plan. Michael didn't look quite so convinced, but he didn't say anything.

They agreed to meet the following morning at 7:30 and drive to the church together. Thankfully, Kate managed to talk Luke out of bringing all of his film equipment. Since they had such an early morning ahead of them, Luke bid them goodnight and left shortly thereafter, though Kate could have sworn she noticed him wink before letting himself out.

"We should probably get some sleep too," she said once she and Michael were alone. "Gotta wake up bright and early for another fun filled day of ghostly adventures."

"Oh, yay," Michael quipped. Kate grinned and kissed him lightly. "So are you going to be all right? I mean, do you need to stay here tonight? You know, after this afternoon and everything?"

Kate could tell he was trying his hardest not to sound like he was expecting anything from her. It was sweet.

"I think I'll be okay. Gavin should be out of it by now." By then, it was almost midnight. Even if Gavin had fallen asleep on the couch waiting for her, he slept so heavily, she was sure she'd be able to sneak in without waking him. "But thank you."

"No problem."

He walked her back to her apartment, and after a sweet kiss goodnight, Kate slipped silently into her apartment. Inside, it was so dark that she could barely see a thing, but she heard Gavin snoring softly from the couch and realized she'd been right about him staying up to wait for her. Under normal circumstances, she would have found the gesture touching, knowing that her big brother worried about her, but at the moment, she was still angry at him for conspiring with their parents. She crept silently past his sleeping form and into the bathroom, where she brushed her teeth and changed into her pajamas.

Climbing into bed, she let her thoughts drift back to Michael, and she realized just how drastically her life had changed over the course of just a few short days, and mostly because of him. So far, the changes were all good. But the sound of wandering footsteps just outside her door reminded her that it wasn't over. Another change was coming.

And this time, it was going to affect everyone.

CHAPTER EIGHTEEN

Gavin was still asleep on the couch when Kate dragged herself out of bed just a few hours later. She showered and changed into a skirt and blouse before meandering into the kitchen to brew a pot of coffee. She was so tired, she was sure it would take at least five cups before she was suitable for any sort of social interaction.

Around the same time she downed her second cup, Gavin came shuffling into the kitchen with disheveled hair and dark circles under his eyes.

"Are you just getting home?" he mumbled gruffly. Kate didn't answer him. Part of her wasn't awake enough to talk. The other part was still mad at him. He knew it, too. "Look Kate, I'm sorry about yesterday. But I told you not to tell them about your imaginary friend."

"You make me sound like a toddler," Kate snapped, her voice rough from her lack of a full night's sleep.

"Well, for the record, I don't want you to move out. But if Mom and Dad think it's for the best - "

Kate didn't want to listen to his excuses. Breezing past him, she sought sanctuary in the bathroom, where she brushed her teeth and applied a light layer of makeup. When she emerged, Gavin had disappeared. She guessed he'd given up trying to be nice and had gone back to bed in his own room. Good. She wasn't in the mood to deal with him.

Without leaving a note or poking her head into his room to tell him where she was going, she grabbed her purse and walked out the door and across the landing to Michael's apartment.

He answered the door and greeted her with a sleepy "Hi."

"Hi, yourself," she replied. She had been worried that her confrontation with Gavin would leave her surly and unpleasant for the rest of the morning, but just being around Michael, she felt her spirits begin to lift. Of course, that may have had something to do with how handsome he looked in a pair of sand-colored slacks and a button-down shirt the color of clouds. He also smelled good, like *Old Spice*. "So, are you ready to get this show on the road?"

"No," he remarked.

Kate laughed.

"Everything is going to be fine. You'll see."

He didn't look like he believed her, but he didn't contradict her. Instead, he took her hands and pulled her closer to him. "You look beautiful."

Even though they were kind-of-sort-of-dating (or so she thought; they hadn't really talked about it), Kate still felt her heart skip a beat. It was amazing, the effect that the simplest sentiment from the right guy could have on a girl's entire day.

"Thank you," she smiled, rising up onto her toes to kiss him. Lost in his touch, she felt airy and light-headed and she found herself wondering why she'd ever worried about a thing in her life. She'd just wrapped her arms around his neck when suddenly, he pulled away, almost like her touch had burned him.

"What's wrong?" she asked.

"Um... Brink just appeared," he replied, blushing furiously. Kate felt the blood rushing to her cheeks as well. "And he's um... he's not very mature..."

Oh God... Kate could only imagine.

"Do I want to know?" she asked.

"Probably not."

Luke arrived a few minutes later, as energetic and ready to go as ever.

"Good morning, friends," he greeted them with a chipper smile. He looked good, too. In dark jeans, a button-down shirt the same color as Michael's, and a vest the color of a thunderstorm, he easily could have stepped out of a copy of *GQ*.

"You're very awake," Michael observed.

"I'm a morning person. Always have been."

"I didn't know that," Kate said.

"Oh yeah. During the first season of the show, I needed a *lot* of carbs and sugar to be able to stay awake to film at night. Now I've sort of trained myself, but I still enjoy mornings."

"Good. That means you get to drive," Michael told him.

"Fine by me," Luke agreed.

Once they were on the road, Kate felt herself perking up a little more. She'd volunteered to sit in the back seat thinking she would want to take a nap, but as they sped along the highway toward downtown, the combined effects of the coffee, the lure of adventure, and the classic rock blaring through Luke's car's stereo had been enough to keep her awake and alert and able to enjoy the ride. Michael, on the other hand, was either still half-asleep or deep in thought. Kate guessed it was probably the latter.

The ride seemed to be going smoothly until they hit a massive traffic jam halfway through downtown. With traffic at a standstill and no real escape, Luke whipped out his iPhone and checked the conditions.

"There's a lot of road work about two miles ahead of us," he announced.

"Are we going to be late?" Kate asked.

"Probably," Luke muttered. "But as long as we get there by the time the service lets out, we should be okay."

"Isn't it kind of rude to walk in in the middle of a service?" Michael asked.

"Depends on what kind of church it is. I grew up Episcopalian and we were always late," Luke responded.

"I'm Presbyterian and we have people walk in late all the time," Kate said. "Do we know what Calvary Hill is?"

"As far as I can tell, they're non-denominational," Luke answered. "Why?"

"Just curious," Kate replied as she glanced out the window at the stationary cars lining the highway. The driver in the car next to them seemed to have abandoned all hope of getting anywhere any time soon. He'd pulled out what was either a Kindle or an iPad and was flipping absentmindedly through the tabs. The woman behind them looked frantic and angry and depressed all at once as she yelled into her cell phone. The driver in the car catty-corner kept glancing around, like he was looking for some sort of escape route. Luke seemed to be of a similar mindset.

"God, does this just never end?" he griped. "This is ridiculous. If they're gonna do this, they need to give people a heads up. Or a way out."

"Welcome to Dallas," Kate muttered.

They pulled into the parking lot of Calvary Hill at 9:18, almost twenty minutes after the service began. It had taken them thirty-seven minutes just to get past the road work that had shut down two of the three interstate lanes, and although Luke had sped like a madman to reach the church on time, the highway patrolman who'd pulled him over just as he was getting ready to exit wasn't as understanding (or as big a *Cemetery Tours* fan) as Luke had apparently hoped he'd be.

The small parking lot was full of cars, several of them rather new. The church itself was a modest white building with blue doors and a steeple. It sat atop a slight hill overlooking an open field. Climbing out of the car, Michael noticed the young man, looking discouraged and forlorn, sitting on the steps leading up to the chapel's porch.

"Daniel?" Michael called.

The ghost looked up at him.

"You came!" His astonishment was apparent in both his eyes and his voice.

"Sorry we're late. We hit some pretty nasty traffic on 75," Luke apologized.

Daniel looked surprised.

"Can he see me?" he asked Michael.

Michael shook his head.

"So, what's the plan?" Kate asked. "Should we just go in?"

"I'll go see where they are in the service," Daniel offered before disappearing through the closed doors.

"Daniel's going to check where they are," Michael relayed, stuffing his hands into his pockets and taking a deep breath. He'd never known exactly how he felt about church, or the idea of God for that matter. He knew that something had to exist beyond the physical realm, but church had always taught him that the spirits of those who'd died either went to Heaven or Hell. There was no in-between. Yet the countless number of souls left wandering the Earth indicated otherwise.

"You gonna be okay?" Kate asked, linking her arm through his.

"I'll be fine," he assured her.

"Just let me do the talking," Luke told him. "Remember, you're only here so you can tell me who I need to talk to. And to back me up when these people don't believe that I host the greatest paranormal investigation show on television."

Daniel returned before Michael could think of a snide remark that may or may not have been altogether appropriate for church grounds. He informed them that the congregants were singing and that they should be able to sneak in before the sermon began.

Inside, the church was a lot more open than its exterior would have led Michael to believe. The twenty or so rows of pews were full of people, from small children to young adults to elderly couples. The white, sunlit walls were decorated with an assortment of blue and gold crosses and the simple wooden altar at the front of the chapel bore a large book, the cover of which looked to be cast in gold and silver.

"Do you see them?" Michael muttered to Daniel as he, Kate, and Luke slipped casually into the back pew.

"My mom's the one in the teal dress. Second row. My dad's sitting next to her. He just got through with chemo," he replied.

Michael spotted them instantly. Although he couldn't see their faces, he knew the last two painful years of their lives would be reflected there. Mr. Ford looked shaky and feeble as he bent over and coughed into his hand. Mrs. Ford, in turn, rested a reassuring hand on his shoulder as she leaned in and whispered something in his ear.

Meanwhile, a distinguished man with a head full of silver hair made his way to the front of the altar. He was dressed in a simple white robe and he walked with his hands held out.

"Welcome friends, family," he announced. "And a special welcome to those of you just joining us."

Michael didn't realize he was addressing them until he noticed several pairs of eyes glancing around to look at them. A few of them chuckled. One person sneered. But overall, the general consensus seemed to be that the newcomers were not all that interesting.

That is, until one of the three teenage girls sitting in front of them took a second look at Luke.

Her eyes widened, a lot like the way Kate's had the first afternoon he'd shown up at their door. With a sharp gasp, the girl turned to her friends and whispered, "That's Luke Rainer!"

"Who?" one of the girls whispered back.

"You know, that hot ghost hunter guy from the Discovery Channel?"

The third girl looked around very indiscreetly.

"Nuh-uh, that's not him," she whispered.

"It is!" the first girl insisted.

"What would Luke Rainer be doing all the way out here?"

"I'm on a top-secret mission," Luke leaned forward and answered her.

That was a mistake.

The girls dissolved into a disruptive frenzy of giggles and excited whispers. A few adults, one of whom looked to be the first girl's mother, shushed them. They quieted down, but they kept stealing glances at Luke over their shoulders.

"It seems there's something rather exciting happening in the last few pews," the pastor observed.

Michael glared at Luke.

"Sorry, Father. Continue," Luke announced.

A few members of the congregation chuckled. Most, however, muttered their disapproval before turning their attention back to the priest.

"Are you insane? You're going to get us kicked out!" Michael hissed at Luke.

"Relax. No one is going to kick us out of *church*."

But the woman who turned and shushed him certainly looked like she wanted to.

"Michael's right, Luke. This is a place of worship for these people," Kate whispered.

"What, God doesn't have a sense of humor?" Luke asked.

But he seemed to understand what they were trying to tell him, because he didn't say another word for the rest of the sermon, which turned out to be a passionate, if not slightly unnerving lecture about faith, words, and actions that set true Christians apart from the rest of the world.

"Now, it is easy for a person to say that he believes in God, that he believes in the power of Jesus Christ," the pastor said. "Talkin' is the easiest thing in the world, because we all know how much we love to hear ourselves talk. But being a Christian, a true follower of Christ, isn't about sayin' stuff. It's about doin' stuff. Reachin' out to our brothers and sisters in the Lord. Helpin' them. Not bein' afraid to do the right thing, no matter the consequence. Those who do so, *they* are truly the ones who walk with our Lord and *they* shall be the ones who inherit His Kingdom.

"Now there are folks out there who will try to tell you that everyone goes to Heaven. There are folks out there who will tell you that believin' that God died for your sins is enough to get you into Heaven. They are all *wrong*. Jesus Christ in the Gospel of Matthew states that many will call out to Him, 'Lord! Lord!' but that is not enough. Those who speak His name, but do not *live* out

His words will not inherit the Kingdom of Heaven. Christ will cast them out Himself."

"This is a little different than the church I grew up in," Kate muttered, her eyes fixed and her brows furrowed.

Michael hadn't been raised in a specific denomination like Kate or Luke, but he had to admit that he'd never heard such harsh words or accusations from any of his religious friends.

The members of the congregation, however, appeared enthralled by the man standing before them. One man scribbled down notes in a journal while a woman next to him clutched a handkerchief to her chest and stared at the pastor with wide, awestruck eyes. Even the girls who, moments earlier, had been starstruck by Luke seemed enraptured by their pastor's words.

"That's Pastor Augustus Cannon," Daniel informed Michael. "He's... a little out there. But everyone in the congregation just loves him."

A little out there was putting it lightly, Michael thought, as the man lost himself in a prayer, raising both hands to the ceiling and invoking the power and might of the Lord.

"If that guy starts speaking in Tongues, I'm out," Luke remarked quietly.

"Oh, that's where you draw the line?" Michael asked.

Fortunately, Augustus Cannon ended his prayer in English.

As the service progressed, Michael began to grow more and more agitated. He knew Luke had volunteered to do the talking, but that didn't make him any less nervous. Kate seemed to sense his agitation, because she reached over and took his hand, lacing her fingers through his.

"Everything's going to be fine," she assured him.

He glanced back at the Fords, who looked so small and meek in the second row, and prayed to the God he didn't know that she was right.

CHAPTER NINETEEN

The service ended with a fast-paced contemporary Christian song that Kate thought she may have recognized from her days in her church's youth group. Immediately after the song ended, the three girls sitting in front of them flocked to Luke to beg for autographs and pictures. Watching them fawn over him made Kate realize how silly she must have seemed the day she met him. While he obliged, signing autographs and posing for pictures, four more girls meandered over to find out what the fuss was about.

"What's going on?"

"It's Luke Rainer! You know, from *Cemetery Tours*?"

"The TV show?"

"What are you doing here?" one of the girls getting an autograph asked.

"Classified," he grinned.

"Is it for the show? Are you guys here filming?"

"Not right now. It's more of a personal favor."

Speaking of that personal favor, Kate looked up at Michael. She followed his eyes to the front of the sanctuary, where a man and a woman stood talking with the preacher. Kate couldn't help but think they didn't look like they were doing very well. In spite of the bright color of her dress, a veil of sadness hung over the woman, so heavy Kate could almost feel it. The man looked sickly and tired as he shook the preacher's hand, unwittingly reminding Kate of Gavin.

"Is that them?" she asked.

"Yeah," Michael replied, glancing back to look at Luke, who was still caught up in the small swarm of fans and curious onlookers. Kate, meanwhile, kept her eyes locked on the Fords.

They exchanged pleasantries with a few other couples before Mrs. Ford took her husband's hand.

"Michael," Kate said. "I think they're getting ready to leave."

Michael turned his attention back to the Fords who, sure enough, were making their way not toward the front doors where Michael, Kate, and Luke had entered, but toward a side door next to their seats.

"We're gonna lose them," Michael said.

And without bothering to tear Luke away from his fans, he took off, making his way through the congregants who lingered to catch up and reflect on the service. Kate followed, unsure if he would need her or not, but wanting to be there in case he did.

"Are you Mr. and Mrs. Ford?" he was asking as she caught up with him. She kept her distance, far enough away to remain inconspicuous, but close enough to be able to hear what he was saying. They didn't even seem to notice her as they answered him, all the while eyeing Michael with confusion and curiosity. "My name is Michael. I uh... I'm sorry to bother you like this..."

"Come on, Michael. You can do it," Kate whispered.

"Are you new here?" Mr. Ford asked. His voice rough and hoarse, like he had an upper respiratory infection.

"Um... no, sir. I actually came here to talk to you. I have a message. From your son, Daniel."

Mr. and Mrs. Ford stared at him with heartbreaking disbelief.

"Daniel?" Mrs. Ford whispered.

"That's impossible," Mr. Ford informed him. "Our son is dead."

"I know. But you've got to hear me out. Daniel told me about everything that happened two years ago. He - " Michael tried to explain but Mr. Ford cut him off.

"Young man, I don't know what you thought you were going to accomplish by coming here and throwing all of this back in our faces - "

"Hi!" An unexpected and cheerful voice in Kate's ear startled her so much, she nearly leapt a foot off the ground. She turned to see a young woman around her age, with hair the color of honey and eyes the color of the sky, smiling at her. "I don't think I recognize you. Is this your first time at Calvary? Or as we call it, 'Cool-vary?'" she giggled.

"Yeah..." Kate replied, hoping the girl wouldn't notice her unease.

"Oh, you don't have to be shy. We're always so happy to welcome new members to our big, happy, church family. My name is Chastity Cannon. I'm Pastor Augustus' daughter."

"Oh, was he the one speaking today?"

"Yes. Wasn't he wonderful? I am so blessed to have such a wise, godly man as my father."

"He was something," Kate acknowledged.

"So what is your name?"

"Oh, right. Sorry. I'm Kate. Kate Avery."

"Kate. Is that short for Katherine?"

"Yeah, but no one calls me that."

"I don't see why. It's a lovely name."

"Thanks, but I don't really like it."

"That's a shame. I believe we should all go by our true names. They are, after all, the names God intended for us."

"Huh. You'd think the guy who designed the universe would be a little more creative," Kate remarked with a quick grin. When Chastity didn't respond, she added, "You know, because there are so many people named Katherine?"

"I don't think that's funny," Chastity replied sternly.

Kate was taken aback. It almost sounded like the girl who moments before had been so friendly and welcoming was scolding her.

Before she could respond, a commotion broke out behind them. Kate whirled around to see sickly Mr. Ford, clutching the front of Michael's shirt and shoving him up against a wall, knocking down several crosses in the process.

"John!" Pastor Augustus was with them in an instant, trying to pry Michael away from Mr. Ford's grasp. Mrs. Ford watched helplessly with a hand clamped over her mouth and tears streaming down her weary face. "John, let him go!"

Finally, the older man relinquished his hold on Michael, who stumbled backward, looking aghast. Kate raced forward, abandoning Chastity and her contemptuous look of disapproval, and pulled Michael away from the scene.

"Are you all right?" she asked, taking him by the shoulders.

"Yeah..." he replied, obviously still shaken.

"Now what is going on?" the pastor demanded.

"Ask *him*," Mr. Ford sneered, pointing a shaky finger at Michael. "Him and his devil speak!"

"His what?"

"My son is dead. You know my son is dead. And here he comes, trying to tell me that he didn't do what he did..." Mr. Ford choked as he dissolved into tears. His wife stepped forward and tried to comfort him, but he shook her off, and, with one last disdainful look at Michael, walked out the door.

Mrs. Ford made to follow him, hesitated for a moment, and then turned her tearstained face back to Michael.

"Thank you," she whispered. Then, she slipped silently out the door after her husband.

Kate looked up at Michael, who stood staring at the door like he wasn't sure he understood what had just happened, and moved in closer to him.

"Well, I believe introductions are in order," Pastor Cannon said, eyeing the couple with great interest. "My name is Augustus Cannon. I'm one of the pastors here at Calvary Hill. I believe you've met my daughter, Chastity." He smiled as Chastity walked over and stood faithfully by his side.

"Yes, Daddy," Chastity beamed. "This is Katherine Avery and her friend, um..."

"Michael."

"Good to meet you, Katherine and Michael," Pastor Cannon said. "Now why don't you tell me what that was all about."

Kate and Michael exchanged glances.

"It's kind of a long story," Michael began.

"I assure you, I've got the time," Cannon replied.

"Well, you see - "

"Hey, guys," Luke interrupted, bounding forward with just as much energy and enthusiasm as he'd displayed earlier that morning. Kate had been following him long enough to know the positive effect that meeting fans had on his mood. "Hey, Father. Great sermon."

"Thank you, young man. But I'm not a Father. I'm a Pastor."

"Oh, sorry. I'm Episcopalian," Luke told him as though that cleared everything up.

Cannon didn't seem to understand, but he didn't pursue the matter.

"And I seem to be the only person in this building who doesn't know who you are."

"Luke Rainer. Host and lead paranormal investigator of the highly rated television series, *Cemetery Tours*. Good to meet you."

"*Cemetery Tours*? What do you do? Do you travel to different cemeteries and study their history?"

"We're ghost hunters," Luke explained. "But every location we investigate has a ton of dark history and we try to learn as much as we can about what went on there. We try to convey as much of that as we can to our viewers, but with commercials, we only get about forty-two minutes of actual screen time. To be honest, we could probably take every location we've ever investigated and do an entire season on every single one of them."

"Well, it sounds like you're very passionate about what you do," Cannon observed.

"Yes, sir, I am," Luke answered proudly.

"But that still doesn't tell me what *you* - " he looked back at Michael, " - said to a very sick and elderly man to make him angry enough to pin you to a wall."

"Whoa, seriously? You pissed him off that bad?" Luke asked. Cannon and his daughter both glared at him. "Oh, sorry. You pissed him off that badly?"

Cannon turned his attention back to Michael. "Maybe we should talk alone."

Michael looked like that was the absolute last thing he wanted, but he didn't object. Leaving Kate and Luke with his daughter, Augustus Cannon took Michael by the shoulder and directed him through a door back behind the altar and out of sight.

Michael reluctantly followed the pastor through a short and narrow hallway and into a small room that seemed to serve as an office, a dressing space, and a storage closet all in one. In the far-left corner of the room sat an old wooden dresser, and just to the right of the dresser hung a full-length rectangular mirror. The opposite side of the room was a cluttered mess of books, boxes, filing cabinets, and even a few potted plants. There was just enough space for the simple wooden desk, covered in scattered papers, pens, and a miniature portable fan, to fit in the center of the mess and confusion. Michael couldn't imagine having to work in such a tight space.

But the ghost standing in the midst of the boxes and plants didn't seem to mind at all.

The first thing Michael noticed about him was that he wasn't Daniel Ford. In fact, Michael hadn't seen hide nor hair of Daniel Ford since before he'd talked to his parents. Perhaps it didn't matter to him that his father didn't believe him as long as he'd heard the message.

This guy looked younger than Daniel, Michael guessed around twenty, with longish light brown hair and chubby features. He was wearing tight jeans and a green T-shirt. He looked up as Cannon and Michael entered the room. Michael quickly averted his eyes. He wasn't about to acknowledge another ghost around these people. Not after the fiasco with the Fords.

He wasn't sure what it was that had inspired him to run after them when Kate pointed out that they were getting ready to leave, why he hadn't just torn Luke away from his adoring fans and reminded him why they'd come there. Maybe it had just been a reflex. Maybe it was because he knew Kate was there. Or maybe he wanted to do something, not just for Kate, but for himself. To prove he wasn't some coward who needed his famous friend to bail him out of situations he'd rather avoid altogether.

No matter what had driven him to speak with them, nothing could have prepared him for Mr. Ford's violent reaction. In the years before he'd sworn off spiritual communication, he thought he'd seen it all, from tears of mirth to overwhelming displays of gratitude. But he'd never once been physically attacked or verbally assaulted. Even now that he'd been able to take a few deep breaths and think it through, he still didn't understand what it was that had caused Mr. Ford to lash out at him like that.

"Sorry this place is such a wreck. We've been having some technical difficulties over in our offices." Cannon's voice pulled Michael from his own mind and back into the tiny room. The older man stood in the corner of the room, unbuttoning the clasp on his long, white robe. "Last week, every bathroom in the whole building decided to flood, leaving us with a lot of damage and not a lot of space."

"Oh, it's fine," Michael replied, trying to distract himself from the ghost's curious gaze. He picked up a Bible that had been left on the desk, flipped it open, and read the first verse that stood out to him.

"Do not be anxious about anything, but in everything, by prayer and petition, with thanksgiving, present your requests to God. And the peace of God, which transcends all understanding, will guard your hearts and your minds in Christ Jesus."

"Well then," Cannon addressed Michael casually after he hung his robe up in the dresser. "Let's talk."

Michael swallowed nervously, only too aware of the ghost listening to their every word.

"Can we maybe go outside? It's pretty stuffy in here," he said and prayed that the ghost wouldn't follow them.

"Sure."

Cannon led Michael through the hallway to a back exit and finally, outside to a small garden, full of ill-tended shrubs, flowers, and vegetables.

"A Sunday School project. This hasn't been our best year, partly due to the horrible drought we've been experiencing," Cannon explained. "Now then. Tell me. What happened between you and the Fords?"

"I was just... giving them a message," Michael explained, sounding like he was somehow trying to prove his innocence while knowing full well that he could not.

"A message from whom?" Cannon asked.

"From Daniel."

"Daniel Ford is dead, son."

"I know."

Cannon's eyes bore so deeply into him that Michael looked away.

"Then surely you know that it is impossible for you to have had any sort of communication with him." Michael didn't respond. He recognized the pastor's tone. It was the same one that teachers used in elementary school whenever they were about to lecture a kid for bad behavior. "That's something I don't understand about you young people today; that you have to go out of your way to hurt other people just to make yourselves feel superior. John and Deborah have suffered more than you can fathom and yet you seek them out here at this holy place of worship, a place where they are supposed to feel loved and protected, and you come here intent on taking that peace away from them. Now tell me, what were you thinking?"

"I was trying to do the right thing," Michael mumbled.

"I find that very hard to believe." The pastor's eyes were cold. "I don't know what you were expecting to gain here, but you listen and you listen good. This is sacred ground. The members of this church are good, holy people of God, and I will not have troublemakers like you and your arrogant friends inflicting pain on any member of this congregation, especially a man who has lost his only son to sin and death. You need to abandon this path of evil and destruction and return to the Light of God. Until you do, you have no place in this church."

With that, Augustus Cannon walked away from Michael and back toward the building.

"There's a ghost in your office," Michael announced to the pastor's retreating back. The man stopped in his tracks. "He's young. He's got long brown hair. Sort of stocky." Slowly, Cannon turned to look at him, his expression torn between shock, hatred, and pure terror. "Maybe you know him."

Cannon took a deep, trembling breath. "You get out of here," he hissed through gritted teeth. "And don't come back."

Michael was only too happy to oblige. After today, he didn't want anything more to do with the small-town church or its ghosts, and he was certainly through with trying to play the hero. The barrier between the realms of the living and the dead existed for a reason, and the ability to breach that barrier did not give him, or anyone else, the right to do so.

Regardless, Michael felt a twinge of guilt when Kate took his hand, kissed him on the cheek, and whispered, "I'm so proud of you," as they made their way through the parking lot and away from the weary souls of Calvary Hill.

CHAPTER TWENTY

"Where have you been?" Gavin demanded as soon Kate walked through the door.

"Church," Kate answered. Of course, that wasn't the entire truth. After church, she, Michael, and Luke had stopped for a quick lunch at a roadside barbecue joint which, at first glance, had struck Kate as "iffy," but had turned out to serve the best chopped beef sandwich she had ever tasted.

There, Michael filled them in on his confrontation with John Ford as well as the lecture he'd received from Augustus Cannon. Although he didn't say so, Kate could tell the morning had left him shaken and she hoped that he didn't resent her or Luke for convincing him that they should go. As much as she wanted to believe that they had done the right thing, she couldn't deny the remorse she felt over upsetting Mr. Ford, nor the nagging voice in the back of her mind that told her they'd made a mistake.

Luke, who'd been in such a good mood earlier that morning, seemed equally disappointed by how their time at Calvary Hill had played out. Of course, being left alone with Chastity Cannon may have had something to do with that.

Chastity Cannon was, to put it lightly, sort of a downer. Unlike the other girls in the congregation, Chastity hadn't been impressed by Luke's celebrity status. In fact, she had gone out of her way to try to make him feel as small and despicable as she could, to the point where Kate had felt like smacking her. Luke didn't seem as bothered by it and he handled her harsh criticism with a lot more maturity and reason than Kate would have been able to muster, but he had looked awfully relieved when Michael finally reappeared and announced that they could leave.

Later, when Luke dropped them off at the apartment complex, he announced he probably wouldn't see them again before he headed back to L.A., but he promised to keep in touch. Watching him drive away, Kate wished that their adventure could have ended on a more positive note, but she knew that he would be back doing what he loved soon enough. Michael was the one who needed time to recover. After being assaulted by John Ford, she knew he wouldn't be convinced to interfere with ghosts or their business for a long time. And maybe he had been right all along. Maybe it was for the best.

Even if that meant she'd never find out who Trevor was, or what he wanted.

"And you couldn't be bothered to tell me you were leaving?" Gavin's angry voice reminded Kate that while Michael might not hold her accountable for everything that had happened that morning, her brother wasn't about to let her off the hook that easily.

"You saw me this morning. You knew I was going somewhere." Kate tried to keep her tone calm and steady, but her nerves were running short.

"I thought you were just getting home! I even asked you and since you didn't respond, I assumed I was right!"

"Well, you know what they say about making assumptions," Kate remarked lightly.

"Kate, you can't keep doing this! You can't just keep running off!"

"I'm a grown woman. I can do whatever I want."

"Oh, that doesn't sound childish at all," Gavin snapped as Kate brushed past him into the living room. "Look, I know you're still mad at me for yesterday, but we've got to be able to trust each other. And right now, you're not doing a very good job of convincing me that I can."

"You know what, Gavin? I really don't want to hear this from you right now. You're the one who went behind *my* back. And don't you *dare* lecture me about trust when you've been keeping secrets from me for months!"

180

"What is that supposed to mean?"

"You know what it means," Kate hissed.

"No, I really don't," Gavin insisted.

Kate looked him dead in the eye.

"Trevor."

"What?" Gavin looked taken aback.

"Trevor. Who is Trevor?"

"How should I know?" Gavin tried to sound like he truly didn't know why she was asking, but a small tremor in his voice betrayed him.

"Because this guy is royally pissed at you. There's no way you can make someone that angry without knowing who they are. So tell me."

"Why would you think he's mad at me?"

"Look at you, Gavin! Look at what he's done to you!" Gavin took a deep breath and closed his eyes. "Please, just tell me who he is. Maybe we can figure out what he wants from you."

"Kate, stop. There is no - "

"Gav, there's nothing you can say. I know he's here. Michael's seen him." The words were out of her mouth before she could stop them.

"*What*?" Gavin asked.

"Michael... can see them. He can see ghosts. And he's seen this guy. He's tall and muscular with a buzzed haircut. And he's angry with you, Gav. Please. Let me help you."

By now, every remaining ounce of color had drained from Gavin's already pale complexion, and Kate was stunned to see tears shimmering in her brother's eyes.

"Kate... I'm so sorry. I'm sorry for everything that's happened in the last six months. I'm sorry for everything that you've had to go through. But I *can't* tell you."

"Why not?"

When he finally answered her, his voice was barely a whisper.

"Because I don't want to hurt you anymore."

Kate was so stunned by his words and the raw guilt with which he spoke them that, for a moment, everything inside her mind short circuited. She couldn't remember where she was or what they were arguing about. All she could think about was Gavin, her smart, protective older brother who had always been there for her, who would never let anything bad happen to her. The man standing before her with weary, guilt-ridden eyes wasn't her brother. He was a stranger, one with a secret so terrible that he couldn't even confide in his family, or look to them for help or advice.

"Gav," Kate whispered in a shaky voice. "What did you do?"

But he didn't answer. And before she could fully register what was happening, something ran toward them from across the room. The sound sent an icy wave of dread coursing through Kate's body and she braced herself for impact.

It never came.

Instead, a burst of energy, akin to a cool electric shock, traveled through her like a gust of wind, leaving her breathless, but stable. Suddenly, there was nothing but stillness and a near-deafening silence. For a brief moment, Kate thought it was all over. Then the temperature in the room began to drop. The air grew tense and heavy. A lamp on the coffee table flickered once and died. Kate wanted to run, but she felt welded to the spot.

"Kate..." Gavin whimpered.

The next second, he was hurtling backwards through the air, knocked off his feet by a powerful and invisible force. And Kate could only watch in horror as her brother crashed into a wall of framed photographs and slumped to the floor, unconscious in a mess of shattered glass and pooling blood.

This has got to stop.

That was the only thing Michael could say, or even think, after he'd received a phone call from a hysterical Kate, telling him that Gavin had been attacked.

After the disastrous events of that morning, he hadn't considered that the day could possibly get worse, but by now he should have figured that things never went as expected. Grabbing his keys off of the kitchen table, he dashed out the door and across the landing to Kate's apartment.

Inside, he found Kate hovering over Gavin, who was lying bloodied and semiconscious in a field of broken picture frames and shards of glass at the base of their living room wall. Although Kate was obscuring most of Gavin's body, Michael could see smears of red on her hands and clothes.

Trevor was nowhere to be seen.

"Gav? Gavin, look at me," Kate was saying over and over again. "Gav, please. Come on, stay with me."

"What happened?" Michael asked, kneeling down next to her.

"We - we were having a fight. And I started asking him about Trevor. It was him. I felt him. I felt him run straight through me. And then, the next thing I know, Gav is flying across the room..." As she spoke, Michael noticed the blood seeping out from a wound behind Gavin's ear, and an open gash down his right arm. "We've got to get him to the hospital."

"Do you want me to call an ambulance?"

"No." This time, it was Gavin who spoke.

"Gav? Gav, what is it?" Kate asked.

"No ambulance," he murmured.

"Okay. But you're still going to the emergency room," Kate told him. Gavin closed his eyes and took a deep breath, but he made no objection. "Gav, I need you to stay awake. Michael, will you watch him? I'm going to get our first aid kit."

"Sure."

After she disappeared into the bathroom, Gavin opened his eyes and looked at Michael.

"Can you really see him?" he murmured.

"What?" Michael asked.

"Trevor," Gavin looked like he was having a difficult time staying conscious, but he spoke clearly and rationally. "Kate told me you can see him."

Under any other circumstances, Michael would have felt compelled to deny it. Maybe it was because he knew something needed to be done, or maybe it was because for the first time, he was speaking with a victim who was still alive. Either way, he answered, "Yes, I can see him."

"Is he here now?"

"No," Michael replied, though he knew for certain that he'd be back. "Gavin, what does he want from you?"

But before Gavin could answer, Kate sprinted back into the room carrying a white kit and a wet wash cloth. Carefully, she cleaned Gavin's wounds and patched them up with gauze and a lot of medical tape.

"I hope this will hold until we get to the hospital," she said. "Do you think you can stand?"

Together, Michael and Kate lifted Gavin to his feet, but he got so dizzy that he had to lean back against the wall to keep from passing out again. Once he was on his feet, they carefully helped him wrap his bandaged arms around their shoulders before they turned and directed him to the front door. Michael took one step before he stopped dead in his tracks and stared ahead.

Their friend was back.

He stood in the entry hall, a dark, looming shadow, watching with utter resentment as Kate and Michael assisted his limping victim.

"Michael, what's wrong?" Kate asked.

"Nothing," he lied. She knew it too. If all the crap Luke had spouted out about sensitivity was true, then she could sense the ghost in the room almost as easily as he could. She just couldn't see him. "We just need to get Gavin out of here."

Kate drew in a shaky breath and Michael knew she understood what he was trying to tell her.

Down in the parking lot, Michael assisted Gavin as he climbed into Kate's Land Rover. He wished more than anything that he could accompany them on the ride over to the hospital, but something inside forbade him from leaving. He wanted to deny it was his conscience, but he couldn't come up with any other reason for the cold knot gnawing away at his stomach. Knowing what he had to do, Michael took Kate by the hand and asked, "Do you think you can handle getting him to the emergency room by yourself?"

"I think so. Why?"

"There's something I need to take care of. But I'll meet you there," he promised.

Michael stayed behind in the parking lot and watched them drive away. Then, summoning up every ounce of courage he had, he climbed back up the stairs, walked across the landing, and began pounding on Kate and Gavin's door.

"Trevor!" he called, sounding a lot braver than he felt. "Trevor, I know you're in there."

He appeared on the landing almost instantly, glaring at Michael with visible disdain. However, Michael could swear he also detected the slightest hint of curiosity. It was for that reason alone that Michael was able to stand his ground.

"What?" Trevor growled. His voice was low and gravelly. It fit his rough, intimidating exterior perfectly.

"What did he do?" Michael demanded.

For the first time, Trevor's expression faded from one of intense hatred to one of genuine and outright shock. As a result, Michael felt oddly empowered. Now, instead of feeling afraid of the ghost standing before him, he felt angry and annoyed for everything he had put Kate through in the last four months.

When Trevor failed to answer him, he asked again, "What did Gavin Avery do to you to deserve this?"

"You – you can really see me?" Trevor asked.

"Yeah," Michael answered shortly.

"Have you always been able to - "

"Yeah. Stop changing the subject. What did Gavin do to you?"

Trevor gave a snort of derision.

"It's not what he did to me," he answered. "It's what he's doing to *her*. It's what they're all doing to her!"

Suddenly, Michael felt his irritation begin to ebb, only to be replaced by a fresh wave of concern.

"To Kate?" Michael asked. Trevor looked as though hearing him say her name made him sick. "What are they doing to Kate?"

"They're lying to her! They say it's to protect her. But they have *no idea*!" Trevor growled and punched the wall. The result was a barely audible *thump*, like a small rubber ball being bounced against a surface.

Michael waited for him to calm down before he spoke again.

"Then talk to me."

"What do you care?" Trevor snapped.

"I care about Kate. And I don't want to see her or Gavin suffering anymore because of you. Do you have any idea what you've put her through?"

Michael instantly regretted his words. Trevor threw him a look of such vile contempt that for a moment, Michael thought he was going to send him flying over the railing. Instead, the ghost heaved a heavy sigh.

"I never wanted to hurt her," he said. "I just don't know what to do. It wasn't supposed to be this way."

"I know," Michael tried to choose his words carefully. He didn't want to antagonize him further. And he really didn't want to be punched in the face. "But taking it out on Gavin isn't going to make things better." Trevor looked like he very much wanted to dispute that, but he remained silent. "Talk to me. Maybe I can help you."

Trevor gave a short, mirthless laugh.

"That's the thing. If I talk to you, you're not going to want to help me."

Michael didn't doubt that. In fact, he would have liked nothing better than to turn his back, walk down the stairs, drive off, and never speak to Trevor, or any ghost, ever again. But that wasn't going to happen. No matter what Trevor had to say, Michael was going to listen.

"Try me."

CHAPTER TWENTY-ONE

Sitting alone in the waiting room of Medical City Plano reminded Kate of how much she hated hospitals. Everything about them resurrected bad memories, from the heavy smell of medication mingled with dying flowers to the bare, colorless walls to the sounds of wheelchairs and gurneys being pushed down long, narrow hallways, that, for so many, held no escape. Kate had been one of the lucky ones. She'd walked out of that very building. But knowing how close she had come to death unnerved her. Now, waiting for Gavin, she couldn't imagine how her family must have felt during their three-week stay, not knowing when or if she would ever wake up again. It made her feel guilty for being so short with them.

Pining for any sort of distraction, Kate pulled out her phone. It had been almost an hour since they'd left Michael in the parking lot. She hoped he was all right.

Just as she was pressing the call button on her phone, the door to the waiting room swung open and Michael appeared. It took only a second for him to locate Kate. When she stood to greet him, he took her in his arms and held her for a long time. She didn't mind at all. His embrace was warm and his arms were strong and comforting. But she did find it a little peculiar. The way he held her, it was almost like he expected her to disappear and he wanted to savor her.

"Is everything okay? I was starting to worry," Kate said after he finally let her go.

"Yeah, I just got caught up," he replied half-heartedly. He didn't sound at all like things were actually okay, but before she could press him further, he asked, "Where's Gavin?"

"They took him back for X-rays about twenty minutes ago. He seemed to be talking a bit more clearly, but he was still pretty dazed."

"Do you think he has a concussion?"

"I don't know. He hit the wall pretty hard."

"Do your parents know?"

"No. And unless there's something critically wrong with him, I'm not going to tell them."

"That's probably a wise decision," Michael said, but he still sounded distant and his eyes were fixed on a spot on the floor.

"Are you sure you're okay?" Kate asked.

He glanced up at her.

"Yeah, I'm fine."

"You look like you've got something pretty heavy on your mind."

"It's nothing," he told her.

She didn't believe him.

"Did you talk to Trevor?" Michael didn't answer her. She knew him well enough now to know that when he didn't answer her questions, she was usually correct. "What did he say?"

Michael blinked, and when he finally did answer, his words surprised her. "I'm not sure I should be the one to tell you."

Kate wasn't sure what to make of that.

"Is it bad?" When he fell silent again, she realized she wasn't going to get anything more out of him. "You know what, never mind. Maybe I don't want to know."

That was about as far from true as she could possibly get. But as long as Gavin was still with the doctors, she didn't need anything else to worry about. She already felt guilty for the way she'd behaved earlier that afternoon. Maybe if she hadn't gotten so upset with Gavin, if she hadn't forced him to say those things about Trevor, then none of this would have happened.

"Are you all right?" This time, Michael asked her.

No, Kate wanted to say. *No, I'm not all right. There's an angry ghost haunting my apartment, he put my brother in the hospital because of the way I egged him on, and neither one of you will tell me what's actually happening.*

Instead, she just muttered, "Yeah, I'm fine. I'm just..."

"What?" Michael asked.

"I'm just worried that this was all my fault. You know, if I hadn't been antagonizing Gavin, then maybe Trevor wouldn't have attacked him."

Michael didn't respond immediately. The longer it took him to contradict her, the more convinced she became that she was correct.

"It wasn't your fault," he told her. "It was only a matter of time."

Oh great. That made her feel a *lot* better.

Time wasn't moving fast enough. Why hadn't she heard anything yet? And *why* wouldn't Michael tell her what Trevor had said? She was so sick of not knowing, of being left in the dark. To make matters worse, whatever Trevor had told Michael had left him detached and distant, right at the moment she needed him most.

"I'm not sure I should be the one to tell you."

Thinking back on Michael's ominous words reminded Kate of what Gavin had said to her just moments before the attack.

"I don't want to hurt you anymore."

Kate wracked her brain, trying to figure out what could have happened that would make both Gavin and Michael so determined to protect her. Maybe Gavin really had done something horrible, something that he knew would devastate her, so he kept it a secret. If that was the case, then what? Would he live the rest of his life in Trevor's shadow? Turn himself in? Would she have to -

No. That wasn't it. There was no way. She knew Gavin better than anyone else on the planet. He wouldn't hurt a soul.

But then what else could it be?

190

Before she could dwell on it any further, the door opened and a doctor appeared. He was tall with thinning hair and a thick mustache. He smiled and held out a hand as he approached them.

"I'm Dr. Morchower. Are you with Gavin Avery?" he asked.

"Yes." Kate and Michael both stood to greet the doctor. "Is he okay?"

"Oh yes, he's going to be fine. We're releasing him now. He had some pretty nasty cuts and some glass embedded in his right arm, but we cleaned him out and stitched him up. We'll need him back in about two weeks to take the stitches out. He has a mild concussion and he did chip a bone in his left elbow, so I'm sending him home with a prescription for painkillers and he'll have to ice the bone every three or four hours for the next few days. Make sure he rests that arm for at least a few weeks, and if it's not better in month, he'll need to see a specialist."

"Thank you so much, Doctor," Kate said, nearly trembling with relief.

Gavin appeared moments later, sporting a row of dark, thin stitches on one arm and a sling the color of a sapphire to support the other.

"Have that prescription, son?" Dr. Morchower asked.

Gavin held up a slip of paper.

"Hey," Kate smiled. "How are you feeling?"

"Kind of achy," Gavin admitted.

"Well, let's get you home and then I'll run and pick up your prescription."

"Why don't I take him home?" Michael asked. Both Gavin and Kate looked at him. "That way, you can just go straight to the pharmacy."

Kate realized that Michael intended to talk to Gavin alone, so she didn't argue. "Gav, are you okay with that?"

"Fine," he grimaced.

Kate knew he was hurting, and as much as she wanted to know exactly what Gavin and Michael were now both hiding from her, she hoped that whatever Michael had to say wouldn't put too much pressure on him. After all he'd been through, what he really needed was to rest. But, she realized with a sinking feeling, that wasn't going to happen as long as Trevor was around. Gavin needed to be free of whatever bound the ghost to him. If anyone could help him now, it was Michael.

"Okay," Kate agreed. "I'll see you boys at home."

"Thanks for all this," Gavin muttered roughly as Michael drove him home.

"Don't mention it," Michael replied. Gavin exhaled slowly and rested his head back against the seat. "You okay?"

"Yeah," he muttered. "It's funny, I didn't even realize my elbow was hurting until they told me it was chipped. Now it hurts like hell."

"Yeah, I broke my arm falling out of a tree when I was seven. It's not fun." Michael made his best attempt at casual conversation while simultaneously trying to figure out how to steer it back to Trevor. "So, what did you tell them? When they asked what happened to you? I mean, I'm guessing you didn't tell them the truth."

"What, you don't think they'd believe that a freakin' ghost threw me into a wall?" Gavin asked wryly and sniggered at his own joke. "I told them that I was helping my sister bring in a box of old picture frames and fell down the stairs."

"So what exactly did happen? I didn't really get a lot out of Kate. She was kind of freaking out while she was trying to explain it."

"Yeah, she does that," Gavin remarked. "We were just bickering. I was pissed because she'd run off *again* without telling me where she was going and she's still mad about everything that happened yesterday. Then she asked me about Trevor and *BAM*." Gavin clapped his hands for emphasis. "You know, we used to argue when we were younger, but we never had full blown fights until we moved here."

"Really?" Michael was surprised. He thought all siblings fought. He and Jonathan certainly had.

"Yeah. And it's my fault. I never listened to her when she said that there was something in the apartment. I just thought she was being paranoid, like always. I mean, I like to think I'm pretty open minded, but ghosts?" Michael glanced at him. "Well, I guess you'd believe it. But think for a moment if you didn't have your spectral vision or whatever. You'd think it was just her imagination."

"I don't know what I'd think," Michael admitted. "I guess it all depends on whether or not a ghost would have a reason to be there."

Gavin sighed. "I didn't even consider it until she said his name. God, that scared the living hell out of me. After that, I just didn't know what to believe. Until today, anyway."

"And now?"

Gavin was silent for a few brief moments. "I think he really wants to kick my ass. And I guess he has a pretty good reason to," he acknowledged.

Michael didn't dispute him.

"You know, he was the one who ransacked your old apartment."

"Are you serious?" Gavin asked. Michael nodded. "What else did he tell you?"

Michael hesitated.

"He told me everything," he finally answered. Gavin closed his eyes and rubbed his forehead with his unslung hand. "It's none of my business. This is between you and Kate. But Gavin, I think you know now that he's never going to leave you alone until she hears the truth."

Gavin stared pensively out the window. "I was trying to do what was best for her."

"I know."

They didn't speak for the rest of the car ride home. Gavin remained transfixed inside his own mind. Michael honestly didn't know what he would decide. He wasn't even sure what to hope for. A huge part of him didn't want Kate to find out. But the small, rational voice in the back of his mind reminded him that she had a right to know. She needed to know.

Trevor was waiting for them inside Kate and Gavin's apartment. Gavin breezed past him and disappeared into his bedroom. Trevor looked up at Michael.

"Well?" he asked.

"I don't know," was all Michael had to say.

"Ow! Dammit!" Gavin suddenly cried.

Michael sprinted down the hall and into his room. Gavin was kneeling next to his bed, wincing in pain.

"You okay?"

"Yeah, just forgot these were here." He indicated the stitches that ran down the outer side of his right arm. The area around his wound was red, and Michael realized he must have put pressure on them. "Hey, do you think you could give me a hand?"

"Sure."

"There's an old suitcase under here. It's about as far back as it can possibly be. Do you think you can reach it?"

Michael obliged, but he wasn't happy about it. Crawling around the tight, dusty space beneath Gavin's bed reminded him of the summer his uncle had managed to talk him and all of his cousins into retracing a path that had led to the discovery of some underground caverns in San Antonio. That path included tunnels, sometimes barely a foot high, that required them to slither along their bellies like snakes. Michael had become so claustrophobic that he'd almost blacked out. He'd avoided cramped, suffocating spaces ever since.

Finally, after reaching and shoving several boxes aside, he found a tattered brown suitcase and dragged it out from beneath the bed.

"Thanks, man," Gavin said.

"Don't mention it," Michael replied as Gavin unlocked the case and pulled out a large black photo album.

"Look, I know this probably won't be a lot of fun for you, but would you mind staying? I think it will be better if you're here."

Honestly, Michael thought his presence would make it a lot worse, but he agreed just the same.

Kate arrived home about thirty minutes later, clutching a small white pharmacy bag and sack full of groceries. She didn't seem at all surprised to see Michael still there.

"I had twenty minutes to kill, so I did a little shopping," she explained. "How are you doing?"

"I'm okay," Gavin assured her.

"Good. The pharmacist said you'd need to get something in your stomach before you take this, so what would you like?" She asked all of this as she was putting the groceries away. Michael realized just how hard she was trying to act nonchalant. She knew that they were going to talk to her, but Michael couldn't tell if she was hoping to initiate it or trying to deter away from it.

"In a minute, Kate. There's something that we need to talk about," Gavin said.

"Okay," she replied and joined her brother and Michael in the living room. She took a seat on the couch next to Gavin. Her eyes fell almost immediately onto the photo album in his lap. "What's that?"

"I'll show you in a minute. First, I want you to see this." He handed her a single photograph of a tall man with dark buzzed hair, warm eyes, and a winning smile. Kate stared down at his handsome face and frowned. "Do you remember him?"

"No, but... I think I had a dream about him."

"His name is Trevor Hanson," Gavin told her. "And he was your fiancé."

CHAPTER TWENTY-TWO

January 6th of That Year

Gavin Avery was content.

No, he was more than content. It was a gray winter day and with a rare layer of fresh snow on the ground outside his apartment, a fire crackling on the hearth, and a beautiful girl in his arms, he had to admit he had it pretty damn good.

"You know what sounds really yummy right now?" Tiffany Stanford asked, nuzzling his neck.

Gavin could think of several responses, none of them very appropriate, but the last time he'd made a dirty joke, it had ended up as Tiffany's Facebook status. It might not have been as embarrassing if she hadn't tagged him in it, but what was done was done.

"What's that?" he asked.

"Eggnog," she sighed and wrapped her arms around him.

"That *does* sound good," Gavin agreed with a huge stretch. "Too bad I haven't been to the store this week."

Even if he had, he wouldn't have picked up eggnog. Not that he had anything against eggnog. But given the choice, he'd almost always pick something else.

"We could go right now," Tiffany suggested.

"Uh..." Gavin glanced out the window. It was snowing again. Although he was fairly certain he could handle driving to the grocery store at the end of his street, there was a reason all of the businesses were closed that day. Most Texans were bad enough drivers without the threat of ice on the road. Snow made the streets of Dallas downright hazardous. "Sorry, Hon, but I don't feel like risking my life for a cup of eggnog."

"Gavin, there is a Wal-Mart at the other end of the block."

"Yeah, and there are lunatics out there who think they know how to drive in snow."

"So does that mean we're canceling on Kate and Trevor tonight?"

"Yeah, I guess so," Gavin replied.

They were supposed to meet his sister and her new fiancé at some fancy Italian restaurant that evening for a belated New Year's/engagement celebration. Although Gavin thought she was a little young to be engaged, he had to admit that he was happy for Kate. Trevor was a good guy, and anyone could see how much they loved each other.

Kate had met Trevor during her senior year of college. He was the friend of another friend's boyfriend, and they had actually been trying to set him up with someone else. One look at Kate, however, and Trevor never looked away.

Their parents weren't quite as enthusiastic about the relationship. They thought Trevor, who was twenty-five at the time, was too old for their daughter. And they didn't think much of his occupation as a part-time construction worker, part-time college student. But Trevor was determined to make something of himself. Within a year of meeting Kate, he had spent a semester at the University of Texas at Dallas, studying to become an engineer. Their parents had warmed up to him a little, but recently, in the midst of their divorce filings, they'd both been pretty distant. Gavin guessed that needed to change, considering Trevor was about to become their son-in-law.

"Well, since we're going to spend the evening in, why don't you go open a bottle of wine while I change into something sexy?" Tiffany grinned.

"But you didn't bring any other clothes."

"I know," she winked.

That Gavin understood.

Hours later, the persistent ringing of Gavin's cell phone stirred him from a wine-induced slumber. He opened his eyes and looked around the living room, trying to remember what had happened before he fell asleep. A quick glance at the brunette lying across his chest answered all his hazy questions.

It was worth it, he decided, despite the pounding headache that plagued him every time he drank too much red wine.

His phone rang again. Who the hell was calling him? He was pretty sure most of his friends were spending the day inside, warm, maybe even the way he was spending it. Who would want to be out on a night like this? Unless...

Oh, God. He'd forgotten to call Kate and Trevor to tell them that he and Tiffany were opting out of dinner. Man, Kate was gonna be pissed.

Miraculously, he managed to slip off the couch without waking his girlfriend. He stumbled hastily into the kitchen where he'd left his phone and answered without checking to see who was calling.

"I'm sorry, I'm sorry, I fell asleep. Please don't be mad," he mumbled.

"Gavin?" his mother whimpered. It sounded like she was crying.

"Mom?" Gavin asked, instantly sobered by the sound of her tears. "Mom, what's the matter?"

"It's K-Kate..." She was crying so hard, she could barely get the words out. "She was in an accident."

In that moment, time stood still. Suddenly, it felt like everything in Gavin's body was shutting down, as though it had somehow forgotten how to exist. He couldn't tell one sense from another. He was numb and in excruciating pain and for a few seconds, he was certain he was going to throw up. He took a few deep breaths and waited for the world to set itself right. A few seconds ago, everything was fine. If he could just figure out how to go back to that moment, then maybe this one wouldn't have to happen.

And then, just like that, he found his voice again.

"What happened? Is she okay?"

"I don't know. They won't tell us anything," Terri sobbed. "I'm so scared, Gavin..."

"Mom, where are you? Is Dad with you?"

But his mother didn't answer. A few seconds later, his father's voice was on the line.

"Hello?"

"Dad? What's happening? Where are you?"

"Medical City Plano." His father wasn't crying, but he was clearly shaken.

"Okay, I'll be right there," Gavin assured him. He'd begun to tremble. He needed to get to the hospital. He needed to know that Kate was going to be okay.

"Gavin," his father implored. "Please be careful out there, son."

As soon as he hung up the phone, Gavin dashed into his room and threw on a ratty pair of jeans and the first T-shirt he found lying around. Then, he grabbed his phone, keys, wallet, and a jacket and was almost out the door before a sleepy voice from the couch asked him what was going on.

Tiffany. He'd completely forgotten she was there.

"I have to get to the hospital," he announced hastily. "Kate was in an accident."

"Oh my God, is she okay?" Tiffany asked.

"I don't know. I just have to get there."

"Wait, Gavin! What about the roads?"

"I don't *care* about the roads, Tiffany! My sister might be dying! I need to be at that hospital!" Tiffany paled and her blue eyes widened. Gavin was stunned himself. He had never yelled at a woman before in his life. But that didn't matter now. All that mattered was getting to the hospital to be with his family. "Look, I'm sorry. You can stay here. I just need to go."

"But, Gavin, - "

He was out the door before she could finish.

He arrived at the hospital ten minutes and two run red lights later. One of them had probably caught him on camera, but

199

he didn't care. He rushed into the hospital where a nurse pointed him in the direction of the Trauma ICU waiting room.

There, he found his distraught parents waiting with two people he'd never met before. They introduced themselves as Ted and Arlene Hanson, Trevor's parents.

As soon as she saw him, Terri Avery threw herself into her son's arms and wept. Gavin held her, smoothed her hair, and tried his hardest not to break down himself.

"What happened?" he asked.

"We got the call about an hour ago," Rex told him. "Kate and Trevor hit a patch of black ice and ran head on into a tree. Thankfully, someone witnessed it and called the paramedics, but we don't know how... how bad it is."

In other words, they didn't know if either of them was going to survive.

An hour ago... That would have been the time Gavin was supposed to meet them for dinner. And he'd never called to tell them that he didn't want to risk driving in the ice and snow...

This time, Gavin knew he was going to be sick. Letting go of his mother, he ran across the hall to the men's room and threw up. His dad appeared a few moments later. Gavin retched again. When he finished, he wiped his mouth and his father grabbed him and crushed him against his chest.

"It's going to be okay, son," he muttered as Gavin finally broke down.

"It's my fault..." he whispered, his voice quivering.

"What?"

"It's my fault!" Gavin cried, shoving away from his father. "Tiffany and I were supposed to meet them tonight, but we decided to stay in, and I fell asleep before I could call them..." By now, tears were flowing freely down Gavin's face. "It's my fault."

"No, Gavin. It was no one's fault. It was an accident."

"But if I had just called them - "

"Gavin. I need you to listen to me. It was *not* your fault. Now I need you to be strong for your mother. And for Kate."

Gavin wiped his eyes with his sleeve and nodded.

200

"Okay."

"They haven't told us anything yet. For all we know, Kate and Trevor are back there asking when they can go home." His father didn't sound at all like he thought that was what was actually happening, but Gavin needed to believe that it was. The thought of his little sister being hurt, *really* hurt, was more than he could handle.

They returned to the waiting room where they sat in silence until about twenty minutes later, when a doctor in green scrubs approached them. One look at the grim expression on her face told Gavin everything he needed to know. Suddenly, he couldn't breathe. He didn't want to hear what this woman had to say. He just wanted to run. As far away as possible. But for some reason, he stayed planted in his seat. He felt his mother's cold fingers grip his wrist. She remained seated next to him, her face white as a sheet. Rex, Ted, and Arlene, however, rose to greet the doctor.

"Mr. and Mrs. Hanson?"

"Yes?" Arlene asked, tearfully.

"My name is Dr. Harper. I operated on your son."

"Is he all right? Can we see him?"

Dr. Harper took a deep breath and began to explain Trevor's extensive injuries. A rush in Gavin's ears drowned out the doctor's words. The news wasn't about Kate. She was still in surgery. Although he didn't want to admit it, he felt the tiniest sliver of relief. As long as they didn't know what was going on, there was a chance that she was okay.

That relief was short lived, however, as he tuned back in to hear the doctor say, "I'm so sorry to have to tell you this, but he didn't make it."

"Oh no. No. No!" Arlene moaned and collapsed, weeping into her husband's arms. Ted held her tightly and cried with her.

Gavin watched the sad scene unfolding before his eyes, but he was having trouble processing it. Trevor was gone. It was unthinkable.

Somewhere through the haze of disbelief, Gavin heard his father ask, "Doctor. Do you know anything about our daughter?"

"I'm sorry. She's in another O.R."

"Okay. Thank you."

Shortly thereafter, the Hansons were escorted back to spend a few final moments with their son's body. Gavin didn't see them again for the rest of the evening.

He didn't know how much time had passed. Word had somehow gotten out about the accident. Maybe Tiffany had posted something on Facebook. Regardless, Gavin's phone had been lighting up with missed calls and text messages from concerned friends and family member so much that it had almost run out of battery.

By that point, the shock had worn off and the truth of what had happened was beginning to sink in. Gavin no longer felt like running. He just wanted answers.

Moments later, a man who, in Gavin's opinion, looked far too young to be a doctor, appeared. All three Averys rose to greet him.

"I'm Dr. Singh. Are you with Kate Avery?" he asked.

"Yes. We're her family," Rex answered.

"Please, tell us she's all right, Doctor," Terri pleaded.

"She's stable. It was touch and go for a while, but her heart beat is strong and she's breathing on her own."

"Thank God," Terri began to cry.

Gavin felt weak, yet almost giddy, with relief.

"When can we see her? Has she asked for us?" Rex asked.

"Mr. Avery, your daughter suffered a severe brain injury. Now her vital signs are normal, but it will take an indefinite amount of time for her to recover from that trauma."

"What are you trying to tell us, Doctor?" Rex asked.

The doctor's answer was direct and to the point. "She's in a coma."

She wasn't brain dead. That was the good news. Brain dead meant the body wouldn't survive without a machine to keep it alive. A coma, the doctor explained, was a natural part of the recovery process. The body remained unconscious while the brain healed itself. That meant there was a good chance that she would wake up. They just didn't know how long it would take. Even the doctors couldn't accurately predict it.

For the next few days, they all took shifts sitting next to Kate's bedside. They wanted to make sure that she was never alone. The doctors told them to talk to her, that there was a good chance that she could hear them. One day, Gavin brought in her favorite book, *Harry Potter and the Prisoner of Azkaban*, and read to her.

Although Kate remained stable and the doctors were optimistic about her recovery, the rest of Gavin's life was crumbling around him. His boss wasn't very understanding about Gavin missing so much work, and although he wasn't fired yet, he had been given his warnings. On top of that, Tiffany was beginning to get on his nerves. At first, she'd been a source of comfort and strength for Gavin. But after a few days, life at the hospital began to bore her. Gavin guessed he couldn't blame her. She was young and energetic and she wanted to spend her evenings out and enjoying herself. Since they hadn't been dating long enough for him to expect any real dedication from her, he told her to go out and have fun. But Tiffany seemed to think she had some sort of obligation to be there, and she made her displeasure at being holed up in a hospital room only too known.

On the last morning of their relationship, she threw a fit because Gavin told her that instead of spending his afternoon with her, he was going to stay with Kate while their parents paid their respects at Trevor's funeral. Gavin had volunteered to stay behind. He didn't want to face the hundreds of people who'd loved the man his sister was supposed to marry.

The man who'd still be alive if only he'd remembered to call.

In spite of his father's constant assurance that it wasn't his fault, Gavin was haunted by Trevor's memory and a terribly guilty conscience. How could he face any of Trevor's friends again? Many of them his own friends? And Kate... What was he supposed to say to her when she woke up and learned that her fiancé, whom she loved more than life itself, was dead and it was all because of him? He didn't want to think about it.

"Baby, come on. You need some time away from this hospital," Tiffany insisted.

"I don't care. I'm not going to leave her."

"Why not? It's not like she knows you're here." Her words stung.

"You don't know that."

"Gavin, she's in a *coma*. I don't think two hours will matter much to her."

"What if she wakes up? What if she wakes up and no one's here?"

"I seriously doubt that's going to happen."

"Well then, I guess I'll just spend a few more hours of my life in a hospital."

Truth be told, Gavin really wasn't too sad to see things end with Tiffany. Sure, she was beautiful and fun to be around, but Gavin needed someone a little more grounded in his life. After she stormed out, Gavin glanced down at Kate. She had declared Tiffany a "dingbat" from the start, but she'd tolerated her for Gavin's sake. Now, looking down at his sister's peaceful form, Gavin couldn't help but smile a little.

"You were right, Sis," he told her. "She was kind of crazy."

CHAPTER TWENTY-THREE

January 30ᵗʰ

Three weeks and a few days later, life at the hospital had become almost routine. Gavin didn't like that at all. He didn't want it to become his new normal. He'd done some research on brain trauma and comas. Apparently, it could take as long as several months for a brain to recover, and since no two brain injuries were alike, it was almost impossible to predict how long a coma would last. That was the discouraging part.

Although the doctors assured them that Kate was healing, the fear still lingered that she might never wake up. The thought of his sweet, crazy, beautiful sister never opening her eyes again was excruciating and to be honest, Gavin wasn't sure how much longer he could handle not knowing.

Then, just like that, the nightmare ended.

It was around one in the afternoon. Gavin and Rex sat reading in Kate's room while Terri ran down to the cafeteria for a quick lunch. She hated being away from Kate for too long and more often than not, Gavin and Rex had to remind her that she needed to eat.

Gavin noticed the movement first. A slight twitch of Kate's fingers. At first, he thought he'd imagined it, but then it happened again.

He tried not to get too excited. Her fingers had twitched on occasion before and nothing had happened. But there was something different this time. He found himself holding his breath as the fingers on her left hand slowly bent, like she was trying to make a fist.

"Dad," Gavin said.

They both watched with anxious anticipation as Kate moaned softly and moved her head from one side to another. As she did, Terri walked into the room to find Gavin and Rex hovering over her daughter's bed.

"What's going on? Is she okay?" she asked.

"Just come here," Rex urged her. As she approached the bed, Kate's face scrunched up in a grimace. Terri gasped. "Kate?" Rex whispered gently. "Pumpkin?"

Slowly, Kate opened her eyes. Terri began to cry. Rex heaved a happy sigh of relief. As for Gavin, he'd never felt more thankful for anything in his life.

For a brief moment, Kate looked completely lost, like she had no idea what was going on. Then, her eyes focused in on the faces of her family, and although it took her a moment to recognize them, she smiled.

"Hey," she whispered, her voice raspy.

"Hi, Baby," Terri whispered tearfully.

"What happened?"

"You were in a car accident. You hit your head. But you're going to be just fine." Kate looked confused, like she had no idea what her mother was talking about. "Do you remember the accident?" Kate shook her head. "That's probably for the best."

Slowly, Kate's eyes drifted from Gavin to Terri before finally settling on Rex. "Daddy," she whispered.

"Yeah, Pumpkin?"

"What happened to your hair?" She sounded almost amused.

"My hair?" he asked.

She nodded.

"It's all gone."

It was then that Gavin knew that something wasn't right. Their dad had started losing his light blond hair the summer before Kate's senior year of college. He'd finally accepted it and shaved it off the following April.

"I shaved it, Sweetheart, remember? Right before your graduation," Rex answered.

"What?"

"I wanted to look nice for your graduation. So I shaved it."

"What graduation?" By now, Kate was visibly distraught. Terri saw it too.

"Your college graduation. From SMU."

Kate's eyes widened as it became apparent that she remembered no such event. Before anything else could be said, Dr. Singh appeared, looking cheerful.

"Well, look who's awake," he grinned.

"Doctor, something's wrong," Terri announced frantically. Gavin wanted to shake her. Didn't she know that kind of tone was only going to upset Kate more? "She can't remember anything."

"Oh, I'm sure that's not entirely the case." He walked over to Kate's bed and shone a flashlight into her eyes. "Can you tell me your name?"

"Katherine Elaine Avery."

"When's your birthday?"

"February 3rd."

"What are your parents' names?"

"Rex and Terri."

"And your brother's name?"

"Gavin."

"Tell me, Kate, what is the last thing that you remember?"

Kate thought about it.

"I was getting my books from the school bookstore. A lot of them weren't in, so I had to order them online," she answered hesitantly.

Terri began to sob all over again.

"Mrs. Avery, perhaps you should wait outside while I talk to your daughter," Dr. Singh suggested.

Gavin knew his mother didn't want to leave Kate, but she cooperated and left the room.

"Gavin," Rex said. "Go with her."

Together, Gavin and his mother watched through the window on the door while Dr. Singh sat on the edge of Kate's bed and talked to her. Rex stood at the foot of the bed, arms crossed, listening intently to what the doctor was saying.

About ten minutes later, Rex joined Terri and Gavin outside Kate's room.

"The doctor's still with her," he explained needlessly.

"What did he say?" Terri asked.

"He thinks Kate has some retrograde amnesia... estimates she lost about two years. He says it's fairly common after her kind of injury. But he doesn't know whether she'll ever get those memories back."

"Oh, my baby," Terri moaned.

"How is she taking it?" Gavin asked.

"Better than your mother," Rex answered matter-of-factly as the door to Kate's room swung open and Dr. Singh appeared.

"You can go back in now. I'm going to order some follow-up tests for the next few days, but for now, I think it would be best for you to spend time with her and talk to her about what's happened. She's going to have a lot of questions."

"Wait a minute," Terri grasped her son and husband as the doctor disappeared down the hall. "I think we need to talk about this."

"About what?" Gavin asked.

After a long pause, Terri answered, "I don't think we should tell her about Trevor."

"What?" Gavin asked.

"Ter, we have to - "

"Why?" Terri cut Rex off. "Why do we have to tell her? If she lost that much memory, then she probably doesn't remember him. Why should we tell her something that's only going to upset her? That might even hinder her recovery?"

"Because she loved him," Gavin said.

"How could she love someone she doesn't even remember?"

"How can we keep someone who was such a huge part of her life a secret?" Gavin countered. With all the various online social networks, it seemed a near impossible task to permanently erase a person from someone else's life. Wouldn't she see all the pictures that were tagged of them? And what about her friends? How would they react? Knowing that group of gossip mongers she'd met in college, someone was bound to say something to her.

"Destroy the evidence. Talk to her friends. Email them. Do whatever you have to do. Say that because of the trauma that she experienced, her doctor thought it would be for the best not to remind her of everything she lost. Just make sure they know that as far as Kate is concerned, there is no such person as Trevor Hanson."

For the next few days, Gavin scoured Kate's apartment for pictures of her and Trevor. He searched every nook and cranny, collected every photograph he could find, and stored them all in a large black photo album, which he stuffed in a suitcase and stashed at his apartment. Then, he removed every item that could possibly remind her of Trevor; the souvenir double decker bus that he'd bought for her in London, the Tiffany heart necklace that he'd given her for Valentine's day, her collection of ticket stubs of all the movies they'd seen together. The doctors had removed her engagement ring sometime in the midst of her surgery and had since returned it to her parents.

Then, Gavin was faced with the ridiculous feat of getting rid of all traces of Trevor from her computer. That included pictures, emails, and her Facebook account. That proved to be the most difficult. Hacking into her page was easy enough. She'd had the same password for everything since she was seventeen. The hard part was seeing all the messages people had left not only on her wall, but on Trevor's.

It was horrible, reading post after post, expressions of shock, sympathy, and utter sorrow that had been left for the world to see on Trevor's page. Gavin knew he shouldn't be reading them, particularly the more personal ones, but for some reason, he couldn't tear his eyes away. It was like some strange form of self-punishment.

Finally, after he'd gone through every message, he began the process of deleting Trevor from his sister's life.

It turned out that Facebook posts and photos weren't the only thing that needed to go, at least as far as his mother was concerned. The family had gone out of their way to tell Kate that she had been driving her car when she'd had the accident. Of course, in actuality, it had been Trevor's Corolla, not Kate's old Jeep, that had been totaled. But Kate wasn't supposed to know that. So, one day after work, Gavin went with his father to sell his sister's beloved vehicle. Instead of buying a new one on the spot, however, they decided to wait and let her decide which car she wanted next.

The final step in their attempt to shield Kate from anything that might pose a negative effect on her recovery was for Terri and Rex to call off their divorce. Gavin had mixed feelings about his parents' decision. Although he hadn't wanted to see his parents end their marriage, he knew how unhappy they'd been, especially in the months leading up to the filing. Part of him was afraid that their trying to stay together might create unnecessary tension that would be harder on Kate than learning that they had planned to divorce. But then, both Terri and Rex seemed dedicated and determined to put their personal issues aside to create the best possible environment for Kate. Maybe, just maybe, something good would come from these last few weeks of hell after all.

Unfortunately, not everybody was convinced that the Averys truly had Kate's best interests at heart. Trevor's family in particular. The Hansons had loved Kate like a daughter, and to be told that they wouldn't be able to see or speak with her had hurt them terribly. They argued extensively with the Averys, saying that Kate deserved to know about the man she loved, that they needed to have that connection with their son, but Terri wouldn't budge on the issue. She even threatened legal action should the

Hansons attempt to contact Kate without their consent. Finally, Ted and Arlene left, tearful and defeated.

A lot of Trevor and Kate's friends were angry too. It was bad enough that they'd lost Trevor. Now, unless they wanted to be cut off from Kate, they had to act like their friend had never existed. Several of Kate's older friends understood and agreed that it was for the best, but some expressed concern about not being able to keep Trevor a secret. A few of them also said that they would feel guilty keeping something so substantial from her. In the end, however, they all committed to the lie. They didn't really have another option.

Over the next couple of weeks, Rex, Terri, and Gavin took baby steps in reintroducing Kate to her old life. They brought in Valerie, the interior decorator who had hired Kate right after she'd graduated from SMU. If Kate not being able to remember her was difficult for Valerie, she didn't let it show. Instead, she walked into Kate's room with a bright, cheerful smile and announced, "Hi, Kate, I'm Valerie. How are you feeling, Sweetheart?"

"A lot better than I have been," Kate replied.

"I'm glad to hear that. We've missed you at work."

"I'm sorry that I haven't been there," Kate answered diplomatically.

Gavin and their parents had filled her in on her job with Val.

"You have got nothing to be sorry for. I'm just glad that you're going to be all right."

After a brief visit, Valerie told Kate that her job was still waiting for her if she wanted it. Kate thanked her and accepted, but Gavin thought there was something off about her response.

While Rex and Terri escorted Valerie out, Gavin took a seat on the edge of Kate's bed.

"Everything okay?" he asked her.

"Mm-hmm," she nodded. "Why?"

"You just seem a little distracted."

"I guess I'm just tired," she shrugged.

"Are you happy to have your job back?"

"I don't really have it back," she reminded him. "I mean, I guess I technically do. But I might as well be starting a new job."

"Val will help you out. I know you don't remember her, but she is a really great person. And she loves the hell out of you." It was true. After Kate first started working for her, she and Val had become fast friends.

"Okay," Kate replied, still looking despondent.

"You sure you're okay?" Gavin asked.

Kate took a deep breath and bit her lip. Gavin suddenly realized she was trying not to cry.

"I don't know what this is," she finally admitted and held up her pale blue blanket.

"Your blanket?"

"No, I know it's a blanket. But I don't know what color it is."

Gavin was confused. The blanket was obviously blue. Had the accident somehow impaired her vision?

"It's blue," Gavin told her.

Kate blinked and two tears ran down her cheeks.

"I don't know what that means," she said.

Now Gavin was alarmed. Trying not to panic, he grabbed a get-well bouquet of pink stargazer lilies off her window sill and held them up.

"Do you know what color these are?" Kate shook her head. Gavin didn't know what to do. Should he call a doctor? Track down their parents? "Do you think - are you colorblind?"

"No, I can see the color. I know that it's the same color as a Valentine heart. But I - I don't know what it's called."

"Do you know what any of the colors are?" Kate trembled and shook her head. "Is this a new thing? When did you notice it?"

"I don't know. I had so much going on inside my head that I didn't really think about it. Then, when you guys told me about the decorating job... I don't know. I looked around the room and realized that I didn't know what anything was called. I tried to shake it off, thought maybe I was just tired and that if I slept, it would get better..." Kate explained. "And Valerie was so nice to me, offering me my job back. How am I supposed to do that job?"

"You'll figure something out. The doctors told you it would take some time, right? You're going to have to relearn some stuff. Maybe this is just part of it."

Kate didn't look so sure.

"Why did this have to happen?" she asked, resting her head back so that she was staring at the ceiling.

Gavin didn't want to answer that.

"I don't know," he finally replied, hoping she wouldn't detect the raw guilt in his voice. "But I swear to you, it will be okay. I know everything seems like a nuisance right now, but Kate, you have no idea how lucky you are just to be alive."

Although he'd intended his words to be comforting, something in his tone betrayed him and he found himself locked under Kate's curious gaze.

"I was the only one, right? I mean, you'd tell me if someone else was hurt, wouldn't you?"

Gavin looked his sister square in the eye.

"I promise, you were the only one. No one else was hurt."

Kate seemed to relax a little after that. Gavin was relieved. He realized then that his mother had been right. Kate was struggling with her new life enough as it was. If she'd found out about Trevor, about how much she'd really lost in that crash, it would have been more than she could handle.

Gavin remembered that day specifically, not only because of the conversation he'd had with Kate, but because it was the first time he went home to discover that the temperature inside his apartment had inexplicably dropped about twenty degrees.

CHAPTER TWENTY-FOUR

Present Day

Kate had managed to remain calm, even neutral, as Gavin recounted to her the details surrounding the accident. Maybe it was the overwhelming abundance of new information, or maybe it was her brain still trying to protect her, but for whatever reason, the story had left her feeling numb, like she was listening to a plot that characters would act out on television. It didn't resonate with her that what Gavin described had actually *happened*.

"So, when Mom and Dad said they didn't want me thinking about Trevor, they weren't afraid it would impair my recovery. They were afraid it would advance it... That I was starting to remember him."

"Yeah." Gavin didn't try to deny it.

Kate was stunned. Not that her parents would go to extremes to try to protect her. She supposed every parent would. But to go so far as to try to hinder her recovery? That just seemed so... wrong.

"What's in the photo album?" she asked.

"Everything," Gavin replied as he handed it to her.

Kate was surprised by how heavy it was.

With a deep breath, she set the book on her lap and pulled back the front cover. Inside, she found images of herself smiling, with her arms around the same tall, dark-haired man in the picture that Gavin had given her earlier. One picture showed her dancing with him in the middle of a crowded room. In another, they kayaked across a lake. In one, he gave her a piggy-back ride on the beach. In another, she kissed him on the cheek. Kate was struck, not only by the massive accumulation of moments that she couldn't remember, but by how incredibly happy she appeared to be. Still, there was something bothering her.

"What was he really like?"

"What do you mean?" Gavin asked.

"I mean, the way you talk about him and the way he looks in these pictures, he seems like this wonderful, amazing guy. But he's been draining you for months. He made you sick. He threw you into a wall! What kind of person does that?" Kate realized that Trevor was probably listening in, but she didn't care. She was angry at him. He'd made Gavin's life, and her life for that matter, an absolute hell for the past five months. And *that* she couldn't forget.

"He says there's no excuse for everything he did, and that if he could take it all back, he would." Michael spoke on Trevor's behalf. "He just needed you to know who he was. He couldn't move on without you knowing how much you meant to him."

"Kate, he loved you more than anything," Gavin told her. "We should never have tried to keep him a secret from you. You know, to be honest, I can't really blame him for wanting to punch my lights out."

Kate still wasn't entirely convinced.

"He says he wants to talk to you," Michael told her.

She glanced up at him. As usual, his dark eyes were a source of reassurance and comfort. This time, however, she could swear she also detected the slightest hint of regret. Kate was ashamed. She'd been so caught up in Gavin's revelation that she hadn't considered how Michael might be feeling.

"Michael, I can't ask you to - "

"Kate, it's okay," he assured her. "I think you both need this."

Kate looked at her brother. He just nodded. She could tell his pain was beginning to get to him. He needed to take his medicine, but she was fairly certain that wouldn't happen until everything was resolved.

Finally, she relented.

"Where is he?"

"He's been sitting next to you this whole time," Michael said.

His answer sent chills racing across Kate's entire body. She turned to face the empty air to her left. She strained her eyes for a glimpse of the man in the pictures, but he never appeared. Just then, a strange sensation like a cool winter's breeze grazed the fingers on her left hand. She couldn't be sure, but she got the feeling that Trevor had just reached for her.

Blinking back tears, she looked into thin air and whispered, "Hi."

⁂

Michael felt a sick, sinking knot in his stomach as Trevor reached over and took Kate's hand, but he tried not to let it show. After all, they were the victims here. They were the ones whose lives had been torn apart. Not him. Though self-pity would have been an exceptionally easy route to take at that point.

No. For once, he wasn't going to think about how hard or uncomfortable the situation was for *him*. Kate and Trevor had both lost something precious, something irreplaceable. As had every ghost who had ever contacted him. Up until that point, Michael had only ever thought about how he felt. For someone who was supposed to be so "in-tune" with other people's spirits, he had a pretty selfish disposition.

"I miss you," Trevor was saying to Kate as he reached out and tried to touch her hand.

Michael took a deep breath and hoped he wouldn't live to regret what he was about to do.

"He says he misses you," he translated.

"I'm sorry," Kate said. "I'm so sorry about everything that happened."

"No, Baby, no. It's not your fault." Trevor reached up and touched her cheek. Kate shivered and pulled away. Michael repeated what he had said to Kate. "I know this is going to be the last time I talk to you until... whatever's next. And I'm not sure what I say is going to mean all that much to you. But I just couldn't leave without you knowing that loving you, being with

216

you, was the best thing that ever happened to me, and that I wouldn't trade my time with you for anything. I love you so much, Kate." He paused for Michael to translate. As he spoke, Kate dried the tears pooling in her eyes with the back of her hand. "I know this is a lot to take in, but I hope you can forgive me for being such a jerk these last few months."

"I do," Kate whispered.

Finally, for the first time since Michael had known him, Trevor smiled. Then, he leaned forward and placed a gentle kiss on Kate's lips. Michael averted his eyes and tried to remind himself that none of what had happened or what was going to happen had anything to do with him.

Remember, this is for Kate.

"Whatever happens next, I'll be with you," Trevor promised her. "I love you, Kate."

Michael relayed his message. And then, just like that, Trevor was gone. The atmosphere inside the room suddenly seemed very still and empty. Kate sensed it too.

"Did he go?" she asked.

"Yeah," Michael answered. He could tell by the look on Kate's face that she wasn't sure how she felt.

"Will he be back?" Gavin asked.

"I don't know," Michael answered, though he honestly didn't believe he would. He'd said all that he needed to say.

Gavin nodded, the look on his face one of great discomfort.

"Gav, you need to take your medicine," Kate told him. She tried to sound nonchalant, but Michael could hear the tremor in her voice. "Let me make you a sandwich so you can get something in your stomach."

"No Kate, you stay here. I'll grab something out of the cupboard."

With Gavin gone, Kate turned hazel eyes on Michael.

"Are you okay?" he asked.

"Yeah," she replied. "Just a little overwhelmed. None of this seems real. It feels like something I saw in a movie, not

217

something that really happened to me." She paused. "That makes me sound like a terrible person, doesn't it?"

"No," Michael assured her. "It's going to take some getting used to."

"That's for sure," Kate agreed. "I just have so many questions. I don't even know where to begin. I was engaged? How long did we date? What were our plans? And my parents... They were going to get divorced? And then they acted like I was going crazy when I mentioned Trevor's name. They said they wanted my memories to return but what they really wanted was to get Trevor out of my mind so I wouldn't remember him..."

"They thought they were doing what was best for you."

"I know," she sighed. "But now I can't help but wonder what else they've been keeping from me. What else happened in the past two years that they think I'm too fragile to know about?"

"I don't know," Michael admitted as Gavin reappeared with a box of Lucky Charms.

"Are you sure that's going to be enough?" Kate asked him. "You know painkillers can make you nauseous if you take them on an empty stomach."

"Well, at least she still sounds like her old self, huh Michael?" Gavin remarked, shoveling a handful of cereal into his mouth.

Michael grinned wryly.

"You know, it's getting late. I should probably be going," he announced.

"I'll walk you out," Kate offered.

Outside, the night air was still and humid. A thin layer of clouds obscured the waxing moon and the chirping of a hundred crickets filled the silence between Michael and Kate as they walked across the landing toward his apartment. When they reached his front door, they stopped and turned to face each other. Kate spoke first.

"Thank you for everything, Michael," she said. "Not just for helping me with Gavin, but for what you did this afternoon. For Trevor."

"You're welcome," Michael told her.

"I guess things are going to be kind of different now," Kate mused. "I mean, with Trevor gone, Gavin will get better. He'll be able to go back to work. I'll stop waking up in the middle of the night afraid that someone's wandering around my apartment..."

She tried to make it sound like having Trevor gone would be a good thing, but Michael knew that a part of her was mourning his loss. He also knew that she wouldn't have been sad if Trevor had been just some random person with a grudge against her brother.

"Kate," Michael stopped her.

She looked up at him, her eyes glistening with tears.

"I'm sorry. I don't know why I'm crying," she murmured, wiping the tears away with the heel of her hand.

"It's okay. You've been through a lot," he told her.

"You know, I should feel so relieved that I don't remember him, because I know it would hurt so much more if I did. But at least I would still have something to look back and smile on. And I'm so sorry to be going on about this to you. I'm just... I'm so confused."

"I know," Michael said, trying his best to figure out how to comfort her. Gently, he pulled her into his arms and let her cry. He stroked her hair and whispered, "I wish I had answers for you."

Kate pulled away and looked up at him.

"Michael, you've done more for me in one afternoon than I think I've done for anyone in my entire life. And I will never be able to thank you enough for that."

"You don't have to thank me. I think I owed it to you." Kate smiled and wrapped her arms around his neck. Holding her in his arms, savoring the sweet floral scent of her hair, Michael hated himself for what he was about to say. "I also think you're going to need some time to... to really get over him."

Kate stepped away and gazed up at him with curious eyes. Although neither of them spoke the words, she seemed to know what he was trying to say. She didn't need to be in a new relationship. Not with the knowledge and loss of Trevor still fresh in her mind. And though she didn't look like she wanted to agree, she nodded.

"You're such a good guy, Michael," she told him. Then, with a swift kiss on the cheek, she turned and walked back to her apartment, leaving him alone on the landing.

As he watched her disappear, he knew he'd done the right thing. But why did the right thing have to leave him feeling so lousy? It was like throwing away the winning lottery ticket.

He tried to remind himself that he wasn't losing Kate. She was still his friend. And they did live just across the hall from each other. And maybe one day, when she was ready, they'd be able to pick up where they'd left off.

Until that day came however, Michael was just going to have to get used to feeling like an idiot.

Brink appeared almost immediately after the lock on Kate's door clicked.

"Dude, what the hell?" he asked. "Do you realize what you just did?"

"I'm aware," Michael replied wearily.

"Well, then would you mind explaining it to me? Because last time I checked, that girl was the best thing that has ever happened to you and you're just letting her walk away, right out of your life!"

"She's not out of my life. I'm just giving her some time."

"Time for what?"

"You mean you weren't listening?"

"Well yeah, I was, but I don't understand it."

"She was *engaged*, Brink! She was supposed to get married. She may have even been married by now if it weren't for that accident!"

"But she's not married. She doesn't even remember him," Brink argued.

"I know."

"Okay. So why are you so upset?"

"Just forget it," Michael muttered, digging around in his pocket for his key.

"No, I'm not going to forget it. You're my best friend and you're hurting, so the last thing I'm going to do is *forget it*," Brink insisted. "You love her, don't you?"

"Brink, can we *please* just drop it?"

"Don't you?" Brink repeated.

"Yes, I love her! That's why I have to give her time! Because I care about her and I want to do what's best for her, even if it means letting her go." Michael expected Brink to come up with some sort of witty response, but his friend's eyes suddenly flickered to something over his shoulder. "What?"

"Michael - "

But before Brink could say anything else, Michael felt a cold grip at the base of his skull.

Pressure.

Dizziness.

Then everything went black.

Inside their apartment, Gavin was finishing up his cereal so Kate went to fetch his painkillers and a glass of water from the kitchen.

"How are you feeling?" she asked him.

"You know after a while, you really get tired of hearing that question," Gavin remarked, swallowing the two pills that Kate handed him.

"Tell me about it," Kate muttered.

Gavin observed her.

"Do you want to talk?" he asked. "You know, about Trevor or... anything?"

She did. She had a hundred questions she wanted to ask. But after such a stressful day, she didn't know if she or her fragile mental state could handle any more emotional strain. That, and any conversation about Trevor was bound to go on for hours. Neither of them needed that now. Gavin needed to rest and recuperate. She needed a chance to clear her mind and let everything sink in.

"Later. You just take it easy."

Gavin nodded and shut his eyes. If he was anything like her, the painkillers would render him useless for the rest of the evening.

Kate thought about helping him into his bed, but decided instead to run into his room to fetch him a pillow and blanket. Every time they were sick or injured as kids, they always camped out on the couch. That way, they were never too far from the important things like the kitchen or the TV.

"Here Gav." She nudged him and handed him the pillow and blanket.

"Thanks, Sis," he murmured.

"Do you need anything else?"

"No."

She could tell he was already almost out. Regardless, she decided to refill his glass of water in case he woke up. She knew he probably wouldn't drink it, but at least it would get her mind off of everything, even if only for a minute.

In the kitchen, she stopped at the freezer, grabbed a handful of ice, and dropped it into the empty glass. She was almost at the sink when a loud THUD from the living room startled her so badly, she dropped the cup, sending ice chips sliding across the tiles on the kitchen floor.

"Gavin?" she called and raced into the living room, expecting to find her brother sprawled out on the carpet.

He still slept peacefully on the couch. Whatever had made that noise hadn't disturbed him in the slightest.

Kate felt her heart thudding as she waited for the sound to come again. When it did, she flinched. It was mostly out of surprise rather than fear, but there was a little of that, too. The noise, which seemed deliberate, was louder this time and much closer. It sounded like someone pounding on the wall directly behind the couch. Kate stared at the spot where she thought the noise originated. It happened again. This time, two knocks instead of one.

She couldn't be certain it was a ghost. Buildings shifted, pipes rattled around, and neighbors did things that could all be misinterpreted as unexplained or supernatural noises. But considering her newfound connection with the paranormal, Kate couldn't help but feel that someone was standing right in front of her. And whoever it was desperately wanted her attention.

"Hello?" she called softly.

One knock.

Her first thought was that it was Trevor. Maybe he'd forgotten to tell her something. But if that were the case, why hadn't he gone to Michael? Why come to her directly when he knew she wouldn't be able to hear him?

"Trevor?"

Two knocks.

Kate didn't know why she'd asked. It wasn't like a ghost could give her a yes or no answer.

Unless...

There was that thing they were always doing on television when there was a communication barrier, like on medical dramas when a person couldn't move or talk. The doctors always told them blink once for yes, twice for no.

Is that what this ghost was doing?

"You're not Trevor?" she asked.

Two knocks again.

"Does that mean no? Once for yes, twice for no."

One knock.

So it wasn't Trevor. Who else, then? She didn't know anyone else who had died. At least, she hoped she didn't. After today, she had no way of knowing for sure. But even if she did know someone else, why would they seek her out? Why not go across the landing to Michael?

Wait a minute. She *did* know another ghost. Michael's friend. The one who'd interrupted them earlier that morning.

"Brink?" she asked.

One knock.

"What's going on? Is everything okay?"

Two knocks.

Kate felt the blood drain from her face as realization dawned on her. Brink had no reason to come to her. The only reason he would be there, trying to communicate with her, would be if the person he normally talked to wasn't there.

"Has something happened to Michael?" she asked, dreading his response.

One knock.

Without a second thought, Kate dashed out the front door and across the landing. She tried opening his door, but it was still locked.

"Michael?" she called, pounding heavily on the door. "Michael, are you all right?"

No answer.

Willing herself not to panic, Kate pulled out her phone and dialed Michael's number. She listened impatiently to the dial tone.

"Come on, please answer," she begged.

Just then, a cell phone went off. Kate pulled her own phone away from her ear and listened carefully, trying to pinpoint the new phone's location. It took a moment for her to realize that the sound was coming from somewhere below her.

By that point, the call had gone to Michael's voicemail. Kate hung up and dialed again. As she waited for the call to connect, she made her way down the stairs, listening intently for the other phone. When it began to ring a few seconds later, she followed the sound to the bed of grass next to Michael's driveway, where his car sat untouched and the screen of his phone lit up with the glow of two missed calls.

CHAPTER TWENTY-FIVE

Pain.

All sorts of pain.

Body aches, nausea, scrapes, and a splitting headache all plagued Michael's transition back into consciousness. He felt like he was waking up from a bad dose of anesthesia. Or from being run over by a truck. Or maybe both. And it was hazy. Everything was hazy. He was dizzy and lightheaded. He wasn't sure if he was lying sideways or upside down. Sounds were far away and when he tried to open his eyes, everything was blurred.

Then something changed. The world stopped.

No. He stopped. Whatever he was lying on stopped.

Then there were whispers. The indistinct voices echoed inside Michael's mind, but he couldn't understand what they were saying. If they were saying anything at all.

He peered forward in the direction of the voices. Everything was still a blur, but he thought he could make out a red light in between two dark shadows.

Then the light changed to green and the world started moving again. The sudden forward motion threw Michael back against a cool, cushioned wall and intensified the pounding inside his skull. He squeezed his eyes shut, held his breath, and waited for the pain to subside.

I'm in a car. Why am I in a car?

Meanwhile, the whispers in front of him were growing louder and becoming somewhat clearer, though Michael still couldn't understand what they were saying. One voice, distinctly male and unfamiliar, muttered something under his breath. His companion didn't respond. In spite of every rational voice in his mind screaming at him not to do so, Michael slowly opened his eyes.

One of the dark, blurred figures seemed to be peering around at him from the front seat. It muttered something in an indistinguishable hush and reached forward. Michael watched in slow motion as a hand emerged from the shadows. Then, he felt the cool pressure at the base of his skull and the world once again descended into darkness.

Kate tried not to panic as she paced back and forth from her kitchen to her living room where Gavin was still passed out to the front door then back to the kitchen. Luke was supposed to arrive any minute with his equipment. Hopefully, they could talk to Brink and figure out exactly what had happened to Michael. As much as she tried to convince herself that she was worrying over nothing, that Michael may have simply gone for a walk and accidentally dropped his phone, her gut instinct told her that something was very, very wrong.

Making her way back to the front door, she stepped out onto the landing and stared down at the street, hoping, praying for a glimpse of headlights. She was about to head back inside when the sharp squeal of tires echoed through the night. Seconds later, Luke's Ferrari came to a screeching halt in front of Building 17. Kate breathed a sigh of relief as Luke leapt out of the car and sprinted up the stairs.

"What happened?" he asked, breathless. Quickly, trying not to sound too paranoid, Kate told him about the mysterious knocks and finding Michael's abandoned phone lying in his driveway. "And you think it was his friend trying to tell you all this?"

"Yes."

"What about Trevor?"

At the sound of his name, Kate felt her heart sink, but she tried not to dwell on it.

"It's not Trevor. Did you bring the recorder?"

"Yeah, but I thought Spirit Box would be more helpful so I grabbed that too."

"You're probably right."

"Should we go inside?"

Kate shook her head. "My brother's asleep on the couch and he's had a... really stressful day." She didn't feel like going into detail.

"Okay, then let's go down to the car. I don't want to make a racket and disturb the neighbors."

"Okay. Brink, follow us to Luke's car," Kate announced, feeling sort of silly. She didn't even know if Brink was around, though she was fairly certain he hadn't left her side all evening.

Once they were inside the car, they shut the doors and turned on the Spirit Box. The roar of the static and sweeping radio stations seemed even louder inside the tightly enclosed space. Kate fought the desire to cover her ears as she asked, "Brink? Can you hear me?"

"*Yes.*"

"What happened?"

"*Michael... gone.*" Kate felt the already cold knot in the pit of her stomach tighten as a whole new wave of fear and concern washed over her.

"Where did he go, Brink?"

"*Don't know... taken.*"

"Taken?" Kate asked. She was suddenly so terrified that she barely noticed Luke furrow his brow. "Who would take him? Did you recognize him?"

"*No.*"

"I think I know," Luke announced, switching off the SB7. "Buckle up." In the blink of an eye, his keys were in the ignition and the Ferrari revved to life. Seconds later, they were tearing out of the parking lot and speeding toward the highway at almost ninety miles an hour. Kate stared at him, waiting for some sort of explanation. "After this morning, I did some research. Turns out our friend Pastor Cannon was supposed to be the officiant at

Grace Bledsoe's wedding which, as we all know, didn't exactly go down the way it was supposed to - "

"Wait, I don't understand. What does that have to do with Michael?"

"I'm not done. Before he became the Pastor at Calvary Hill, Cannon was a Reverend at a little church in Oklahoma. During his five years there, two members of his congregation committed suicide and his son was killed in some sort of accident. Then he gets to Calvary Hill and the bride of a wedding he's supposed to perform ends up murdered."

"So does Daniel Ford."

"And so does Daniel Ford," Luke repeated. "That makes five unnatural deaths under this guy's watch. And these are tiny congregations. It's not like a mass random sampling where X number of people will be predicted to die prematurely."

"You think he did it?"

Luke didn't answer right away.

"Michael was taken for a reason," he finally said. "I mean, it is possible that this was just a random abduction, but think about it. Michael isn't a cute girl. He's not a kid. He's not just another faceless person on the street. He's a guy who can talk to dead people. Now, I'm not saying that Cannon is responsible for all those deaths. But if he *was* and Michael comes around telling him about his little talent - "

"Then Michael becomes a liability," Kate finished Luke's train of thought.

"I was going to say a 'threat,' but yeah, pretty much."

"Oh my God, we've got to hurry." Kate had long surpassed full-out panic mode. All that mattered now was getting to Michael. "Where do you think Cannon would take him?"

"I have no idea. But I'm going to start at the church. Maybe someone will be there."

"At this time of night?"

"At the church I grew up in, there always seemed to be someone working late. I snuck in once, back when I first started investigating. We have a columbarium in our courtyard where a lot of parishioners are buried and I was hoping I could capture some EVPs. I wasn't there five minutes before one of our office ladies found me and kicked me out."

"Do you think whoever's there will know where Cannon is?"

"No, but they might be able to give us some idea of where he's gone."

As he spoke, Kate realized that their entire rescue mission was, to put it lightly, insane. If Luke was right and they were chasing down a *murderer*, just what in the world were they going to do about it? Luke was a hot TV star and she was an interior decorator. Neither of them was even remotely qualified to track down a killer. Luke may have had a slight advantage because he was really buff and he'd communicated with criminals before, but all of the murderers he'd encountered on his television show were, well, *dead*.

"Maybe we should call the police," Kate suggested.

"What are the police going to do?"

"I don't know. If we tell them that we suspect foul play, they might be able to conduct a more thorough investigation of the scene, file a missing person's report, get a more accurate search going..."

"Call them if it will make you feel better. Just make sure they don't need you around for questioning."

He had a point. How were they supposed to explain to the police that their friend who could see ghosts had been taken by someone that they thought wanted him dead for that very reason? They wouldn't believe the first part, let alone the second. And neither Kate nor Luke would ever convince them to engage in a wild goose chase all the way to Waxahachie.

Maybe they could somehow alert the police there. Ask them to keep an eye out...

By that point, they were flying down the highway. At the rate they were going, they'd make it to Waxahachie in a little under thirty minutes as long as they didn't hit traffic. Normally, Kate would have been petrified of going so fast, but at the moment, her concern for Michael far outweighed her intense fear of crashing on the highway. Fortunately, there weren't too many cars out (it was Sunday night, after all). That, and she couldn't help but feel that this wasn't Luke's first time driving at the reckless speed of 94 MPH. She just hoped they were going the right way.

"If this is Cannon, how do you think he found out where Michael lived?" she asked.

"He probably followed us."

"This morning?" Of course. When else would he have followed them?

"Yeah."

"But that's impossible. We would have noticed."

"Not necessarily. He probably stayed a few cars back, pulled over when we stopped for lunch, and started tracking us again when we left," Luke replied grimly.

"So you think Cannon's been watching him all day?"

"Probably," Luke answered. Kate felt sick. "You'd be amazed at what some people are capable of. One of the reasons I stopped talking about our film locations on social media is because we've had some legitimately crazy fans track us down. Turns out it is really easy to stalk in this day and age."

"Great," Kate murmured.

"Hey, good news for us," Luke told her. "If some lunatic priest from Nowhere, Oklahoma can find Michael in one of the biggest cities in the nation, then you and I should have no problem tracking him down in the boonies."

Less than thirty minutes later, Luke and Kate pulled into the parking lot of Calvary Hill. With no street lights overhead, Kate could barely see through the pitch darkness. Only a single light from one of the windows inside the church's main building provided any sort of illumination.

"Come on." Luke didn't need to tell her twice. Together, they ran up the steps to the chapel. The door, as expected, was locked, so Luke reached into his wallet and pulled out a credit card.

"You know that trick?" Kate asked.

"I told you, Babe, I've picked a lot of locks," Luke reminded her as he knelt down and slid the credit card through the crack between the doors. Seconds later, the lock clicked and Luke gave the door a slight push. It opened with a loud *creak*. "Oops," Luke whispered.

Kate grabbed his shoulder.

"Wait a minute, what's our plan?"

"What do you mean?"

"Are we just going to barge in and demand to know where Michael is or are we trying to stay quiet and sneak up on him?"

"Well, I think any and all chances of staying discreet sailed with this door, so I guess we'll go with the first one."

"But what if he has a gun? Or a knife? We're completely unarmed."

"Oh no we're not." Luke flexed his muscles. "You asked me what I do in my spare time? I work out. And not just because it makes cute girls weak at the knees. I've met a lot of shady characters over the years and I've learned you never know when you're going to need to defend yourself. But, if he does come after us with some kind of weapon, I've got this." He held up his keys to reveal a Swiss army knife keychain. "But Kate, listen to me. If anything happens, you get out of here. You turn, you run, and you don't look back, you understand?"

Kate wanted to argue that she would stay and help him, but given her limited experience in physical confrontations, she knew she'd be about as helpful as a caterpillar in an actual fight. She might even make things worse if she tried to stay.

"Yeah, I understand," she replied.

"Good. Now, let's go find Mikey."

CHAPTER TWENTY-SIX

When Michael woke up for the second time, he was sitting upright in the dark. He blinked a few times, wondering briefly if he'd gone blind, before his eyes began to adjust. Everything hurt just as badly as it had before, and on top of that, his back was pressed against something so hard it sent little sparks of pain shooting through his vertebrae. Everything was blurry and distorted and he was so dizzy that he was sure the world had spun right off its axis and was freewheeling through space. He closed his eyes, rested his head back against whatever was behind him, and took several deep breaths.

Slowly, the misery began to subside and his senses began to pick up on little things that previously had taken a backseat to the pain and nausea. Things like the slight breeze toying with his hair, the crickets chirping around him, and the tickling of grass against his ankles. He was outside... but where?

He opened his eyes again and tried with all his might to make them focus. It was difficult enough to see in the dark without the blurred vision and shaky disposition. Instead of depending on what little he could see, he thought about what his senses weren't picking up. There was no sound of passing cars or horns blaring through the night. That meant he wasn't close to a highway, or any road for that matter. The total absence of any source of artificial light was even more unnerving.

The only good news was he could neither see nor hear whoever had dragged him out there. He hoped that their mission had been fulfilled by leaving him out in the middle of the field. He didn't want to think about what they had in store for him should they return.

Michael didn't want to take any chances. If they were coming back, he didn't want to be there when they arrived.

He needed to get out of there. His mind was clear enough so that he thought he'd be able to stand without falling over. But try as he might, he couldn't seem to figure out how to move his arms. A few moments later, he registered that his hands were stuck, bound together, behind the wooden pillar.

"Oh, this is not good," he muttered, trying to wriggle his wrists free from whatever his captors had used to tie them together. It didn't feel like rope or string. It felt more like some sort of plastic, but for the life of him, he couldn't figure out what that might be.

He constricted his hand as tight as he could and tried to slip it through the plastic shackle. For a split second, he thought he might be making progress. He could feel the plastic ring around the heel of his hand. But that was as far as the binding would allow him to go. He pulled harder, so hard that he felt the sharp edge of the band digging into his skin. Moments later, his fingers were covered in a hot, sticky liquid. The sting of the fresh cut made him flinch.

God, he thought, *if you're there, now would be a great time for a miracle.*

A rustling in the tall grass behind him startled him. As he listened to the heavy footsteps approaching, he felt his stomach sink with dread. That wasn't exactly the kind of miracle he'd had in mind.

He waited, wracking his brain for something, anything that he might use to bargain. Maybe he could reason with them. Surely every person, no matter how damaged, had the capacity for some sort of empathy or understanding.

Right?

Finally, the two shadowed figures came into view. One of them was carrying a flashlight. Michael couldn't make out their faces, or even what they were wearing, but the taller one seemed to be holding something in his arms... almost like a baby. He set the bundle down a few yards away from Michael. Then, the shorter of the two turned and shone the flashlight straight into Michael's face. Instinctively, he closed his eyes and turned his face away from the searing white-blue beam.

"Oh good. You're awake."

Kate tried not to think as she followed Luke through the center aisle of the church. If she thought too much about where they were or what they were doing, there was no way she'd be able to take another step. The church was eerie at night; dark, quiet, and far too still. If Kate hadn't known better, she'd swear the eyes of Christ Himself were watching her from behind the altar, following her every move.

For all she knew, they could have been.

Cautiously, they approached the door through which Cannon had led Michael earlier that morning. Kate felt her stomach turning backflips as Luke pushed the door open. The soft *click* of the latch echoed through the silent sanctuary, the sound magnified by the absolute emptiness of the room.

Looking to the left, they noticed light pouring through the crack beneath one of the doors down the hall.

"That's our door," Luke muttered to Kate.

They scampered down the hall toward the light. Kate felt her heart pounding with dread and anticipation. What if they were too late?

Luke got to the door first and pushed it open, fully prepared to defend himself if necessary. But the look on his face, however, told Kate that the room was empty.

"He's not here," he confirmed. "Dammit!" he yelled and struck the wall with his fist.

Although Kate was somewhat relieved that they had not found Michael hurt or worse, she felt her spirit sinking. Where were they supposed to go from there?

"*What are you doing here?*"

Kate was so startled by the harsh voice over her right shoulder that for a moment, her mind went blank. She couldn't move. She couldn't breathe. She couldn't hear the scream that surely escaped her lips. All she knew in that moment was fear.

"Looking for you, as a matter of fact," Luke replied, far less shaken by Augustus Cannon's sudden appearance. "You wouldn't happen to know what happened to our friend, Michael, would you?"

"I told that boy that I didn't want to see his face, or any of yours for that matter, on these grounds again. Why do you think he would be here?"

"Because he disappeared about an hour ago, and we figured that someone who hated him so much... who might have a reason to want him to disappear... might be able to give us some idea as to where he could be."

"And why would you assume that someone is me?" Cannon narrowed his eyes.

"Never said I did," Luke shrugged.

If Cannon was annoyed, he didn't show it.

"Well, if that is the case, then you have no business here. Now get out."

"Hold on a second," Luke countered. "I'm a little disappointed in you, Pastor. I would have thought a man of God such as yourself would be a little more concerned that an innocent man is missing. That is, unless you don't think he's innocent."

Kate held her breath. She knew that Luke and his team sometimes provoked evil spirits to get them to make themselves known, but there was a big difference between provoking a ghost and provoking a man who, even if he hadn't killed all those people, still had the capacity to do a lot of damage.

Pastor Cannon just gritted his teeth.

"If this has something to do with what happened in Oklahoma - "

"Oh, it's not just that. It's about Grace Bledsoe and Daniel Ford, too."

"You are out of line, boy!" Cannon snarled. "You act so smug and clever, but you have *no idea* what it's like to see a young person's life taken, wasted. Especially young people who had so much to live for. And then the whispers, the suspicions, the *blame*... The mere notion that people believed I was responsible for the death of my own son... I wouldn't be able to live with it were it not for the strength and comfort that the Lord gives me."

Kate was stunned. This was a whole different kind of passion than she'd seen earlier that morning during the service. This was pure, unadulterated heartache, and Kate suddenly found herself pitying the man they'd come to accuse. Luke seemed equally unnerved.

"Well if it wasn't you, do you have any idea who it could be?" he asked.

"No," Cannon replied hastily. "Now I respectfully ask that you leave me in peace."

"You answered that awfully quickly, Pastor. Are you sure you don't want to think about it? What about your friend, Mr. Ford? He seemed like he wanted to beat the crap out of Mikey."

"John is a very sick man. To think him capable of what you're suggesting is ludicrous."

"A relative then? Maybe John Ford has a crazy brother or really dedicated nephew."

"This is not the work of John, nor any soul in this congregation. Now for the last time, *goodnight*."

Kate felt more discouraged and humiliated than ever, but Luke wasn't giving up. He stared directly into the old man's steely eyes and asked, "What about your daughter?"

Michael blinked up at the person standing in front of him, certain that his eyes were playing tricks on him. Maybe he'd been unconscious for too long or his brain had been deprived of oxygen. He might have hit his head being dragged to wherever he was. Whatever the reason, he knew he could not be staring into the wide blue eyes of Chastity Cannon.

"Wha - what are - "

"No, shhh. You shouldn't try to talk." Chastity knelt down next to him and stroked his face. "You've been through a lot tonight."

236

Yeah, thanks to you. You and...

Michael didn't recognize the bulky guy who accompanied Chastity. If he'd been in church earlier that morning, Michael hadn't seen him. He couldn't quite make out the expression on the stranger's face, but he got the feeling that he was much more apprehensive than his female companion, whose face still hovered a few inches away from Michael's. He instinctively tried to move away from her, but his bonded wrists prevented him from doing so.

"Oh, I know, it's uncomfortable, but trust me, it's for your own good. How else do you expect me to help you?"

Michael narrowed his eyes.

"Help me?" he asked in a weak, hoarse voice.

"Your life has been overrun by sin, Michael Sinclair." Though hardly significant, Michael wondered briefly how she knew his full name. "But don't worry. That's why the Lord has disciples like me. To guide you back into the light of His redeeming love."

Michael's head was spinning again. He truly did not understand what she was saying. Where was she coming from with all of this?

He cleared his throat and asked, "What did I do?"

"You did nothing, Michael. It is the power of Satan living inside of you that is to blame. Until that power is destroyed, you can never be free."

Destroyed? That didn't sound good.

"I don't understand."

Chastity stared at him, her light eyes full of a strange combination of condescension and pity.

"James, chapter four, verse seventeen." she answered as though that explained everything. When she saw that Michael still wasn't getting it, she continued. "'So whoever knows the right thing to do and fails to do it, for him it is sin.' I am a child of God, Michael. It's my duty to uphold the laws of my Lord and King. That's why I had to see those disgraced sinners put to death. It was the only way to help them. Thanks to me, their sin has been destroyed and they are free to dance in the Kingdom of Heaven."

"Who?"

"The temptress and the idolater. The adulterers. And my brother, the homosexual. All abominations in the eyes of God."

Out of the corner of his eye, Michael noticed the silent man behind Chastity wince at her harsh words.

"What about murder? Doesn't the Bible say that's wrong?" Michael didn't remember a whole lot from his Sunday School days, but he was pretty sure 'Thou shalt not kill' was one of the Ten Commandments.

"It isn't murder if it's God's will," Chastity replied.

You're insane, Michael thought. But he held his tongue, hoping that if he cooperated, he might figure out a way to reason with her.

"So what do you need me to do in order for you to save me?"

Chastity smiled. For a moment Michael felt a sense of relief. If this girl wanted to help him, then by all means, he was going to let her think she was. Especially if he could avoid the destruction part.

"First, you must confess your sin, repent, and ask God's forgiveness. In doing so, you will renounce Satan and all he stands for."

Confess, repent, renounce. Easier said than done. What was he supposed to confess? Every bad thing he'd ever done in his life? That would take a while. And was she expecting formality? Was there an incantation or poem he needed to recite? Hoping he wasn't about to make a mistake, he looked up at Chastity.

"Will you help me?"

Chastity frowned.

Mistake.

"A truly repentant heart shouldn't need help," she told him.

His mind scrambled for a way out of the hole he'd inadvertently begun to dig for himself.

"I'm sorry," he blurted. "I'm sorry for everything. For lying, for being a coward. For not helping people when I should have. I'm sorry I put myself first. And I hope God forgives me. Please, please forgive me."

Chastity was still frowning.

"Aren't you forgetting something?" she asked, arching an eyebrow.

She must be referring to something specific. Michael thought back to earlier that morning.

"I'm sorry for the pain I caused Mr. Ford," he said.

Chastity sighed.

"Unless you confess all your sin, I can't help you."

Michael was nearing the end of his rope. What other sin could he possibly have committed? He hadn't done anything! Meanwhile, Chastity was growing more impatient by the second. Michael hoped that honesty might be enough to save him, but he doubted it.

"I'm sorry, Chastity," he finally told her. "But I don't know what you're talking about."

"Then you leave me no choice," she replied solemnly. Then, she rose to her feet and walked back to her companion, who watched silently with remorseful eyes as she bent down, took something in her hand, and turned back to face Michael.

"No choice about what?" His heart was beating so fast, he could barely form the words. Any pity that had once existed in Chastity's eyes had vanished and had been replaced by a cold, bitter passion.

"Leviticus, chapter twenty, verse twenty-seven. 'Now a man or a woman who is a medium or who consults the spirits of the dead shall surely be put to death. They shall be stoned with stones, and their blood shall be upon their own heads.'"

CHAPTER TWENTY-SEVEN

Though he'd spent his whole life staring into the faces of the dead, Michael realized he'd never once been confronted by the prospect of his own demise. Now he knew what all those countless souls had felt seconds before death had claimed them. Silently, he cursed himself for never taking the time to consider all they'd been through.

Up until that point, his entire existence seemed to have revolved around death, but he'd never stopped to think about what death would be like. Would it come quickly for him or would he be left to suffer for a few hours before his heart gave out? Would there be a flash of light? Or would it be like going under anesthesia? You close your eyes one second, then the next wake up in an entirely different place? He should have spent more time talking with Kate about her brush with death, though at the time, he'd felt so guilty for how he would have treated her had he known she was dead that he hadn't wanted to discuss it.

Michael had always thought that he wouldn't fear death. He'd been wrong. The *idea* of death didn't bother him. The act of dying, however, was a whole different story. It didn't matter that death had never been a mystery to him. He was just as scared of it as any other person would be.

As Chastity posed herself in what vaguely resembled a pitcher's stance, a million thoughts raced through Michael's mind at once.

Stop her! Try to stop her!
What made her this way?
Is there any way I'll survive this?
Will I become a ghost?
What will happen to my mother?

The thought of his mother mourning for yet another son was more than Michael could bear. He felt hot tears sliding down his face and he stared up Chastity with pleading eyes.

"Chastity... Please... You don't have to do this."

She didn't seem to hear him. Or if she did, she ignored him. With a self-satisfied smile on her lips, she raised her arm to cast the first stone. Then, in one swift motion, she threw.

The stone, about the size of a golf ball, hit Michael's chest, knocking the wind out of him. While he struggled to catch his breath, another stone struck his shoulder. Both would surely leave bruises, but Chastity's arm, thankfully, was not as strong as it could have been. She threw another stone that missed him altogether. With a slight frown, she turned to her accomplice.

"Beau, help me," she told him.

No.

Michael could only watch in horror as the strong, sturdy man reached down, picked up a fist-sized rock, and prepared to send it hurtling his way. Too terrified to speak, he shook his head.

No use. Less than a second later, the stone struck his collarbone with a sickening CRACK. Blinded by pain, he cried out and doubled over as far as he could with his arms tied behind the wooden pillar.

"There, there," Chastity called out to him in a soothing voice. "I know it hurts, but I promise, it will be over real soon."

Yes, please. Please be over. Death had to be nothing compared to this misery. Brink seemed happy enough, right? Maybe being dead wouldn't be so bad. No illness, no broken bones...

No Kate.

If he died tonight, what would happen to her? He knew they'd agreed that she needed time to mourn for Trevor, but he'd sort of thought, or at least hoped, that eventually, they would be able to pick up where they'd left off.

It didn't look like that would be happening. Still grimacing from the pain of his broken clavicle, he gritted his teeth and looked up at Beau, who was preparing to pitch another stone.

Unable to speak and too weak to resist, Michael closed his eyes and waited for the next agonizing blow.

It didn't come. No pain, no impact, not even pressure. Michael began to wonder if Beau had even thrown the rock when Chastity's confused and anxious voice ordered, "Again!" This time, Michael heard the stone flying through the air, but again, it missed him.

Curious, Michael opened his eyes. He couldn't see Chastity or her companion. Instead, he found himself staring into a wall of billowy white.

Wait, did I die?!

Alarmed, he tried to account for the last few seconds. His hands were still bound. Searing pain still radiated from his broken collarbone. He was definitely still alive.

Then what was he looking at? Straining against the pain between his shoulder and neck, he lifted his head up. The woman standing in front of him, dressed all in white, turned and looked at him with hard, dark eyes. Michael felt his jaw drop.

"Grace?" he whispered.

She didn't say anything. She just sneered at him and whipped her head back around to stare down Chastity. Michael watched, awestruck, as Grace lifted her lace covered arms out in front of her, then, in the blink of an eye, thrust her left arm out to the side. As she did, the stone Beau had just thrown altered its course midair and flew off to the side, just like a bad curveball caught in the wind.

Grace Bledsoe was protecting him.

Why?

An exasperated growl from Chastity answered his question. Of course. Grace and Daniel were the adulterers she'd "saved." Grace may not have been fond of Michael, or anyone for that matter, but she wasn't about to see another life end at the hands of the woman who'd murdered her.

"What is the matter with you?" Chastity demanded. "Throw straight!"

"I'm trying!" Beau told her.

242

"You're not trying hard enough."

Chastity shifted to the right and into Michael's line of vision. He watched as she wound her arm up and threw yet another stone. Again, Grace raised her arm and the stone deflected to the side.

Michael would have been thankful for his ghost guardian were it not for the fact that Chastity was growing more frustrated by the second. He'd learned enough as a psychology minor to know that provoking the criminally insane was never a good idea.

Sure enough, after yet another failed attempt, something snapped and Chastity began hurtling stones like a mad woman. Beau followed suit. Their attack was so vicious that for a moment, it seemed the stones were literally falling from the sky. But thanks to Grace, none of them reached Michael.

"Enough!" Chastity finally hissed. "This isn't working."

For a split second, Michael thought she was giving up.

Please, just go away. Leave me here. Eventually, someone will notice that I'm missing and come looking for me.

No such luck. Instead of gathering up her stuff and walking away, Chastity dug around in her purse until she found what she was looking for. Then, she dropped the purse and held her hand out at arm's length. The sleek silver gun in her hand reflected the pale light of the crescent moon.

Grace turned and looked at Michael. Her mournful brown eyes told him what he already knew.

I can't help you.

Grace was strong, stronger than most spirits Michael had ever met (at the moment, he could think of only one exception), but no ghost, no matter how powerful, could stand in the way of a bullet. Michael was dead as soon as Chastity decided to pull the trigger.

Michael simply nodded and whispered, "Thank you."

In the blink of an eye, Grace vanished.

This was it, then. He almost wished Grace hadn't come. It would have been better to get death over with than to have it taunt him with false hope. With the gun pointed straight at Michael's head, Chastity approached him.

"Don't want to miss," she explained. "Beau, cut him loose."

"Cut me loose?" Michael asked.

"Well, it'd be pretty difficult for you to shoot yourself with your hands tied behind your back, now wouldn't it?"

So that was her new plan. Chastity was setting the scene for another suicide. Suddenly, every shred of fear, pain, and resignation evaporated and was replaced by a rage unlike Michael had ever known. To be murdered was one thing. A terrible, horrible, awful thing that he would never wish upon anyone. But he would rather die a slow, miserable death at the hands of someone else than have his mother believe for one second that both her sons had taken their own lives.

"No!" he yelled and, summoning every ounce of strength he possessed, fought against his bonds.

Chastity knelt down next to him and smiled.

"Don't worry, Michael. Soon, you too will be a member of God's Holy Court."

"What about the bruises? My collarbone? That'll look suspicious. They'll know they were there before I died. There'll be an investigation."

"They could have been self-inflicted. Perhaps you tripped."

Michael glared at her with hard eyes. "No one will believe it. Kate, Luke, my mother... They'll know I didn't kill myself. I had no reason to."

"There, there, don't get upset. A lot of people take their lives unexpectedly. But in your case, I'd say you did have a reason. Didn't you break up with Katherine tonight?" Chastity, asked, rising to her feet.

Michael's face fell as Beau knelt down behind him to cut the plastic wires that bound him.

"How did you know...?" Of course. She'd been listening. She'd been following him all day. How else would she have known where to find him?

"I know she'll be sad. I think she really liked you. But the Lord has someone special picked out for her. Soon, she'll forget she ever had you."

And then, like an answer to a prayer, a new voice echoed across the empty field. "Don't be so sure!"

There was absolutely nothing surprising about the setting Chastity had selected for Michael's execution or redemption or whatever the hell Cannon had warned them his daughter might be doing. Of course, the pastor didn't know for sure. He'd been hoping and praying that the mysterious deaths that seemed to follow him were just coincidences. Unfortunately, there wasn't a whole lot of room in his belief system for mere chances of fate.

He'd been right.

Following his best guesses, Kate and Luke found themselves in an open field, not far at all from the bridal barn where Grace Bledsoe had been found stabbed to death. They'd abandoned the car once the grass started getting thick and continued on foot through the meadow until they'd heard Chastity's voice.

She was standing over Michael, who sat at the base of a tall wooden cross, and pointing a gun at his left temple. Kate didn't notice the man behind Michael until he stood, startled by their sudden appearance. Kate locked eyes with Michael for only a brief moment before Luke addressed Chastity.

"Chastity, drop the gun."

"Why?" Chastity asked, swinging the gun around so that it was pointed at Luke's heart.

Kate took an automatic step backward, as though half a foot of distance would save her from a gunshot. Luke stood his ground, but he held his hands up and tried to reason with her.

"Look, I'm unarmed. You don't have to shoot," he told her. "Please, just put the gun down. Let's talk about this."

"There's nothing to talk about. I am a servant of the Lord. I have been sent to do His work."

"Hate to break it to you Chas, but I'm pretty sure that killing people isn't part of the job description."

"I don't kill people. I help them."

"And how is putting a bullet through a guy's head helping him?"

"A demon has taken root inside his mortal body. It communicates with the dead through him. The only way for Michael to be free is to separate his soul from his defective body."

"That's why you want to kill him? Because he talks to ghosts? I talk to ghosts too. Hell, I go looking for them. Why didn't you come after me?"

"Yours is not a gift of the devil," Chastity answered, as though that cleared everything up.

"How did you find out?" Kate asked.

"My father told me after you left."

"Then how did you follow us? We should have been long gone by the time he talked to you."

"I didn't need to follow you. You gave me all the information I needed when you told me your full name," she told Kate. "Beau is a computer genius. He was able to track down your personal information in less than a second, and as a result, Michael's."

Kate turned her eyes on the bulky guy standing behind Michael. His eyes were fixed on a spot on the ground. Almost like he felt guilty...

"What about you? Why are you doing this?" Kate asked Beau.

"He's doing this because it is God's will, and the only way to vanquish his past sin from his life," Chastity answered for him.

"Oh. I thought only Jesus could do that." The words were out of Kate's mouth before she could stop them.

Chastity narrowed her eyes.

"You are not a true Child of God, so how can you be expected to understand His ways?"

You know what, bitch? You go ahead and think that. Chastity could say whatever she wanted. All that mattered was getting Michael, Luke, and herself out of that field alive.

Luke seemed to be on the same page.

"So how are we going to do this, Chas? Are you going to let us take our friend home or are we going to have to fight you for him?"

Oh, such a bad idea. Why, why, *why* had he said the word, "fight?" They weren't supposed to fight, especially with a crazy person wielding a gun. Hell, they weren't even supposed to be out there in the first place. Cannon had advised them to wait for the police, but neither was willing to do that; a decision that Kate was beginning to sorely regret.

"My name is *Chastity*. And you will not be taking him."

"Well, in that case, I guess I have no choice." Luke pulled out his phone, pretended to punch something in, and held it up to his ear.

Chastity narrowed her eyes. "Who are you calling?"

"The police," Luke replied casually. Of course, it was all a bluff. If Pastor Cannon was to be believed, the police were already on their way. Luke was simply trying to buy them all a little more time.

Though the longer it took for the police to show up, the more Kate wondered if maybe he'd set them up to die as well. Maybe he and his daughter were more similar than he'd let on.

"Drop the phone!" Chastity demanded.

"Drop the gun," Luke countered.

Chastity's hands began to shake. In that moment, Kate realized why Luke wasn't afraid to go on taunting her. Chastity couldn't kill him. If he didn't have "the gift of the devil" or whatever, then killing Luke would be murder, a sin. And ironically, that was the last thing Chastity Cannon wanted to do.

Luke, apparently having decided he'd waited long enough, said, "Yes, I'd like to report an abduction and attempted murder - "

247

"No!" Chastity screamed as the gun slipped out of her hand and tumbled to the ground. Then, like a hysterical child reaching for a candy bar, she lunged toward Luke's phone. But Luke was too fast and too strong for her. He sprinted off into the thick grass to the left, leading Chastity away from Michael. "Beau, help me!" she cried.

As the bulky man barreled across the field after them, Kate made a mad dash over to Michael. She dropped to her knees, scraping both of them in the process, and took his tortured face in her hands.

"Are you all right?" she asked.

"I am now," he told her.

But Kate could see the awkward way he held himself and the harsh, plum-colored bruise that was creeping up his neck. He was far from all right.

"We've got to get you out of here," she told him and scrambled around to the back of the cross, where his bloody hands were bound by two thick plastic zip ties. One of them had marks in it, like it had been in the process of being cut before something, or someone, had interrupted.

Crap.

There was no time to dwell. Kate reached into her pocket, pulled out her keys, and began sawing away at the bands. The one that had been cut broke fairly easily. The keys barely made a mark in the second.

"Dammit," she hissed through gritted teeth. If only she had Luke's Swiss army knife. Of course, he probably needed it more than she did at the moment.

"Are you okay?" Michael asked.

"This isn't cutting. Do you have anything sharp?"

"No."

Kate thought fast. If she could get the key between his skin and the zip tie, maybe one good tug would do the trick, just like the tiny plastic clothing tags. She'd have to pull hard, and the band would probably hurt Michael even more, but it was her only option.

248

"Michael, this might hurt a little," she warned him.

"I can handle it," he assured her.

With a silent prayer, she turned the key sideways and slid it beneath the zip tie. Then, she turned the key ridge-side-up, took a deep breath, and tugged. Michael inhaled sharply as the band cut into the back of his wrists, but Kate wouldn't let up. Seconds later, the band broke with a gratifying SNAP, but Michael cried out as his arms fell free. Kate was by his side in an instant.

"What's wrong?" she asked.

"I can't - it hurts - " He tried to speak, but he was in too much pain.

"Can you stand?" She had learned back in her lifeguarding day that injured persons should never be moved, but she was pretty sure that rule could be ignored when there was a homicidal she-devil on the loose.

"I don't know."

And then, like music to her ears, distant sirens began to wail. Kate heaved a sigh of relief.

"They came!"

In spite of his pain, Michael grinned too.

Slowly, easily, Kate took Michael's good arm and helped him to his feet. He was still shaking after his ordeal, but with Kate supporting him, he was able to stand.

"Thank you," he whispered.

"No problem. Now let's get you out of - "

Her words died in her throat, as she turned to see the shadowy silhouette of Chastity Cannon standing just a few yards away. Kate felt all the blood draining from her extremities as she stared into the barrel of the gun that Chastity had aimed at her heart.

"Chastity..." she whispered. Her instincts told her to run, but her unwillingness to leave Michael held her where she stood.

"You know why I have to do this, don't you Katherine?" Chastity patronized. "First Samuel, chapter fifteen, verse twenty-three B. 'Because you have rejected the Word of the Lord, He therefore has rejected you.'"

"*What?*"

But Chastity was through explaining. With a wry grin, she straightened her arm and cocked the gun.

Michael didn't have time to think. He didn't need to think. He could hear the shouts and footsteps of a dozen men and women running across the field. It was almost over.

But it wouldn't be over soon enough.

"*Kate, get down!*" Summoning every ounce of strength he possessed, Michael threw himself at Kate.

He felt her falling beneath him.

Then Chastity pulled the trigger.

CHAPTER TWENTY-EIGHT

The last eight hours were a blur, and to be honest, Kate was okay with that. For once, she didn't want to remember.

There had been questions. A lot of them. She thought she'd answered all of them, but she couldn't be sure. The only good news was that neither she nor Luke was suspected of having anything to do with what had happened.

Luke was doing okay. He had an ugly bruise around one of his eyes and he'd sprained his ankle, but he would be fine. He'd had to answer a lot more questions from a lot more people, but that wasn't surprising. He was a good sport about it too, but he was obviously worn out from the ordeal. Kate didn't envy him a bit.

Gavin had called her sometime around 6 A.M. wondering where she was. She didn't tell him the whole story, but assured him that she was fine and that he didn't need to worry. Her mind was so numb that she wasn't sure she would have been able to talk about it even if she'd wanted to. And why would she want to? Living through it once had been enough.

The last few moments before Waxahachie police had finally apprehended Chastity Cannon were the ones that Kate couldn't make go away. Every few minutes or so, she heard Michael yell at her to get down. She heard the gunshot. Then she felt the flow of hot, sticky liquid as she crumpled to the ground beneath him...

Kate shuddered at the memory and tried to force herself to concentrate on something, anything, else. Luke was *still* talking to reporters outside. Kate wished his agent or manager or whatever would tell them to get lost and let him rest, but she seemed to be of the mindset that all publicity was good publicity.

Why would anyone want publicity for this? She didn't. Yeah, they'd sort of helped apprehend Chastity, but at what cost?

A small voice in her mind reminded her that not all hope was lost. Michael might still be okay. The bullet had missed his heart by a few short inches. But she'd seen his pale, lifeless body lying on the ground after he'd pushed her out of the way. She couldn't imagine anyone waking up from that state.

You did, the voice reminded her. Somehow, it brought her little comfort. It was true, she had come back. But that sort of miracle happened once in a lifetime, if that.

Hoping to tune everything out, Kate closed her eyes and leaned her head back against the wall. She'd been sitting in the ICU waiting room at Baylor Waxahachie for what seemed like a millennium. She remembered what Gavin had told her about his time in the waiting room. He'd reached the point where he just wanted answers. Kate didn't want answers. She already knew everything. Now, all she wanted, was to open her eyes and be somewhere else.

She must have fallen asleep then, because the next thing she knew, someone was shaking her shoulder.

"Kate," Luke whispered.

"Hmm?" she asked, rubbing the sleep out of her eyes. "What's going on?"

"He made it."

When Michael woke up for the first time, he was in a white room. It was so bright, he shut his eyes and immediately fell back asleep.

The second time, he was in a new room with soft blue curtains and a television. It was still bright, but not nearly as blinding as the first room had been. He looked around the room and saw his mother sitting in a chair next to his bed, reading a book. She smiled and cried when she saw that he was awake. He was sure they'd talked, but he was so exhausted that he couldn't remember what was said.

By the third time he opened his eyes, the events leading up to waking up in the bright white room were coming back. Some of it was a little fuzzy, but he remembered all the big things. Being kidnapped. Being stoned. Being saved. Being shot. Even the after-effects of anesthesia couldn't dull those memories.

The fourth time he woke up, she was there, smiling at him, holding his hand, and looking more beautiful than anything he'd ever seen before.

"Hey," Kate greeted him, blinking back tears.

He held her gaze for a moment. Then he rasped, "And *that* is why I don't tell people."

She laughed.

"I don't blame you," she told him. "How are you feeling?"

Michael had to think about that one.

"Very medicated..."

"That's probably a good thing." Kate leaned forward and stroked his hair. "You saved my life."

"Returning the favor," he whispered. Kate's smile broadened as she kissed him lightly on the cheek. "So what happened?"

"Chastity and Beau were both arrested. The police are investigating the other murders. And Luke is getting a *lot* of press coverage."

"He's not... I mean..."

"No. No one's said a word."

Michael heaved a sigh of relief and closed his eyes. He felt Kate kiss him once more on the forehead before he drifted back to sleep.

Michael's condition continued to improve until, five days later, he was released. He'd still have to be on pain medication for a while, and his arm would be in a sling for at least six weeks, probably longer to allow his collar bone to heal, but his doctors were confident he'd make a full recovery and felt no qualms about sending him home.

Kate had driven up earlier that morning to help him pack the things she'd brought up for him throughout the week: clothes, books, toiletries. Then, once all the paperwork was done, they'd make the sixty-minute drive back home.

Throughout the week, they'd somewhat been keeping up with the investigation. They learned that Beau Jennings had been a member of Cannon's old congregation back in Oklahoma. Everyone thought he'd followed the Cannons to Texas to be with Chastity, but the truth was that he'd been in love with her brother, Simeon. Chastity had found out about them back in Oklahoma. Instead of killing Beau, however, she'd managed to guilt him into believing that his sin was to blame for Simeon's death and that the only way to earn forgiveness was by "living out God's will." In truth, Michael pitied the guy.

Meanwhile, Luke's costars from *Cemetery Tours* had all flown in to lend moral support to their heroic lead investigator. They'd stopped by to visit Michael in the hospital, though Kate had gotten much more of a kick out of it than he had. Still, it had been nice of them to make the journey and Michael appreciated their being there.

Kate's parents were another matter entirely. Although Kate had not been injured, it was impossible to keep something like involvement in an attempted kidnapping and murder a secret, and when Mr. and Mrs. Avery had found out, they'd gone ballistic. And that was *before* Kate had let it slip that she knew about Trevor. Although they hadn't come to yell at him in person, they'd voiced their concern more than a few times to Kate by telephone. She didn't tell him everything they'd said, but it was enough for Michael to know that if Kate ever wanted to date him again, they would not have her parents' approval.

By the time they'd almost finished packing, Kate's phone was ringing for the fourth time that day. Fortunately, this time it was Gavin.

While Kate stepped out of the room to talk to her brother, Michael did his best to finish stuffing his suitcase with one good arm. It was difficult, but he wanted to be able to do things for himself. It was bad enough that he wasn't allowed to drive. He wasn't going to have Kate or Gavin or his mother tending to his every need for the next six to twelve weeks.

"I think you dropped something." The rough voice startled Michael, even though he probably should have been used to people walking in on him after five days in the hospital. He turned and was surprised to see Trevor standing in the doorway. Trevor ignored his stunned expression. "Your shirt?"

Michael glanced down at the floor and sure enough, one of his shirts had tumbled out of his suitcase and on to the floor.

"Thanks," he told Trevor as he knelt down to pick it up. "I didn't really expect to see you again."

"I know. But it seems that there's something still holding me here. And after everything you went through, I realized what it is."

"What's that?" Michael asked, still a little afraid that Trevor might want to beat him up.

"I never thanked you for everything you've done for her. And for me. I know how easy it would have been for you to let her go on believing I was just some jerk. To be honest, if our roles were reversed, I'm not sure I would have been able to tell her," Trevor admitted. "You're a good guy, Michael."

"So are you."

"Well..." He grimaced good-naturedly. Michael chuckled. Trevor's expression softened. "You take care of her, all right?"

"I will," Michael promised.

With one final nod of gratitude and respect, Trevor walked toward the window and looked up at the sun. Then he disappeared in a flash of white and gold light.

Kate reappeared a few minutes later.

"Do you have everything?" she asked.

"I think so," Michael replied.

"Are you okay? You look a little sad."

"Just ready to be home," he told her.

"Me too. I think I'm ready for things to be back to normal."

"Normal. What's that like?" he asked.

Kate laughed.

"You know, I'm not really sure." She grinned up at him. "Guess we'll have to figure it out."

Moments later, a nurse arrived with a wheelchair. After assuring her they wouldn't need assistance, Kate thanked the nurse while Michael took a seat and set his suitcase on top of his lap. Then, Kate took the handles and pushed him out of the room, through the hallway, and into the elevator. They rode in a comfortable silence down to the first floor, where Kate pushed his wheelchair through the lobby and all the way to the front entrance.

More than ready to be back on his feet, Michael stood and stretched while Kate returned the wheelchair to one of the nurses. When she came back, she took him by the arm and said, "Do you need me to go and get the car? I parked in the spot closest to the door."

"Nah. It feels good to walk," Michael told her.

Kate smiled again and together, they walked through the automatic sliding doors and into the fresh summer air.

"There he is!"

Both Michael and Kate turned in the direction of the shout. A group of two dozen reporters, photographers, and paparazzi were bearing down on them. Before either realized what was happening, they were separated by a frenzy of eager news reporters. Cameras were clicking, flashes were firing, and Michael had about five microphones being shoved into his face at once.

"Mr. Sinclair, Vince McLaughlin from CNN. Would you answer a few questions for me?"

"Michael, Tish Peterson, WFAA. Can I talk to you briefly about what happened a few days ago?"

"Michael, please, just a few questions for CBS."

There were so many people calling his name that Michael wasn't sure which way to turn. Lost in the commotion, he tuned everything out and tried to find a pathway back to Kate.

"Please, um, I'm sorry. No comment," he told them, but there were so many of them, he wasn't sure any had actually heard him.

Above the noise and confusion, Michael could hear Kate shouting, "Get out of the way! Leave him alone! Michael!"

"Mr. Sinclair, are you and Miss Avery dating?"

"Is that what compelled her and TV personality Luke Rainer to attempt such a daring rescue?"

"Mr. Sinclair, is there anything you'd like to say to the people who abducted you?"

What was with all of this attention? Surely there were a lot more interesting things going on in the world. Things that were actually worth reporting. But if he was what these people wanted to write about, maybe he should answer a few of their questions. The sooner he gave them what they wanted, the sooner they would leave, and the sooner he could go home.

"Okay, I'll answer a few questions," he announced. "Just one at a time, if you can."

"Mr. Sinclair! Seth Withers, NBC. I have just one question," an enthusiastic young man addressed him.

"Okay."

"Is there any truth to the claim that you can actually see and communicate with the dead?"

Oh God.

And just like that, the world stopped. No one spoke. No one seemed to breathe. They all just waited silently and hungrily for his response.

Lie! Lie! Lie!

Somehow, Michael managed to pick out Kate's face in the crowd. She looked just as pale and bewildered as he felt. He couldn't speak. He couldn't think. And with every passing second, his silence all but confirmed the curiosity and disbelief in every reporter's eyes.

"I... I mean... Um..."

Wrong answer.

Suddenly, the crowd exploded with more vivacity and persistence than before.

"Is it true then, Michael? Is Miss Cannon telling the truth?"

"How do they find you? How does it work?"

"Can you actually *see* ghosts, Mr. Sinclair?"

Michael wanted to run, but for some reason felt rooted to the spot. He wanted to deny everything, but couldn't form the words. It felt like a nightmare, but try as he might, he couldn't wake up.

Dissatisfied with Michael's lack of response, a few reporters turned to ambush Kate.

"Miss Avery, you spoke with us a few days ago. Why didn't you tell us about Mr. Sinclair's astonishing ability?"

"Did you know your boyfriend had a sixth sense?"

Flabbergasted and overwhelmed, Kate turned wide eyes on Michael. He wished he could help her, but the reporters who had chosen to stick it out with him were growing even more restless. They weren't going away. There was only one way out.

"Yes," he answered.

Time screeched to a halt.

Deafening silence.

All eyes on him.

Then the questions began all over again.

Nightmare begins now.

ACKNOWLEDGEMENTS

First and foremost, I'd like to thank my Lord and Savior for all that He has given me.

I'd also like to thank...

My mother, Susan, for being an ever-abundant source of love, enthusiasm, support, and patience and for her willingness to see me through not four, but six years of expensive higher education only to have me major in the creative arts.

My father, David, for always encouraging me to pursue my dreams, and for teaching me never to settle. He acts as my left brain, as I have none, and is always eager to guide, to enlighten, and to sacrifice for his girls.

My sister, KJ, for reading and rereading all hundred and seven versions of this one book. She is my best friend, my twin soul, and the only person in the world whose opinion I trust 100% of the time, especially when it comes to books.

My amazing editor, Nancy Lamb, for her wisdom and impeccable grammar skills.

My teacher and mentor, Steve Lund, for nurturing countless students' love of reading, writing, and of course, William Shakespeare.

My friend and fellow author, Stephen Harrison, for his guidance, encouragement, and willingness to answer all of my questions about writing and publishing.

My best friends in the world, Hannah, Jessica, Jalitza, Aïda, Bobby… I love all of you more than words can say.

© 2017 by Fervent Images – Tim Malek

JACQUELINE E. SMITH is the award-winning author of the CEMETERY TOURS series, the BOY BAND series, and TRASHY ROMANCE NOVEL. A longtime lover of words, stories, and characters, Jacqueline earned her Master's Degree in Humanities from the University of Texas at Dallas in 2012. She lives and writes in Dallas, Texas.

Made in the USA
Columbia, SC
23 March 2022

58022851R00162